FANTASTIC WOMEN

FANTASTIC WOMEN

18 tales of the surreal and the sublime from Tin House

INTRODUCTION by JOY WILLIAMS

Edited by Rob Spillman

TIN HOUSE BOOKS

Portland, Oregon and New York, NY

Published by Tin House Books, Portland, Oregon, and New York, New York
Distributed to the trade by Publishers Group West, 1700 Fourth St., Berkeley, CA 94710, www.pgw.com

Library of Congress Cataloging-in-Publication Data

Fantastic women : 18 tales of the surreal and the sublime from Tin house / edited by Rob Spillman. -- 1st U.S. ed.
    p. cm.
ISBN 978-1-935639-10-7 -- ISBN 978-1-935639-11-4 (ebk.)
    1. Fantasy fiction, American. 2. American fiction--Women authors. I. Spillman, Rob. II. Tin house.
 PS648.F3F353 2011
 813'.087660806--dc22

                                    2011009695

First U.S. edition 2011
Cover illustration © Juliette Borda
Book design by Janet Parker
www.tinhouse.com
Printed in the U.S.A.

Contents

Introduction by Joy Williams vii

Americca 1
AIMEE BENDER

Whitework 13
KATE BERNHEIMER

Abroad 19
JUDY BUDNITZ

The Young Wife's Tale 35
SARAH SHUN-LIEN BYNUM

The Entire Predicament 51
LUCY CORIN

Five Fictions from the Middle of the Night 61
LYDIA DAVIS

The Dickmare 65
RIKKI DUCORNET

The Wilds 71
JULIA ELLIOTT

Beast 87
SAMANTHA HUNT

Oranges 107
MIRANDA JULY

Light 115
KELLY LINK

Snow White, Rose Red 151
LYDIA MILLET

Hot, Fast, and Sad 163
ALISSA NUTTING

Song of the Selkie 169
GINA OCHSNER

The Doll Awakens 187
STACEY RICHTER

The Seagull Army Descends on Strong Beach 197
KAREN RUSSELL

Drive-Through House 225
JULIA SLAVIN

Big People 245
GINA ZUCKER

Introduction

Joy Williams

All men say "What" to me
but I thought it a fashion.
—EMILY DICKINSON

I once used the word *peculiar* to describe the fabulous Flannery O'Connor and her work and got spanked by a doyenne of the literary establishment. But what's wrong with the word *peculiar*? It means special, distinctive, different from the usual or normal or ordinary. It even means exemption from the power of an authority to interpret and control. (Perhaps the doyenne feared she wasn't peculiar enough.) In any case, the doyenne found the word to be mildly pejorative and condescending while going on to describe all the cool stuff it actually meant.

The stories collected here are peculiar, I say! As well as being witty, spooky, disorienting, and artful. It would be tempting to call many of them surrealistic, but in fact one of the limitations of that movement was that it was so male. WOMAN is the key to man's search, the surrealists cried. The great secret of nature, the incarnation of man's subconscious destiny. Women are manipulative muses. Sweet. Innocent of their mysterious power. Women are the answer. And an answer can't question itself. Meret Oppenheim's fur-covered cup and spoon, *Déjeuner en fourrure*, arguably the most important surrealistic work of all, is actually a notion named by naughty boys. (My favorite surrealism is Aube Elléouët's painting *Le Secret*, in which a woman and her squid lover lounge blissfully in a garret.)

The surrealists were deeply enchanted with transformations and correspondences and were intent on revealing the emptiness and falsity of reasonable discourse. Thoughts became objects, objects thoughts. They sought the emancipation of words from their worn and dreary meanings. They were always more playful and effective in their art than in their writing—with some extraordinary exceptions, of course, all among the poets. Perhaps their reign was so brief—twenty years—because they were forever trying to define their aims; they became pedantic. In the end, the surrealists decided not to be defined as a school at all, but as a way of thinking, of knowledge.

Such knowledge finds wild flowering in *Fantastic Women*, in the unschooledness of these writers, their "unhousedness," in Kafka's term. These ladies don't lunch.

They're also divinely unmaterialistic. So much of American fiction can't seem to crawl out of the hole of stuff, the stuff that defines us, the stuff that codes. The drugs, the labels, the bands, the names of the machines, the foods, the annihilating oppressive numbing stuff of things.

"Things don't happen, it depends on who comes along," Paul Bowles said.

The painter Ivan Albright said, "Things are nothing. It's what happens to them that matters."

Many of the women in these stories are farouche—they're outsiders, they're troubled, they lack polish, they dream too much. But they're quite accepting of the strange whos who come along, bringing the situations that confound and confront them. Husbands and boyfriends are no help whatsoever, although the lawyer in Gina Zucker's "Big People" does help his wife drag the clubfooted midget she's been entertaining in their apartment when the time really has come for the little fellow to go. And the couple in Samantha Hunt's "Beast" do manage to have a serious conversation or two before they both turn into deer:

> "[W]hat's the most adult thing?"
> "Fucking?" he asks.
> "No. Fucking's for kids. Dying is adult."

What begins in Judy Budnitz's "Abroad" as a typical tourist holiday swiftly deteriorates into bedlam as the unnamed narrator's boyfriend brings more and more people back to their room: "The hotel room now is just a mass of bodies, cookstoves, tents, shanties, music, dancing arms and bobbing breasts, boys pitching pennies, stray dogs, the burned smell of someone curling her hair, a bazaar of stalls selling rugs and copper kettles, laundry hanging on lines overhead . . . . The walls are grease-stained, the bare bulb a small sun. He is . . . among them, shaking hands, kissing men on both cheeks, kissing women on the lips, as is the custom here. His face is tanned mahogany brown, though as far as I can tell he never goes outside."

Fathers are no better. No help, no hope of salvation. The dad in Aimee Bender's "Americca" is cheerfully clueless: "Dad lost his job. Then he got a new job. Then he got his old job back and went back to it. They were all in the same building."

In Lydia Millet's no-nonsense update of "Snow White, Rose

Red," the dad's a gray suit, a groom doll, obsessed with business, while in Lucy Corin's "The Entire Predicament," the husband, home from work and making himself a peanut butter sandwich, doesn't notice that his wife is gagged and suspended in the doorway within a network of ropes. The children seem okay. They're outside, playing with the soldiers.

"The Entire Predicament" says it all. Life is so perplexing. Things get strange fast. Chance rules. One second you're listening to the comfy sounds of your dog drinking water from his bowl and the next you're all ransacked. Or you find yourself boiling in a kettle in some god-awful kitchen. You bob around with others for a while but then you're alone, the last to be chosen (Alissa Nutting's "Hot, Fast, and Sad"). "I'm only going where others have already been," you say pluckily.

The new heroine is the superadaptable woman, wanderer, perpetrator and acceptor of illogical action. In Lydia Davis's "Five Fictions from the Middle of the Night," a woman is escorted to a bathroom by a schoolboy: "[I]t's a nice bathroom, with old fixtures and paneled in wood. As I sit on the toilet, the room rises—because it is also an elevator." (Oh, that "because"!) "I wonder briefly, as I flush, how the plumbing works in that case, and then assume it has been figured out."

One can only assume . . . Exactly! Or not . . . The important thing is to be alert to one's surroundings, as we've been taught in these borderland, murderous, drug-crazed, netty, webby, clear-cut, schizoid times, even as those surroundings are morphing, melting, darkening, and shifting before our eyes.

What?

That's right. Birds can swipe your incidentals to feather their omen nests and warp your present into some awful irrefutable shape (Karen Russell's "The Seagull Army Descends on Strong Beach").

What!

Yes. The important thing is to be alert, aware, calm, and resourceful. When there's nothing for miles and miles but pavement and your momma won't sell to the highway department, the only correct thing to do is allow your friends and neighbors to drive through the house, accept donations, and sell 'em cookies, sort of like Toll House cookies but far flakier (Julia Slavin's "Drive-Through House").

When you're kidnapped by the swarm of little boys who live next door, don't struggle, show no fear: "Their chests glowed with fire-fly juice. They had steak knives strapped to their belts and some of them wore goggles. White cats strolled among them, sometimes sniffing their bare feet. 'Move,' yelled a small Wild, no older than six, a butter knife dangling from his Cub Scout belt." (Julia Elliott's "The Wilds")

There's little desperation or rage in these stories. (Kelly Link's Lindsey can get cranky in freaky Florida's "Light," but she's dealing with pocket universes and too many iguanas. Gin can help only so much. The important thing to know is she had a happy childhood.) The angriest female here is Miss Pretty in Stacey Richter's "The Doll Awakens," who, after suffering the final humiliation of penetration of her long-suffering plastic self by two meth heads in a trailer, hauls off and takes a bite "the size of a crab apple" out of one of them.

Nor is there much sex. Oh, a crush or two. A little vampirish nip here or there or a difficulty arising from postcoital good organic dope blessed by monks. Rikki Ducornet does explore longing among the bivales in "The Dickmare," a wildly gorgeous tale told by a . . . what is not exactly clear. We do know that this what once found her husband admirable: "Admirable his thorny cone, his sweet horny operculum, his prowess as a swimmer, the beauty of his sudden ejections, the ease with which he righted himself when overturned." But he's not what he was and our feminine what, really quite attractive in her luminosity, her roundness, her smoothness, finds herself noticed by the somewhat godlike Dickmares, who "are known to unspool and push their pistons forward with such alacrity a subconical cavity will be stunned into service before it has a chance to ignite."

Fantastic!

Writers create the myth of their age's concerns, finding forms in which the concerns can be felt if not understood. These stories do not take up environmental or political or spiritual issues and I'm not going to find excuses for that. That's not their nature. Their take on the psychological viewscape is that it's endlessly curious and exploration is never fatal as long as one is able to keep afloat in the magical waters of the imagination. They are fictions neither moral nor immoral. Rather they are involved contrivances, preposterous in conception, logical in presentation, quite delightful and askew.

In Kate Bernheimer's "Whitework," her elegant retelling of Edgar Allan Poe's "The Oval Portrait," an injured woman rests in a cottage in a deep forest avidly reading from a small book that describes the delicate paintings on the walls of her sickroom. The room is a curious one—a turret, a circle, but with inexplicable corners. In one corner, suddenly illuminated, is a tiny, bizarre, but perfectly executed portrait of a young girl. Concerning this, the little book offers a frightening and wondrous assessment.

Awakening from her reflections and recognitions, the woman finds herself in another place, a hospital room, with a doctor by her side who tells her that prognosis for recovery is good but it depends on one thing alone—she must eliminate every gloomy thought: "He pointed toward a room I had not noticed before. 'You have the key to the Library,' he said. 'Only be careful what you read.'"

We know of course that our woman would rather not "recover" than be limited in what she can read. The fabulous, the otherworldly, the odd, the incomprehensible, the *peculiar*, must be sought out and absorbed. We enter a story, and when it's a good one we emerge, however briefly, as another self.

The world we think we know doesn't exist anyway.

So don't be careful. Read.

AIMEE BENDER

Americca

When we came home from the movie that night, my sister went into the bathroom and then called out to our mother, asking if she'd bought another toothpaste as a hint.

I know I have major cavities, she said. But do we really need two?

Two what? asked my mother.

Two toothpastes, said Hannah.

My mother took off her sweater for the first time in hours and peered into the bathroom, where, next to the grungy blue cup that holds the toothbrushes, there were now two full toothpastes.

I only bought one, she said. I think. Unless for some reason it was on sale.

We all shrugged in unison. I brushed my teeth with extra paste and went to bed. This incident would've been filed away in non-memory and we would just have had clean teeth for longer, except that in the morning there was a new knickknack on the living room side table, a slim abstract circle made of silver, and no one had any idea where it came from.

Is it a present? asked our mother with motherly hope, but we children, all too honest, shook our heads.

I don't know what that is, I said, picking it up. It felt heavy and expensive. Cool to the touch. Nice, Hannah said.

My mother put it away in the top of the coat closet. It was nice, but it felt, she said, like charity. And I don't like too many knick-knacks, she said, eyes elsewhere, wondering. She went to my grandmother and brought her a lukewarm cup of tea, which Grandma accepted and held, as if she no longer knew what to do with it.

Drink! my mother said, and Grandma took a sip and the pepper-mint pleased her and she smiled.

Happened again the next evening when, while setting up for a rare family dinner, my mother stood, arms crossed, in front of the pantry.

Lisa, she said, you didn't go to the market, did you?

Me?

Hannah?

No.

John?

No.

Grandma never shopped. She would get lost in the aisles. She would hide beneath the apple table like a little girl. Our mother, mouth twisted in puzzlement to the side, found soup flavors in the pantry she swore she never would've considered buying. She held up a can of lobster bisque. This is far too bourgeois for me, she said. Anyone else buy this? We all shook our heads. Wild rice and kidney bean? she said. What is this? I would never buy this—lemongrass corn chowder? They sell this stuff these days?

Yum, yelled Dad from the other room, where he was watching tennis.

Who put these here? asked Mom again.

Hannah paused, placing spoons on napkins. I don't really like soup, she said. I shook my head. Not me, I said. I definitely hate soup.

Our mother tapped her fingers against the counter, nervous.

What is going on? she said.

Hannah lined up the spoon with the knife. We've been backwards robbed, she said solemnly.

I laughed but her eyes were serious.

Alls I know is, she said, I did not buy that soup.

Neither did I, said Mom.

Neither did I, called Dad from the other room.

I could tell I was still the main suspect, just because I seemed the most interested in all of it, but as I explained repeatedly, why would a person lie about bringing food and new knickknacks into the house? That is nice. That is something to get credit for.

Dad cooked up the corn chowder after he found an enormous piece of gristle in his mustard chicken. We all watched him closely for choking or poisoning but he smiled after each spoonful and said it was darned good and very unusual. Like Southwestern Thai, he said, wiping his mouth. Like . . . the Empress meets Kimosabe, he said. Like . . . silver meets turquoise, he said, laughing. Like . . . we all told him that was enough. Hannah checked the inside of the can for clues. After dinner, Dad collected water glasses from the rooms, singing.

That night I kept a close eye on the back door, but it stayed locked, and I even fixed a twig at its base to see if it got jigged during the night, but in the morning, the twig was just as before. I was walking to the bathroom to get ready for school when Mom cried out, and I ran over, and she was standing over the kitchen table, which held an extra folded newspaper. Hannah found a third pewter candlestick that matched the previous two, standing tall in the bookshelf. We ate our breakfasts in silence. Although being robbed would suck, there was nothing appealing about getting more items every day, and I felt a vague sense of claustrophobia pick up in my lungs, like I might get

3

smothered under extra throw pillows in the middle of the night. Like I might wake up dead under a pile of a thousand tiny wind-up toys. And we couldn't even sell the new stuff for extra cash because everything we got was just messed up enough to make it useless—the pewter candlestick was flaking into little slivers, and the silver circle thing had a subtle, creepy smell.

For the first time in my life, I cleaned my room after school. I threw out tons of old magazines and trash and dumb papers for school with the teacher in red pen stating: Lisa, we all know you can do better than this. I had the cleanest closet in years, which is why it was once again bad when I found, an hour later, a new mug on my side table of dancing cows holding balloons that said Happy Birthday! that ONLY could've been purchased by Hannah, but when I showed it to her she started to cry.

They're trying to kill us! she sobbed, wiping her nose on her T-shirt.

Who? How? How are they trying to kill us?

The people bringing this stuff in.

But who's bringing it in? I asked. We've been home the whole time.

Ghosts, she said, eyes huge. She stared at the mug. It's not even your birthday, she said, not for months and months.

I stuck the mug in the outside trash can along with the extra newspaper. I kept my eyes carefully on all the doors. The twig stayed put.

We had a respite for a week, and everyone calmed down a bit and my mother went to the market and counted how many cans so she'd know. We ate the food we bought. We stared at the knick-knacks that represented our personalities. All was getting back to normal until the next Sunday, when Hannah opened the towel closet and screamed at the top of her lungs.

What? We all ran to her.

The towel closet had towels in it. Usually it had small, thin piles—we each had a towel and were expected to use it over four days for all towel purposes, and there'd be a big towel wash twice a week, one on Thursday, one on Sunday. We never stuck to the system and so usually I just used my towel as long as I possibly could until the murky smell of mildew and toothpaste started to pass from it onto me, undoing all the cleaning work of the previous shower.

Now the towel closet was full, not of anything fluffy, but of more thin and ugly towels. Tons of them. At least ten more towels, making the piles high. Countless piles of worn towels.

Well, I said. I guess we can cut the Thursday/Sunday wash cycle.

My mother went off to breathe into a paper bag. Hannah straightened taller, and then put one towel around her hair and another around her body, a very foreign experience in our family.

I'm going to just appreciate the gifts, she said, even though her face looked scared. I've always wanted to use two at once, she said, even though her hair was dry and she was fully dressed in jeans and a T-shirt and the towel looked like she was getting a haircut.

At school the next week, it was past Halloween and we had to bring in our extra candies for the poor children of Glendora. Bags and bags came pouring in and, aside from candy, I brought in an extra bag of stuff for the poor children, full of soup cans and knick-knacks I'd salvaged from the trash. Everyone in the family felt funny about it; maybe it was like passing on poison. But at the same time, throwing out whole unopened cans of lobster soup struck my mother as obscene. How often does a homeless woman who lives nowhere near salt water get lobster? she asked, hands on hips, as I packed up the bag. We all shrugged. We liked how her guilt looked in this form of benevolence. I repeated it to my teacher. It's not a Snickers bar, I said, but it's got a lot more protein.

I think I saw my teacher take that soup can for herself. I watched her closely that week, but she seemed healthy enough, and my dad had never had a single negative symptom from his lemongrass corn chowder. I didn't eat any Halloween candy. I didn't want anything from anyone else.

I got a note from the shelter saying my bag was the best.

Hannah got a boyfriend. She didn't tell anyone but I could tell because she was using so many towels, making the bathroom a pile of towels, and for some reason I knew the towels were happening because of a boy. Why did she need to be so dry all the time? I asked her about it, when she came home for dinner and looked all pretty with her eyes bright like that. I had to set the table because she was late, and she apologized and said she'd take dish duty for two days.

It's okay, I said. Who is he?

She blushed, crazily. Who is who?

The reason you are late, I said.

I had to study.

Mom stood in the doorframe, but she wasn't listening. She wasn't out to bust Hannah.

How was your math test? Mom said, brushing the side of her hair with a soupspoon.

Okay, said Hannah, glaring at me. I got an A.

What did you hear? she asked, dragging me aside and cutting into my arm with her budding nails.

Nothing, I said. Ow. I just guessed.

How? she said.

No reason, I said. Towels. Who is it?

She said no one, but then she barely ate at dinner, which is rare for her, and usually I have to fight my way to the main dish to even get any because she is so hungry and that let me know she really liked him.

Dad lost his job. Then he got a new job. Then he got his old job back and went back to it. They were all in the same building.

We didn't get any more items for a few weeks. I started to miss them. I mean, I felt like I would die of claustrophobia and I had become paranoid about all things coming into the house including bathwater and I had made a checklist for market items, shopping items, and all school items, but when I opened the refrigerator and saw all the same old stuff, I wanted to cry sometimes.

I left a few baits: I cleared my nightstand of all things so that it was ready for a deposit. Nothing. I bought a lobster soup with my own allowance, which made my mother shriek, but I assured her I'd bought it and I'd even saved the receipt to prove it. I brought it out of my bedroom, and she stared at the curling white paper and then looked at me, in the way she rarely did, eye to eye.

Are you okay, Lisa? she said. Ten-year-olds don't usually save receipts.

I'm trying to trap a ghost, I said.

Would you like to go to the mall? she asked. Her eyes were tired. She looked pretty with tired eyes, so I didn't mind so much.

We went to the nearest mall, over in Cerritos, which had been built twenty years ago and was ugly. I liked that about it. It was like a relative nobody liked but still had to be related to anyway. We went to the kids' store and she bought me two shirts, one orange, one red, and then I got very attached to a particular cap with an octopus on the cap part and I felt if I left it in the store I might dissolve. I didn't have much allowance left due to the spenditure of the lobster soup, and so I asked my mom as nicely as I could if I could have an advance and get the octopus cap because I loved it very much.

That? She was holding the store bag and trying to stop the salesperson from talking to her by staring out the door. Thanks, she was saying, thanks, thanks.

I love it, I said, putting it on my head. It was too big. I couldn't see well underneath it.

Please? I said.

We just got you two new shirts, she said. Do you really need a cap?

It's good for skin cancer, I said. Of the face.

She laughed. She was tired these days because she was having job trouble too; her job trouble meant she did not know how she could be useful in her life. Dad's job trouble was he had too much to do with his life. Sometimes I just wanted them to even it out but I couldn't think of how. That afternoon, I didn't want to bother her more, but I wasn't certain I could leave the store with that cap still in it. If someone else bought it, I might tear in two.

I will pay you back, I said. I swear. Or we can exchange it for one of the shirts?

She got me the cap because I hardly ever asked for much, and at home, I slept with it on, and I wore my new orange shirt to school and back and I was ready to charge ahead when I noticed the octopus cap on my dresser.

I thought it was the one on my head except then I realized that one was already on my head. So this had to be a new one? I took the one on my head off and held them both side by side. Two octopus caps. I had two now. One, two. They were both exactly the same but I kept saying right hand, right hand, in my head, so I'd remember which one I'd bought because that was the one I wanted. I didn't want another octopus cap. It was about this particular right-hand octopus cap; that was the one I had fallen in love with. Somehow, it made me feel so sad, to have two. So sad I thought I couldn't stand it.

I took the new one, left hand, to the trash, but then I thought my mom might see it and get mad that I'd thrown out the new cap she had bought especially for me, so I put the one I loved on my head and put the one I hated in the closet, behind several old sweatshirts. I went out to play wearing the first one. I played kickball with Dot Meyers next door but she kicks cockeyed and it was hard to see out of the cap and when I went inside, I scrounged in the closet for the second cap and it fit. That's what was so sad. It was the right size, and I put it on, and it was better. The ghosts had brought me the better cap. I put them both on, one after another, because at least by size now I could tell which was which, but it was just plain true that the one I loved did not fit and kept falling off and the one they brought did fit and looked better. Dot Meyers thought I looked dumb in a bad-fitting cap but she's dumb anyway and can't spell America right.

I saw Hannah kissing a boy I'd never seen before outside our house in the bushes.

That night, I put a bunch of stuff in Hannah's bedroom to freak her out but she recognized it all as mine so it wasn't the same as the ghosts who came in with their own stuff, and I had no allowance to buy anything new.

I wore the good new cap to school.

I ate the lobster soup. I liked it. It had a neat texture. I liked it better than the usual plebeian chicken noodle my mom got. I liked the remaining wild rice one that hadn't made it into the Halloween bag; it was so hearty and different. I used the cow cup I'd salvaged from the trash, and the truth was, I liked the cow holding a balloon; it was cute. When I looked in the mirror, I sneered my upper lip and said, Benedict Arnold, Benedict Arnold, your head is on the block.

Mom came home from taking a class called Learning How to Focus your Mind, and she seemed kind of focused, more than usual at least, and she sat with Grandma on the sofa and talked about childhood.

After awhile I sat with them. There's nothing to do after homework and TV and creaming Dot Meyers.

You were a quiet child, said Grandma.

What did I like to do? asked Mom.

You liked to go with me to the store, said Grandma.

What else? asked Mom.

You liked to stir the batter, said Grandma.

What else?

I don't know, said Grandma. You liked to read.

Even as they were talking, I saw it happen on the dining room table. Saw it as they were talking, but it wasn't like an invisible hand. Just one second there was a blank table, and I blinked, and then there was a gift on the table, a red-wrapped gift with a yellow bow. It was in a box, and I went to it and sat at the table. I knew it was for me. I didn't need to tell them, plus they were talking a lot, plus Dad was at work, plus Hannah was out kissing.

It had no card, but it was really good wrapping, with those clean-cut triangular corners, and I opened it up and inside was a toy I had broken long ago. Actually, I hadn't broken it; Hannah had. It was a mouse, made of glass, and Hannah had borrowed it without asking and dropped it in the toilet by accident—so she said—and broken off the red ball nose. I had been so mad at her I hadn't spoken to her for a week and I'd made a rule that she couldn't come in my room ever again and I asked Mom for a door lock but she didn't think I really meant it so I got one myself, at the hardware store, with a key, with money from my birthday, but I couldn't figure out how to put it on. Here was the mouse, with its nose.

What was next? Grandma?

Thanks? I said, to the air.

I took the mouse and put it on the shelf it used to be on, next to the mouse that had no nose, retrieved from the toilet. The mouse without the nose looked pathetic but a little charming, and the mouse with the nose, well. It had never been in the toilet.

When Hannah came home, I showed her. Mom's taking a new class, I said. That's good, she said. Her face was flushed. She seemed relieved, once she paid attention, that the new mouse had arrived. Sorry about the toilet thing, she said, for the fiftieth time. It's cute, she said, patting the new one.

Let's flush it down the toilet, I said.

What?

My eyes were pleading. I could feel them, pleading.

Please, Hannah.

Hang on, she said. She went to the bathroom and splashed her face and spent a minute in there with her crushiness, and then opened up. I brought both mice in.

Both, I said, the old and the new.

Fine, she said. Whatever.

How'd you do it?

I just dropped it in, she said.

On purpose?

Yeah.

I didn't blame her. Right now, it seemed like these mice were just made for the toilet. I sat next to her on the edge of the bathtub and dropped in the new guy. He floated around in the clean white toilet water.

Flush away, said Hannah, her eyes all shiny from kissing.

I flushed. He bobbed around and almost went down but didn't. He was slightly too big. The toilet almost overflowed. But still, the nose.

That's just what I did, she said. She was putting on lip gloss and smacking at herself in the mirror.

I picked up the wet new mouse and broke his nose right off. It took some pressure, me holding him good in one hand and then snapping it off. You can ruin anything, if you focus at it. There, I said.

I put both mice in the trash and washed my hands. Hannah broke up with her boyfriend a few weeks later because he'd started calling her honey, and I got picked for the kickball team, and we didn't get any more gifts. Not for years.

Mom found some work downtown as a filing clerk, and Dad almost got that promotion. Hannah went to college nearby but she lived at home because of the price of rent. Grandma got older and eventually died.

When I was about to graduate high school, I did notice a packet of yellow curry in the pantry while I was rummaging around, looking for a snack. It was in a plastic yellow envelope that just said Curry on it in red letters. I asked my mom if she'd bought it, and she said no. Hannah? No. Dad? No. I don't like curry, I said out loud, although I'd never tried it. As an afterthought, I brought it with me to college, where I had a scholarship, so I was the first one to leave home, it turned out, and it sat in the cupboard in the dorm for four years, alongside the oregano and the salt and my roommate's birth control pills. I took it with me to my first apartment that I shared with the utilities-shirker, and my second apartment with the toxic carpet, and in my third apartment, when I was twenty-seven, living alone across the country, I opened it up one night when I was hungry and made a delicious paste with butter and milk, and then I ate it over chicken and rice and cried the whole way through it.

KATE BERNHEIMER

Whitework

The cottage into which my companion had broken, rather than allow me, in my desperately wounded condition, to pass a night in the thick-wooded forest, was one of those miniaturized and hand-carved curiosities from the old folktales that make people roll their eyes in scorn. This, despite the great popularity of a collection of German stories published the very same year as my birth! As to the justifiability of this scornful reaction: I cannot abide it, nor can I avoid it by altering the facts. This is where I found myself: in a fairy-tale cottage deep in the woods. And I had no use of my legs.

When we came upon the cottage we were certain, by its forlorn appearance, that it had long ago been abandoned to the wind and the night, and that we would be perfectly safe. Or rather, my dear companion was certain of this. As for me, I was certain of nothing—not even of my own name, which still eludes me.

There were but few details for my enfeebled mind to record, as if the cottage had been merely scribbled into existence by a dreamer's hand. Tiny pot holders hung from the wall in the kitchen, beside tiny dish towels embroidered with the days of the week. In each corner of each room was tucked an empty mousetrap—open and ready but lacking bait. At the entryway, on a rusted nail, hung a minuscule locket, along with a golden key. As to whether the locket ever was opened, and what it contained, I have conveniently misplaced any knowledge. About the key I will not presently speak.

My companion placed me onto a bed, though I would not know it was a trundle bed until morning. I had only vague notions as to how we had arrived at the cunningly thatched cottage, but I believe we had walked through the forest in search of safety. Perhaps we sought some gentle corner where we would not perish at the hands of those who pursued us. Or had we been banished from a kingdom I no longer recall?

The room in which my companion put me to bed was the smallest and least furnished of all. It lay, strangely enough, down a long hallway and up a stairway—I say "strangely" because the house was so diminutive from outside. I realized, upon waking in the morning, that I lay in a turret. Yet from outside, no curved wall was visible. With its thatched roof the house had resembled a square Christmas package, a gift for a favorite stuffed rabbit—a perfect dollhouse of a cottage, the sort I had painstakingly, as a child, decorated with wallpaper, curtains, and beds.

Though there was scarcely any furniture in this turret room, the sparse pieces were exactly correct—nothing more, nothing less: the trundle bed, empty and open; and the walls bedecked with no other ornamentation or decoration save whitework, the same sampler embroidered with the same message over and over. It was embroidered in French, which I do not speak: *Hommage à Ma Marraine*. In the center of each piece of linen was sewn an image of a priest holding two blackbirds, one on each hand. The edges of all the whitework were tattered, and some even had holes. To these white-on-white sewings, my foggy mind immediately fastened, with an idiot's interest—so intently that when my dear companion came up to the turret with a hard roll and coffee for breakfast, I became very angry with him for interrupting my studies.

What I was able to discern, looking about me while nibbling the roll after my companion had left, was that some of the whitework contained a single gold thread as the accent over the *a*. Why the gold thread was used, I had no idea; and in considering this detail, along with the remarkable fact that blackbirds had been so expertly depicted in white, I finally asked my companion to return to the room. I called him and called him before he returned—disconcertingly, for it seemed he had returned only by accident, to fetch my empty teacup—and when he took the cup from my hand he gazed into it for a very long time without speaking a word.

At last, he closed the shutters of the windows tight, which was my wish, as it allowed me to see the whitework more clearly: I find I see better in the dark. A candle in the shape of a bluebird sat on the floor beside the bed, and I lit it, and turned it just-so, toward the wall. Luminous! I felt I had not, in many years, experienced such nocturnal bliss—even though the broad daylight shone outside the curtained windows, at least as broad as a day may shine in a deep and thickly wooded forest where real and grave danger does lurk.

This activity transfixed me for hours upon hours and days upon days.

In time, my companion and I so well established ourselves in the cottage that soon we felt that we had lived there our entire lives. I presume we had *not* lived there our entire lives, yet of the event that drove us into the forest to the cottage I cannot speak, and not only because I cannot recall it. But I can tell you that we had so well established ourselves in this cottage that I was shocked one morning to discover, under my feather pillow, a miniature book that had not been there before. It purposed to criticize and describe the whitework on the walls.

Bound in black velvet, with a pink ribbon as a placeholder, the volume fit precisely in the palm of my hand, just as if it had been bound for me to hold there. Long, long I read, and devoutly, devotedly I gazed. Rapidly and gloriously the hours flew by, and then the deep midnight came. (Not that I knew the day from night with the curtains so tightly drawn.) The bluebird was guttering—just a puddle of blue now, with yellow claws fashioned from pipe cleaners protruding from the edges of the blue puddle. I reached my hand out to try to build the wax once more into the form of a bird, but I achieved merely a shapeless mass of color. Regardless, the candlelight flamed up and shone more brightly than ever upon the black velvet book with onionskin pages.

In my zeal to illumine the onionskin, the better to learn about *Ma Marraine* and so on, I had, with the candle's light, also illumined the corners of the room, where sat the mousetraps. Yes, this turret had corners—quite a remarkable thing, as the room was a circle. If I failed to perceive the corners before, I cannot explain . . . truly this architectural marvel of corners was a marvel inside a marvel, since even the turret itself was not visible from outside.

With the corners of the room thus illumined, I now saw very clearly in one corner, behind a mousetrap, a very small portrait of a young girl just ripening into womanhood. I don't know how that phrase comes to me—"ripening into womanhood"—for I would prefer simply to describe the portrait as a very small portrait of a young lady. But, to continue, I could not look at the painting for long. I found I had to close my eyes as soon as I saw the portrait— why, I have no idea, but it seems to be that my injury, rather than being limited to my crippled legs, had crept inward to my mind, which had become more . . . impulsive or secretive, perhaps. I forced my eyes back on the portrait again.

It was nothing remarkable, more a vignette than an exposition. The girl was depicted from top to bottom, smudged here and there, fading into the background, reminiscent somehow of the *Kinder- und Hausmärchen*—yes, you could describe her portrait as an illustration. She was a plain girl, not unlike me. Her eyes were sullen, her hair lank and unwashed, and even in the face and shoulders you could see she was undernourished—also not unlike me. (It is not my intention to plead my case to you or to anyone else, now or in the future; I merely *note* the resemblance.)

Something about the girl's portrait startled me back to life. I had not even realized what a stupor I'd lain in, there in the turret, but looking into her sullen eyes, I awoke. My awakening had nothing to do with the girl herself, I believe, but rather with the bizarre execution of this portrait, this tiny portrait—no bigger than that of a mouse, yet life-size. And it was painted entirely white upon white, just like the embroidery on the walls.

Though I felt more awake and alive than ever before, I found that I was also suddenly overcome with sadness. I don't know why, but I do know that when my companion brought me my nightly black coffee, I sent him away for a pitcher of blueberry wine. I asked for him also to bring me a pink-flowered teacup. My needs felt at once more urgent and delicate, and thankfully he was able to find articles in the cupboards that satisfied them.

For quite some time, drinking the wine, I gazed at the portrait of the sullen girl staring out of miniature eyes. At length, wholly unsatisfied with my inability to decipher the true secret of the portrait's effect (and apparently unaware that I very nearly was standing), I fell into the trundle. I turned my frustrated attentions back to the small book I had found under the pillow. Greedily, I turned its onionskin pages to the girl's portrait. "Flat, unadorned," the page read. The rest of the description was missing—everything except a peculiar exclamation for an encyclopedia to contain:

SHE WAS DEAD!

"And I died." Those are the words that came to my head. But I did not die then, nor did I many days and nights later, there in the forest, where I lived with my companion quite happily—not as husband and wife, yet neither as siblings: I cannot quite place the relation.

Soon, of course, I thought of nothing else but the girl in the painting. Nightly my companion brought me a teacup of blueberry wine, and nightly I drank it, asked for another, and wondered: *Who was she? Who am I?* I expected no answer—nay, nay, I did not wish for one either. For in my *wonder* I possessed complete satisfaction.

It was of no surprise to me, so accustomed to confusions, that one morning I awoke to find the painting vanished—and not only the painting but all the little priests with the little birds from the walls. No whitework, no turret, no companion. No blueberry wine. I found myself in a different small and dark room, again on a bed (not a trundle). An old woman and a doctor sat by my side.

"Poor dear," the old woman murmured. She added that I would do well to take courage. As you may imagine, the old woman and doctor were at once subjected to the greatest of my suspicions; and as I subjected them privately, I also protested publicly, for I knew I had done nothing to lose all I had learned to love there in that mysterious prison or home. No: I should have been very happy to be lame and blurred, to have my companion bring me teacups of wine at night, and in the morning my coffee and rolls. I never minded that the rolls were so tough to the bite that my teeth had become quite loose in their sockets, as loose as my brain or the bluebirds in the forest when their nests are looted by ravens.

Cheerfully, the doctor spoke over my protests. He said that my prognosis relied on one thing, and one thing alone: to eliminate every gloomy idea. He pointed toward a room I had not noticed before.

"You have the key to the Library," he said. "Only be careful what you read."

JUDY BUDNITZ

Abroad

The trip was not going as planned. The train was supposed to take us to the white-sand beaches and white hotels high on cliffs and the burnished tans that we could step into and zip up like a second skin. Instead it deposited us in this place where all the buildings looked covered with smudgy fingerprints and the only water in sight was running in the gutters. The sky was overcast, lumpy, a poorly plastered ceiling.

The guidebook says there's a railroad museum here, I said. And a bone church.

We weren't supposed to stop here, he said. He went up to the ticket agent caged behind a wire grill and spoke with him and came back and said: The next train's in three days.

Three days?

If you don't believe me then you go ask him.

Oh, but I don't want to bother him, I said.

So we went to see the bone church. If you can believe it, that's exactly what it was—a church made entirely of the bleached skulls and preserved leg bones of some very old people. A row of skulls arched over the door. They all looked alike; I would not have thought that people's bones were so uniform you could stack them up like bricks.

He saw my face and said: Don't be sad, I think they were already dead. That was his idea of a joke.

We were the only people there except for the boy at the entrance, who held out his hand for our admission money. His shorts were too short, his sweater too big for him. A cigarette drooped from his mouth. He spoke sharply at us, I could not understand a word. His face was unreadable, hard and perfectly immobile, as if the bones were on the outside.

Don't give him money, I said.

Why not?

How do you know he works here? I mean, he's not wearing a . . . a *badge* or anything. He could be anyone.

So what?

How do we know our money's going to the, the bone-church people? He's probably going to keep it for himself.

So what if he does? He's probably related to these bones one way or another. *Look* at him.

I looked and it was true: the boy's head belonged up there with the others. A face hard enough to break your hand.

We spoke in whispers when we went inside. Because of the boy. We whispered because we did not want him to feel left out.

I was surprised by how white they were. I expected old bones to have the stained yellow of a smoker's teeth. To go inside was like stepping inside the rib cages of a thousand people, hearing their phantom heartbeats fluttering around like moths, or like strolling through the whale skeleton at the natural history museum.

There's a blister on my heel, I said. But these shoes never gave me trouble before.

What are you complaining about now?

Nothing.

Behind the bone church lay a cemetery, which seemed superfluous: why put them in the ground when you could add another wing? I wanted to take a picture but thought it would be rude, like photographing sleeping people. I had bought a camera for the trip, an expensive snouty thing I did not know how to use.

The buses were white and red and did not seem to have any scheduled stops. You had to stand directly in their path to get their attention.

These people, I don't know what to make of them, he said. Their faces are so old, but not in the usual way. They seem to age from the outside in rather than the inside out; rather than a sagging and puckering, it's a buildup of deposits. It's as if anything that life's ever thrown at them has hit them in the face and stuck there.

Your pants are too short, I said.

What's wrong with my pants?

They're wrong. Nobody else's pants look like yours.

I think the problem was in the way he wore them, the set of his hips. They demanded attention, those pants. They were swaggering pants. The men we saw on the streets all had a slow, low-stepping shuffle, as if they'd wet themselves.

We saw no restaurants. What, do these people never eat? That is why they seem so pure and walk so slowly. We asked some local people, who looked at our clothes and directed us to the McDonald's.

Perhaps they misunderstood us. We did not want to be the kind of abrasive tourists who think that if they speak their own language loudly enough the locals will eventually understand. So instead we spoke apologetically, fumblingly, as if our own language was foreign to us.

A place . . . to eat? Food . . . restaurant? Sit down, inside?

He mimed hands to mouth, a waiter with a tray, pulling out a chair, made the universal check-please gesture.

They were not fooled.

The night came down suddenly, like a lid being clapped on. We found our hotel; we had not been looking for it but there it was. Our landmark was the woman in dark glasses with her flower stand across the street.

Why are flower sellers always blind? he said.

They're born that way, I said.

She waved at us and smiled.

We climbed the stairs to our room; they were so steep we had to use our hands. I looked closely at each stair and each one had a different kind of debris: buckles, beads, beetles. I wanted to lie down and sleep right there. I was exhausted. What do these people want from me? To make me climb all these stairs!

Our room was tall, like two rooms stacked on top of each other, and dark. There was a bulb set in the ceiling, but it was so far away its light gave up and died before it reached us where we lay on the bed. There was a long slice of window that ran from floor to ceiling and showed us the spires and towers and crested weather vanes of a city we had never seen before.

It's just a travel poster, he said and tried to scrape off a corner.

We had thought that making love in a strange place, between foreign sheets, would bring us together. But the bed seemed determined to keep us apart. It didn't sag in the middle; it had a sort of hump that kept us sliding away from each other.

I felt more familiar with his body than with his face; his body was finite, known, a region explored and mapped and marked with little dots indicating theaters and hot nightspots and restaurants with easy menus.

What's this? he asked.

You know . . . my appendix scar.

What's *this*?

I don't want to talk about that. Don't touch it.

Did you hear about that woman? he said. Now he was touching

the lump of fat on my hip. The rest of my body isn't so fat, just that one place. Why does he have to touch me there?

What woman? I said.

The train . . . I think she was a tourist.

Was she pretty? Was she thinner than me?

I don't know. It was in the paper. She was waiting for the underground. With her husband. They were on their honeymoon, people thought. She had a yellow dress. They were waiting for the train, and she was a tourist, you know, she didn't understand how fast the trains come, and how close, and this one didn't have its lights on for some reason. And she was holding her husband's hand. She was leaning out.

I bet he pushed her!

Why do you say things like that? She fell, and the train came and sliced her clean in half. And this is the strange part. The conductor realizes what's happened and brakes the train. The husband is standing on the platform, and half of the woman's body is on one side of the tracks, half on the other, and the train in between. All the husband can see are her legs. He knows he doesn't have time to dash around either end of the train to be with her head so he leaps off the platform and runs to her legs and holds them, caresses them. Like this.

Oh don't. That's sick.

And the strangest part, the reason I'm telling you this, is that the people on the opposite platform, the ones that could see her head, they *swore* she could feel him, she knew he was touching her. She said his name. Even though the rest of her body was ten feet away. Isn't that amazing?

Did she die?

Well of course she died. But that's not the point.

I think those people were pulling your leg. They were lying because you're a tourist. Did they try to sell you a watch next?

You don't find that story amazing? The power of love?

I think you got it wrong. I think she jumped. I think she had a sudden glimpse of how miserable her life would be, being married to that man, and she decided the only way out was to end it right then.

Why do you ruin everything? A beautiful story and you ruin it.

We slept, with the humped mattress between us and the window casting a long strip of grayish light across our bodies.

I opened my eyes and the clicking went on. Clicks and flashes of light.

What are you doing? I said.

Did you know you smile in your sleep? he said. His hands were holding the black snout to his face. He changed the focus.

Click. Flash. Blackness.

What are you doing?

Preserving the moment.

What moment? What moment?

It's gone. You just missed it.

Then I must have slept, because the next thing I knew was yellow morning light, sounds of people shouting in the street, smells of bread and garbage. I heard shrill little-girl voices singing a pop song with the words all garbled. He was sitting on the edge of the bed, rubbing his eyes in a way that would leave them red all day.

Clanking, splashes, heavy breathing. Someone was mopping the hallway, right outside the door, ready to burst in on us at any moment. These people, they won't leave you alone, not even for a minute. They're always trying to get in.

Remember when we first met? I said. We used to talk for hours.

Endlessly, he said. Interminably. It still feels like that sometimes.

Guess who, I said in his ear. His eyelashes were tickling my palms. He twisted away and stood up. I got up too.

How long have we been here? I said.

A day? Two days? I forget.

Are you going to the train museum? It's the only thing to see besides the bone church.

I'll see you tonight, he said and was gone. I sometimes wondered why he didn't just grow a mouth on the back of his head since he seemed to do all his talking turned away from me.

I was going to shower but I didn't, the people here don't seem to bathe at all and they are not too offensive; they smell of cedar, of pine straw and smoke. The young women don't wear underpants, the old women don't wash their hair, they just cover it with greasy scarves and go about their business.

The people here all understand English, they just pretend they don't. You can tell.

The blister was even bigger than the day before, an amniotic sac of salt water on my heel. But I *wanted* to wear those shoes.

The train museum was housed in an old station no longer in use, a single room; there were some photographs, maps, model trains; beer served in the back. A big box for donations. All the signs printed in their illegible backward mirror-writing. No one there. I don't care about trains but I made a point to look at everything.

On the wide front steps there were boys dressed in towels and sandals, playing soccer. I walked through the middle of their game; I did not mean to but honestly there was no other way. They were dribbling the ball up and down the steps, shouting to each other, there were complicated rules involved, some had their hair shaved close, others had hair that had never been touched but you would never mistake them for girls. They had not yet discovered Band-Aids there. Each child was a mass of scabs.

One of them came right at me and I thought I should dodge, I was in the way, but he kept coming. Hey, lady, he said. Hey, lady.

What? I said. Yes? The whites of his eyes were yellowish, jaundiced, and so was his skin, and his hair was dark blond too, he was a mustard-colored boy from head to foot. The others stopped running and listened.

Can I see your camera? he said. I thought he wanted his picture taken; I lifted it to my face and stepped back. I bumped into more boys. They had stepped up behind me. Shouldn't they be in school?

No, give it to me, he said. I thought, What kind of town is this where they've never seen a camera before? And I leaned down so I could hand him the camera without taking off the strap. This brought our faces close.

I'll buy it from you, he said. I looked at his mouth; the teeth were brown and yellow at the edges, there were gaps that were not from lost baby teeth.

He gave the camera one sharp yank and the strap broke at some weak link, and then he was off running and the rest of them with him, their cheap sandals slapping the pavement, all of them raising their hands to their throats with monkey grimaces of horror as they ran. I looked down and saw my hands doing the same, felt my face constricting. They vanished down alleyways and I felt grateful to them for at least not laughing while I could hear them.

I was not too sorry it happened, I felt relieved of a burden, until I remembered the film in the camera, the pictures I had taken from the window of the train as we arrived, the pictures he had taken in the middle of the night. So much for preserving the moment.

The sky darkened and I did not recognize anything. I did not want to take out my map, because you are not lost until you admit that you are; until then you are exploring, you are admiring scenery.

Why would I ask for directions anyway, since I can't understand a word they say and if I could I know they would only lie to me. I'd ask them for my hotel and they'd direct me instead back to the bone church, and I'd wander in circles there until I died, unable to find my way out, and with each circuit that boy would charge me more money, an admission fee for each lap around the bone church until I was bled dry and footsore and dead. Then they'd take my bones and add them to the steeple, or the pews, or they'd build a little washroom for the priest behind the altar. It's not a church of their ancestors' bones, it's the church of unwanted tourists. It is where the uninvited and uncomprehending go to die. And they'd sell my clothes as relics, as souvenirs, my shoes made into bookends, my buttons into bracelets, my blister sewn into a little change purse with a picture of the bone church embroidered on it.

I saw a group of people on a corner. Beautiful white clothes, raised voices. A pause, the slow telling of a joke, bursts of laughter. Women shifting their weight from hip to hip, men with their sleeves rolled to the elbows. They were drinking from green bottles, the mineral water which, according to the guidebook, came from a local spring and was supposed to have medicinal properties.

Then I saw the head I knew so well, the curly hair.

He was telling the joke, he was drinking the water.

Even from this distance, I could pick him out of the crowd immediately, the way you always can with a loved one, that sudden rush, that relief. I called his name but I was too far away. The people around him were too loud, they drowned me out. I walked faster and called again.

Hey, I called and started to run.

I was shouting his name now and waving my arms, I didn't care what they thought of me, what did I care? But as I got close a cab whipped around a corner and paused at the curb, and the whole mob of them swept inside, and the door slammed in my face and the car sped away. It all happened in the space of a breath.

There was a moment when my fist was against the window and his face behind it, just inches away. Our breath clouded either side of the glass at the same point. Then he turned away and all I saw were taillights.

But it could not have been him.

It was someone who looked a bit like him.

Your mind will do that sometimes when you want very badly to see someone; your mind will conjure him up before you, will draw your eye to an approximate head of hair, a close-enough pair of shoulders.

The cab was gone but it was all right because suddenly I knew these street lamps, this tobacco shop, that housedress hung out the window to dry. Here was our hotel. The flower seller waved to me again and showed her teeth. God, she looked even older than she had the day before, how did she keep going? And the woman at the front desk glared at me as if to say: What are you doing here now, this place is for sleeping and making love and you're no good at either.

The seasons here are strange and vague. It feels too grotty for spring, too humid for autumn. It's a perpetual waiting, the charged stillness before a thunderstorm. What month is it? But it doesn't matter, we crossed some significant line when we came here, didn't we, so the seasons are the reverse of what they are at home. Or did we lose a day? Gain a day?

I packed my things into my half of the suitcase. We had drawn a line down the middle of it. I wanted to be ready.

I did not hear footsteps on the stairs until evening.

Where have you been? I said.

What? he said. He said: This is Vera.

Vera had the eyes like they all do, and the hennaed hair, and thick white legs. I had never seen anything like them, perfectly smooth, hairless, solid, opaque like marble.

She said something I could not make out.

The room was too crowded, I wanted to rise up and hover in the empty space near the light fixture until I could get my bearings. His face was something I swear I had never seen before. At least the back of his head was familiar.

Come have dinner with us, he said.

Did he say it to her, or me? Which side of *us* was I on?

We drank bottles and bottles of wine, and I was fascinated by the way she ate, pulling things apart with her fingers and sucking out their insides. My throat closed up at the soup, which I swear was full of things still alive and swimming. But the candles were nice, and I felt happy and stroked and squeezed his knee under the table, and he gave me understanding looks all evening.

What are you talking about? I said.

Yes, I know, it's noisy in here, isn't it? he said.

No, I can't . . . I'm not following the conversation.

He smiled at me. You're drunk, aren't you?

He turned back to Vera but that was all right, he and I did not need to talk, we understood each other. He kept talking to her so that she would not start to feel uncomfortable, shut out. He was considerate that way.

It was not until we were leaving that I saw that what I had thought was his knee was the knobby corner of his chair.

When we went back to our hotel room Vera came with us.

She's very tired, he said. And she lives so far away.

That seemed legitimate. It seemed only right to show her some hospitality since we were guests in her country.

I tried to express this to her but she blinked her black-rimmed eyes at me impatiently and waited for him to explain. These people, they have no sense of graciousness. Maybe they have no vocabulary for *please* and *thank you*. She slept heavily, deeply, she filled the room with her breath.

The towers outside the window had grown during the day. They blocked more sky than before. I had never been able to find them when I was out walking on the streets, I could see them only from this window.

I suppose this is because the maps they give tourists are not entirely accurate. They want to steer you to certain areas so they can sell you cheap trinkets and marionettes and overpriced film and toothpaste. They want to force you through the gauntlet of jugglers and dancing bears and street artists.

He seemed very far away on the other side of the bed, I could not even feel his cold feet, or the toenails that usually scratched me during his running dreams. The hump in the mattress seemed to have grown, I could hardly see him. There was a tuft of hair, or it could have been the blanket.

Vera came out of the bathroom and asked me something unintelligible, nostrils dancing.

What?

You should try harder to understand, he scolded me. She's speaking perfectly clearly.

I'm trying, I said. When are we leaving?

I have to check the train schedule. Make some room in the suitcase for Vera.

Why?

She's bringing a few things.

But . . . why?

You can't expect her to use your things all the time, can you?

She's *coming*? What about us?

What about *us*?

His *us* seemed subtly different from mine; his seemed to involve the closed bathroom door. I was not sure, though, and did not ask again.

I did not see him again until evening, when he came back to the room with Vera and Marat. Marat's an *architecture* student, he told me confidingly. She *builds* things.

But *I* used to be an architecture student, I said desperately.

He said: You quit.

Then he said something to the two women that made them laugh. Marat had a black bob and thick bangs that covered her eyebrows and most of her eyes. She was tall and angular, not like most of the women here, but I knew she was one of them.

I watched them talking. The language has such an ugly sound, rough and rattling, they must have crenellated throats.

Marat asked to borrow some of my underwear since she had none of her own. First she asked me, and then when I didn't understand she pantomimed her request with ugly flapping gestures. She and Vera rolled their eyes and snickered.

Why are you being so rude? he said to me.

Why are *you* being so rude? I said.

Now you're just being obnoxious, he said.

Marat snored, and Vera snored. And *he* snored too. I had never noticed that before.

The next night he came bringing Vera, and Marat, and Anna and her twelve-year-old, Lars. The room was too crowded to move, the noise was unbearable. What were they all laughing about?

He moved close to me and breathed harsh gutturals in my ear.

What?

He said: Make some more room in the suitcase.

I said: There isn't any more room.

He said: You could take your things out.

But I don't want to.

Then *make* room.

But what are you doing? What about me?

What *about* you?

Don't you care?

What is it? Are you sick? Do you need a Tylenol?

No! What's going on here? I don't understand!

You don't, do you, he said. And you refuse to try.

I don't even understand anything these people are saying.

If you'd try, you'd learn. You're so self-centered.

But I *am* trying, I said. I looked at him and wondered when he had started oiling his hair and wearing his shirt unbuttoned like that, and where had he gotten that gold medallion? And when had he started speaking with an accent like that? Surely he was putting it on, as a pretension, as a joke, and we'd laugh about it later.

I am trying, I said. Are we breaking up? I whispered.

Break? Break something? he said, and I saw his eyes waver the way the eyes will when a person doesn't quite understand what you're saying but doesn't want to admit it. I know that look, I had it myself in my high school French class: Oui, oui, monsieur, les legumes sont tres cheres, il fait beau, non, non, il pleut, cette fille est belle, non? Oui, oui, madam.

Just keep nodding, smiling.

Marat and Anna lounged on the bed, Vera and Lars leaned out the window, smoking cigarettes. He left to buy wine and came back and passed it around and Marat pointed to the tulip-headed towers in the distance and I suppose she was explaining where they were and who built them and why. She was naming all the gargoyles, and I would have liked so much to know but I had no idea what she was saying.

And the next night they were back, and they brought the blind flower seller and a bartender named Yves and some girls who were too young to be of consequence, and someone's uncle who needed to leave the country right away, and they all crammed their things into the suitcase so that it became an incredible snarl of hair-dryer cords, makeup cases, diapers (because there was a baby some-where—you could smell it), rayon scarves, Walkman radios, bathing suits, rolling papers, uncooked pasta, pearl necklaces, sunglasses.

I suppose I should take out my things to make more room for the others but I don't want to, not yet; I suppose we are leaving any day now, any day. The train schedule, where did he put it? He's always losing things, it's one of his endearing quirks. This is something he and I will laugh about later, I am sure, but for now the noise is get-ting unbearable, the baby crying all night, and these people with their constant talking. What can they possibly have to say to each other?

The room is so crowded that I spend my time walking the streets. But these people everywhere, I don't know them, I don't *want* to know them, it's impossible. It's only natural to want to be with the person who understands you. True communication is the most inti-mate thing there is; you don't want to share it with everyone.

Earlier today, in a small grocery store, I stood in front of a thick-faced cashier for an hour with a package of crackers in one hand and two bills in the other. She would neither take the money nor acknowledge my presence. A standoff. I know my mouth was open, I know sounds were coming out. But I had lost the guidebook, with the native phrases spelled out phonetically. I think some boys stole it to roll homemade cigarettes with its pages.

The cashier's eyes followed a fly beating itself against the window. She was in no hurry. The shadows lengthened. Time passed. *Common cour-tesy*, a voice in my head said over and over. Common courtesy. I admired her head. A big, solid head. It would look good on the bone church.

My own skull, I realize now, would never fit in. It is too oddly shaped. Too pointy.

I suppose if it all gets to be too much I can leave, put my things in a plastic bag, get on the train with the spacious vinyl seats and the empty beer bottle rolling up and down the aisle, go on ahead to the next stop listed in the guidebook, if I can remember it, and he will catch up with me as soon as he can.

But I would hate to leave him here all alone.

The hotel room now is just a mass of bodies, cookstoves, tents, shanties, music, dancing arms and bobbing breasts, boys pitching pennies, stray dogs, the burned smell of someone curling her hair, a bazaar of stalls selling rugs and copper kettles, laundry hanging on lines overhead, the endlessly overflowing toilet. The walls are grease-stained, the bare bulb a small sun. He is still there among them, shaking hands, kissing men on both cheeks, kissing women on the lips, as is the custom here. His face is tanned mahogany brown, though as far as I can tell he never goes outside.

Every time I catch sight of him in the crowd I ask when we are leaving, and he looks past me as a stream of incoherence pours from his mouth. I am sure he just does it so as not to offend the others.

It would make them feel left out.

SARAH SHUN-LIEN BYNUM

The Young Wife's Tale

There once was a king who came to his throne only after a long period of trouble. Everyone, everywhere, felt relief that he had at last returned to them, but no one felt it more keenly than the young wives of the men whom he led. What possessed them was more than relief; it was a deep, mysterious joy that the king's return had set astir. Their husbands would no longer be leaving for war, they told themselves. Their children would grow old under the eyes of their fathers, and the land would prosper, and life would be restored to the rhythms they could not even recall. So they said to one another as they bent their heads and pounded clothes in the cold streams.

In truth, the young wives were stirred by the king's bravery, and his extraordinary beauty. Never before had they seen a man as beautiful as he. They wondered whether it was the years in exile, his time spent wandering despised and alone, that had given him his grace. His eyes said he understood all the sadness in the world, and his worn face said that he would do everything in his power to defeat it. These qualities, combined with his dark, lank hair and his roughened hands, made the young wives almost frantic with a longing they couldn't describe. But they would see it reflected in each other's flushed, stricken faces, and know that they were not alone in what they felt.

The women's love caused them to act in strange ways, some small, some not. One wife awoke in the morning, climbed from the bed, went about her tasks and heated the water, without once opening her eyes. She was reluctant to enter out of her dream. Another, in the early days of winter, would slip behind her house, take off her clothes, and stand turned to the sun, unmoving as stone. Among the youngest of the wives was a girl who disappeared for long spells into the forest. Each time she would eat a little less and roam a little farther, in the belief that she might faint at just the moment the king was striding past, and he would stoop down to the ground, lift her up in his arms, and revive her. Why she believed this was a mystery. The king did not hunt in these woods, nor did he travel alone anymore, nor did he travel on foot. Maybe she was searching for the exiled king, the sorrowful king, and believed she would find him in this forest. But he would be at once the king adrift and the king redeemed, because look, in her dream, how he lifts her from the ground.

In time, the king died and passed into legend. He was remembered in songs and paintings and books, and then for a long while he was forgotten, as the paintings blackened and the books moldered and other, shorter songs came into fashion. Such a very long time went by, it seemed possible that the king and his hard struggles, the peace that followed, would be forever lost, as if his beauty had never existed, and he had never walked this earth or looked up at this sky. But there was an old university where, one night, a scholar discovered the king, either in a trance or in the stacks of the library, and once again his story came to light. First, he appeared in a pair of essays, then a book whose unlooked-for appeal inspired several more volumes, followed by rock-and-roll albums and animated cartoons, underground fanzines and doctoral dissertations, and, finally, a film.

In this last incarnation, the king began again to disturb the young wives of the world. There were so many pleasures to be had as a young wife—the new towels and sheets, the espresso machine, the warm, receptive body waiting in the bed—and at first this seemed merely one of them. Two women together, confessing the terrible love they felt for their husbands, so much deeper and sharper than they ever expected to feel, could then pour fresh cups of coffee, pick up crumbs off the new yellow dishes with the moistened tips of their fingers, and proceed to speak gravely of their feelings for the king without suffering the slightest twinge of foolishness or betrayal. They took it as one of the privileges of marriage. They laughed when other women, their still-unmarried friends, suggested it was a movie actor who provoked in them their peculiar hunger. Because hadn't they seen him a hundred times before, as a cowboy drifter, an army sergeant, a sidekick, a painter having an affair? It was not an actor they thought of. Their thoughts belonged wholly to the brave, ravaged, beautiful king.

Eva believed in the beginning that he reminded her of her husband, and she told him so. He smiled at her in such a way to show he was grateful, but also that he disagreed. Don't you see it? Eva asked. She was full of adoration for him. For the way his feet sounded coming up the stairs, the way he kept himself so clean-smelling and neat, for the solo dances he'd perform on the carpet when he was happy. Countless ways and things she adored, innumerable as the stars. Things that of course existed before they were married, but to which she could now fully surrender, abandoning herself to wonder. How did she ever. How did she ever. She could not account for her fortune. She could only note that she had, unaware, held part of her self in suspension before, and now she had let go. The fall was slow, luxurious, and seemingly infinite. It refused to be described. She was reduced to murmuring, almost against her will: You are the best. Words impoverished of their meaning, used most often to thank a person to whom one's not truly indebted, but when Eva uttered them to her husband, she asked the words to carry the full weight of her astonishment. She wasn't ever confident they did.

A paradox of growing so close to another person was the doubt that you could impart to them the very closeness that you felt. Eva would awake in the night, feeling someone's breath on her forehead, hearing someone beside her ask, Do you know how much your husband loves you? Do you know?

Eva would sigh and burrow more deeply next to him, then descend into a dream about the king. He was drawing his sword from his belt. He was turning to face an enemy. The look on his face was grim, and the circle of motion his body described—rough hand on hilt, arm sweeping up, torso pivoting in the direction of danger—had a poem's grace, its balance and frugality. There was the clang of metal meeting. The hissing sound of tempered weapons slicing through the air. More enemies, their black helmets dull in the brilliant sunlight, came swarming down the wooded slope. They yelped and they whooped, they beat their drums and bared their rotting teeth like dogs, but the expression on the king's face did not change. One by one he felled his enemies, pressing in on him from all sides, with a bleak patience and determination. Eva flattened herself against a tree and quaked. Not once in her dream did she fear for the king, but she felt acutely the overwhelming odds against him, the extreme peril, the thrill. He would not die, but he might come close. The bark of the tree bit into her skin, her fingers were sticky with pitch, the pine needles yielded beneath her feet. The next time that Eva awoke, in the darkness of the bedroom, her heart was beating very fast.

The mornings made her sad. She didn't like saying good-bye to her husband when he left for work. She held on to him tightly, and he said to her, We'll see each other tonight. I know, she sighed, but that seems far away from now. And it was true, the days were long. He was a resident in emergency medicine. He was a lawyer for legal aid. He wrote articles about changes in technology, for which he was paid, and also articles about wars in Africa, for which he was not paid. He worked in a record shop and composed strange, haunting music. It didn't matter. He was doing something good. Eva, also, had a job. She had high hopes for herself. For both of them. They were traveling the distance, in very small, sometimes imperceptible increments, between where they found themselves now and where they desired one day to be. Soon. It wasn't happening quickly enough. You're getting there, they told each other. With brightness in their voices, a true conviction. Over and over they told one another, You're a rock star. Fuck them. What do they know. You're kicking ass. I mean it. We're getting there. Soon.

Eva would see the king when she stepped onto the bus in the mornings. Then she would see him again in the lap of the little boy sitting across from her on the aisle. She would see him behind the glass at the newsstand, and as he flew raggedly down the length of a block. When she walked to the bank she saw him, hair tangled and sword raised, looking out across the city from the top of an office building. Somehow he remained irreducibly himself, even when miniaturized on a lunch box, or multiplied in the pages of a magazine, or flattened and stretched across the side of a bus. Though she saw him everywhere, her spirit would still leap in surprise at the sight of him. Then her heart would unfurl, in petals of flame, and she would burn with a clear, consuming light.

At its peak, before it extinguished itself, the fire made Eva's vision sharpen. She perceived what was beautiful and fierce in the man who drove the bus, his supple fingers tapping against the wheel, and the man beside her in the elevator, who nodded at her kindly, almost caressingly, before he stepped off at the seventh floor, and the man she saw from her window, crossing the street against the traffic light, a small limp in his step. She stared at each of them and realized, I could love you. The thought filled her with courage.

She wondered if everyone around her might feel it, her valor and love, radiating off her like heat. But as quickly as it flared up, her insight faded, and all that remained were the ashes, the unremarkable faces of men.

The nights also made Eva sad sometimes. She tried luring her husband into staying up late, with the promise of movies or cake batter or card games. I don't want to go to sleep yet, she'd say as her eyelids grew heavier and heavier. Yet the new sheets were so exquisitely soft. And the blanket her cousins had brought back from Wales. Their bed was an abyss into which she could not help but precipitously fall. She clasped his arm, knowing that to sleep was to leave one another for a while. I'll be right here, he said. I'm not going anywhere. And she said wistfully, I know! Sleep well. I'll see you in the morning.

Her husband shook his head. She could hear his hair rubbing back and forth on the pillowcase. I'll probably see you before then, he said. You have a funny habit of showing up in my dreams. You're always hanging around.

He said it with exasperation, but he didn't mean it. Together they had developed a talent for hanging around. How else could they have built their wealth of solace and closeness and ease? They lived surrounded by the dear familiar. Eva had been folding laundry when he asked her to marry him. He had been warming leftover noodles on the stove. On the television played a spooky show that they liked, whose characters and conflicts they knew so well, had seen so many times, that they could drift in and out of conversation, or become absorbed with the task of mating socks, of stirring pans, to still return and feel they hadn't missed anything at all. When Eva turned around to glance at the screen, she nearly fell over her husband, who was on his knees among the washcloths and the turtlenecks still spread across the floor. He opened his hand, like a magician about to make a coin disappear, and there sat a ring. Her grandmother's ring; she recognized it at once. But how did it ever end up in his hand? There had been forethought, conspiracy! Her very soul rushed forward to meet him. She dropped to the floor and they held one another, laughing and weeping, with all the beloved things of their life arrayed about them, the butter popping in the pan, the detective muttering on the television, the water stain from the leak last winter floating on the ceiling above their heads.

Recounting the moment later, she shivered at the possibility that it could have happened differently. I would have been embarrassed! she cried. A dimly lit restaurant, a horse-drawn carriage? A banner pulled by a propeller plane across the sky? Some women she knew had become engaged on faraway beaches, strolling underneath the moon. Ugh, she said. It was horrible to contemplate. There were so many opportunities for the process to go awry. She felt lucky her husband had asked the right way, the solely acceptable way, which was exactly the way that he had.

But saying so was obvious. For if he had asked in a different manner, if he had taken her to the top of a mountain, or buried the ring in a chocolate dessert, then he would be a different person, and she would never have married him, now would she.

Would she?

With a pang she remembered the dizzying sensation she had felt while walking through the city. Anything was possible. Anything, more dangerously, was imaginable. Why was it so easy to feel the bus driver's hand holding her own, as he led her up the crumbling stoop to meet his father? And how did she know that the man on the elevator preferred his eggs soft in the middle, served on little dry triangles of toast? Every glance, every encounter, contained within it a dark, expanding universe of intimacies, exploding like dandelion fluff at her slightest breath, flying up and drifting about and taking stubborn root somewhere. Which was why she understood, with absolute certainty, that the slightly lame, foolhardy fellow, the one riskily crossing the street, would, if given the chance, bury his head between her legs, inhale, and utter indecipherable words of joy, making every inch of her vibrate with the sound.

Did you hear me?

Yes, yes, I heard you, she says and sinks her hands into the damp head of hair, lightly closing her eyes, feeling her body hum, wondering how did she ever—

Eva?

Her husband was propped up on his elbow, looking at her curiously.

You asleep? he asked.

That night she dreamt once more of the king. He heaved open the oaken doors to the hall and hung there, his bent figure thrown into shadow, before he staggered through. The men gathered in the great hall stopped what they were doing and turned to him and stared. They seemed hardly to recognize their king, his face filthy, his eyes haggard, his lean body stooped with exhaustion and pain. It was as if they could scarcely believe he was not dead. A young boy was the first to come to his senses and run forward to the king, who hesitated, then laid his hand, with a sigh, upon the child's shoulder. Rousing themselves from their disbelief, the men sent up a shout. The king had come home. His enemies, who had snatched him from the battlefield, could not keep him. The voices of his men echoed through the hall, but the king did not share in their rejoicing. He smiled at them faintly. Leaning on the boy, he limped to a dark corner, sank down on a bench, tipped his head back against the stone, and closed his eyes. Eva stood pressed behind a pillar, close enough to see how his face twitched with grief. She looked down and found she was carrying a basin of water, its cool weight trembling slightly in her hands. The water, she knew, was meant for the king. But before she could move to him, a hush fell over the hall, the men parting as another walked slowly through their midst and with quiet steps approached the body resting on the bench. The man was tall, his hair gray, and when he stood before the king, he seemed to cover him with light. My lord, the man said, in a voice of such gentleness that the king then opened his eyes. His face showed his struggle to understand what he saw. You fell, the king whispered. The older man looked at him with love. Yes, the man said, but I did not die. And from the king's face his pain dropped away, and wonder took its place, for his old friend had been returned to him.

The moment was broken by the sound of water dripping. Eva gazed down at the bowl in her hands. Then she woke, in the darkness of the bedroom, feeling wetness on her cheeks, pooled in the cups of her ears. She heard a voice beside her, whispering. Eva, it said. Eva, it asked in soft dismay, why are you crying?

In the morning, it was her husband who held on tightly. He looked back up at her as he circled down the stairs. When he reached the bottom, out of sight, he called to her, as if he wasn't sure she'd still be there. He told her to have a very good day. He told her to say hello for him to her friend. I will, she shouted into the stairwell, I will. The front door scraped open, lingered a moment, and then swung shut with a gasp.

As her husband had asked, Eva delivered his special hello to her friend. She was a young wife herself, and pregnant. Her doctor had offices in the part of the city where Eva worked, so after her appointment they would sometimes meet at a restaurant and eat together. Generally speaking, her friend had an exceptional appetite, but now she stared down sadly at her food.

She said, I bet this looks delicious to you.

Eva shook her head.

What? Her friend lit up. Are you pregnant too?

Eva shook her head again, and smiled.

Oh, her friend subsided. You got my hopes up. I thought for a minute I wasn't alone.

You're not alone, Eva said.

She found her friend disturbing to behold. Her face appeared both drawn and puffy at the same time. Tiny blossoms of burst blood vessels had broken out along her cheeks and the delicate skin above her breasts. Her hair—all over, she said—had turned coarser. All day she stroked her stomach without knowing it, though her belly had only just emerged.

We have a favorite, she said. I want to know what you think. Alice.

I like it, Eva said. And what if it's a boy?

Her friend spoke the musical name of the king, and a shudder passed between them.

Can you imagine? her friend asked, for a moment on fire. She remembered herself. No, really it's Jack.

I like that too, Eva said.

The waiter took their plates away, untouched.

Her friend dropped her head into her hands. I'm tired, she said. How did this happen to me? I'm tired all the time.

Eva didn't know what to say. She reached across the table and rested her hand on the woman's arm.

Her friend glanced up, brightened, and began to scold. You didn't eat anything. That's unforgivable. You're going to disappear before our eyes. Don't you dare do that when I'm blowing up like a balloon.

After they had finished wrapping themselves in their coats and their scarves, her friend kissed her on both cheeks. One is for you, she said, and the other is for him.

As her friend had asked, Eva bestowed a kiss upon her husband. He was already asleep when she came home. She lit a candle and studied him as he lay sleeping in their bed. He too possessed his own share of beauty, or so she had thought in the beginning, and so she was repeatedly still told. Many people, men and women both, found his looks worth noting. But she could no longer see what they spoke of. She saw only the face most familiar to her, the most dear. It was as if, over time, her tender stare had sifted over his face and settled there—on his forehead, his eyelids, his cheekbones, his mouth—hiding from her what was beautiful in him.

She had thought, like Psyche, like all the other curious young wives, that she might creep up on her husband while he lay unconscious, a small circle of light hovering in her hand, and spy the secret face that had for so long remained invisible to her. Psyche had believed she would find a serpent. Another wife, a troll. And what did they find but Beauty. Their fair husbands had vanished like smoke. But why should Eva think of those old stories? The magnificent castles, the unseen servants. Imagine those wives in an apartment! Could enchantment take hold among the recycling bins, the sickly houseplants, the student-loan letters? When the match sparked and the wick flared, all Eva saw was her husband's face, neither stunning nor monstrous. The face that she loved. Wax did not drip from her candle; the spell went unbroken. He stayed right where he was, fast asleep.

For the first time, the king appeared alone in Eva's dream, standing atop a dry and windy hill. His cloak flapped roughly about his legs, and above him the sky glowed with a strange luminosity. Heavy gray clouds moved low and swift over a scrim of sheer, pearly, roseate light. The clouds were edged in gold and vermilion, and seemed to portend that some stirring, unknowable change was on its way. But the king did not gaze at the mysterious sky, the dark gilded clouds sweeping overhead. He kept his eyes fixed on the barren ground. He ran his open hand over a brittle tuft of grass, he turned a small stone over with his boot. Suddenly he fell to his knees, his cloak gusting up behind him, and brought his face close to the turf. What he found excited him. Hurrying on in an urgent, uneven gait, half scrambling, half running, trying to stay low to the ground, the king followed a path of signs discernible only to him. Eva could not guess what he was seeking. Her perspective was puzzling: in one blink she saw the king as a distant figure, stark against the toiling sky, and in another she could see the tiny flecks of brightness in the stone he overturned. Where am I? she wondered, and at the very moment the question arose, she felt beneath her palms the cool, papery surface of a birch. She was lost in a stand of ravishingly white, naked trees. And at the very moment she knew she was lost, she also understood she would be found. It was she the king was searching for. Stepping through the pale trees, their white arms touching her, she drew closer and closer until at last she appeared on the edge of the wood, the wind filling her nightgown like a sail. The king looked up from the ground and saw her.

Then Eva awoke, in the darkness of the bedroom. Her heart had slowed to a languorous throb. She felt as if she were surfacing from a sleep that resembled, or perhaps preceded, death. She wanted to reach for the hand of her husband, but found herself too entranced, too abandoned, to do so. Though she could not lift her head, she became dimly aware of a reddish gleam at the foot of the bed, and wondered if, having dreamt this dream, she was destined to go up in flames, the bed a pyre, a shimmering blanket of fire enfolding her. But she was not. Through the lowered veil of her lashes, she made out embers burning in a grate; through the remnants of her dream, she smelled the ancient scent of wood smoke, she heard the ticking of cinders falling into ash. Opening her eyes, she saw above her a low ceiling, black beams of wood, a small window hanging bright and faceted as a jewel. The room was not her own. Her husband was not beside her.

In the first days of the king, there was a girl who wandered far into the forest. At dusk she would come home, with scratched face and torn skirts and brambles stuck like pins in her hair, to find her husband sitting before a hearth gone cold, a dirty pot caked with gruel. But how his eyes would shine when she appeared! He draws out her seat, he brings in water, he makes her a thin soup, which she plays with, with her spoon. She smiles at him shyly, saying, I think I lost my sense of time.

One evening, the dusk turns into darkness and still the girl has not returned. Her husband runs to the edge of the forest, a torch in his hand. All night he searches for her, the legions of trees looming around him, and by morning he stumbles out from the woods, bewildered and afraid, having found no sign of her. The other wives are washing clothes in the stream. They bend down farther over their work, as if by doing so they might make themselves invisible.

The young husband approaches them, his face a wound, his voice hoarse when he asks them, Have you seen her? The women, up to their elbows in cold water, shake their heads. They are silent.

Eva imagined the silence into which her husband would awake. She imagined his voice in the empty room, saying her name. She heard, clearly, the variations he would use—Evita? Evuncular?—time's elaborations, the joyful, thoughtless ornamenting of the word he most liked to say. The names would chime and shiver in the air. Evel Knievel? he would ask, and there would be no answer. She had been taken too far away.

In a strange bed, in a strange room, she felt the anguish of her husband as her own. It felt like knives, like rats gnawing, like broken glass, like poison bubbling—no, it felt like something else. Exactly. All it took were two slippery pills, swallowed at the clinic, and then a bus ride home and straight into bed. The pain began as a little pang in her gut, and then—whoosh!—she was possessed by it. Her husband (not yet her husband) knelt beside the bed with a cool washcloth in his hand as she writhed around like a snake, sweating through the sheets. And just as swiftly it was over. The pain disappeared and the bleeding began. The whole thing lasted only an afternoon. In the evening the two of them walked around the neighborhood, eating ice cream. To say they had made a decision would suggest that they had needed to have a conversation. Neither one had said, Given the smallness of our apartment, and the narrowness of the stairs. Considering where we are in our lives . . . She didn't even have to mention her wedding dress, which was already paid for, already fitted, sitting hugely and steadfastly on her credit card. It was made of silk organza and floated up behind her when she moved. It was the color of champagne.

In this strange bed, in this close room, beneath the tiny jewel of a window, she thought of her husband and felt again the ache of that dreamlike afternoon. Or at least she did for a little while. A shockingly, shamefully little while. For how could she stay sad when the king himself was watching her, sitting alert by the fire? As she saw his dark eyes gleaming in the light, her sorrow for her husband dwindled into a low, melancholy note above which her false heart trilled. The king! The brave and ravaged and beautiful king. What might he say to her? What might he see? There was always the possibility he could love her, wasn't there? There was always the possibility. If her young marriage had taught her anything, it was that. The surprise, the stark miracle of love, bent in her direction. So why not the king, watching silently from his chair?

She felt his eyes move over her, touching each part of her deliberately, like a hand.

The next time Eva awoke, in the darkness of the bedroom, her heart was brimming, beating lightly as a bird's. The heaviness that had pulled on her was lifted. She yawned enormously, stretching her limbs to the far corners of the bed. At the end of the room a ruddy light glowed, but rising up onto her elbows, she saw that it belonged to the unsteady street lamp outside her apartment window. And above her was her ceiling, still haunted by the water stain. The crooked blinds. The seething radiator. Did the sound of its spitting mean she was back? The dream over? More likely, more tormenting, the dream continued, and she had simply been ejected from it. For there sat her umbrella, her shoes. There lay the novel she was reading, prostrate on the floor. Her crumpled socks. His swaybacked boots. His corduroy pants, upright and perfectly accordioned. They spoke of the lovely, unflustered motion with which he had loosened them, allowed them to drop down the length of his legs, neatly stepped clear of them, and then plunged into the bed. Her husband. His watch resting on the bureau. His stack of hermetically sealed comic books. The photograph of his mother and father and sisters on the wall. His harmonica glinting. His collection of fortune cookie fortunes in a jar. All the things about him she adored, infinite and ordinary as the stars.

She reached for his hand. She slid her foot across the sheets, seeking his leg. She rolled over voluptuously, in anticipation of the warm obstacle that would stop her. But she rolled, unhindered, all the way to the edge. Nothing prevented her, nothing held. She had the cool expanse entirely to herself. Her husband was no longer there.

He's coming right back, she thought. He'll be here in a heartbeat.

Because maybe he wanted a glass of water, or else drank too many before he went to bed. Maybe he heard footsteps on the stairs, and was waiting, dictionary raised, behind the door. Maybe he was saving them. Maybe he was thirsty. Or maybe, like her, he had fallen in love—with the gypsy queen and her raven hair. The tiny girl tucked inside a tulip. The mermaid, the shield maiden, the daughter crying from the tower. Maybe it was the siren who had called to him. And maybe he had answered, and was gone.

LUCY CORIN

The Entire Predicament

My head hovers over the floor, and my hair dangles, and my foot teeters near my ear, and my backside is exposed. I'm separated. I'm gagged and behind my gag I can't feel my voice. Homebound, on my very own threshold, I am of two minds or more about most things. I am of no mind about the rest, suspended, here in the doorway, within a network of ropes. I'm dangling upside down, one foot bound to the door frame, an arm bending somewhere behind my back, another hip rotated, thigh stretching toward my ear, knee bent, a foot hovering somewhere above it. I have never felt so asymmetrical.

A bird yaks from a tree in the yard behind me. Bright air moves like a thousand singing bees as I breathe. I can release my head and look at the floor or I can raise it and gaze across my house. I can see beyond the living room, past the breakfast bar, into the shining kitchen, and beyond that, through the glass doors to my pool fuming with chemicals. Expensive house, cheaply made. Inside, the doors are hollow, the knobs brass plated. Nick a wall and it crumbles.

I've lost the education I worked so hard for, or at least, it turns out I know nothing. My money is down the drain; I can see my last dollar from here, where I swing in the doorway, shifting my weight enough to revolve; I can see it blooming in the kitchen sink. My dog caught two rabbits in the backyard, finally, after years of failure. He slung them in a bundle over his shoulder and went packing.

My country's at war, and I don't mean venereal disease.

I swing here, hung, dumb, limb after limb, by hook and crook, bound, naked, open. I'm also turning. I moon every direction I don't face as I turn. I moon the blank world out my front door, and then I moon the desirable open floor plan inside. I moon my living room and its seven broad windows, and I moon the kitchen beyond it, mirrored deep in the appliances. I moon the patio set beyond the sliding glass doors. Sunshine hums in the windows and gushes along the walls, bounces and lolls on the flanks of my overturned furniture, the coffee table warming its belly, the sofa slashed, stuffing bulging, books like fallen moths, bits of china and glass from the buffet doors fairy-dusting my Pergo floors and tasseled throw pillows. How many hours has it been since my sunny eggs winked from their squares of toast? Since the tongue of my dog splashed in his water dish, since I sprinkled confetti for the fish, since my daughter donned her red boots and tromped to the school bus with bows in her hair and my husband, the dumb lug, backed over the roses on his way into town for the bacon? Enough hours for my hands to grow rubbery in their rope cuffs, for blood to fill my ears to bursting, my eyes rolling in their humble sockets, my brain rocking in its everlasting bath. How many hours since my dear withdrew himself from my cozy body and flopped onto his back in the moonlight, his grin sliding about his face, the silhouetted dots on the dotted bedroom curtains swaying in the breeze as I am swaying now, the motion moving them like a galaxy in a planetarium, night insects cruising and making their soft landings on the sill and on the branches of the tree that drags its nails across our shingles—

And before that the sleeping in feathers—

And before that the dog curled with the daughter in the wooden bed—

And before that the peace of nothing happening that I even thought to know of—

And before that the lives I could have led, and the cells that made me.

Anyone could see I can do nothing, nothing, but there's nobody that I can see to see me. As I turn I can look across the planks of my porch and if I tuck my chin I can see my lawn above me and the broad black band of the street with no cars parked along it because everyone's taken all their cars to work, and on errands and vacation. Or else the neighbors are cowering in their houses, cars tucked into garages with the doors squeezed shut, or else they're peeking through their windows and they can see me and I make them afraid to come out. All I can see through my windows as I pass one and then the next are boiled reflections of the ideas of the colors of things like flowers, like hedges, like lampposts, like a cloud here and then there, and that's all.

My vertebrae push at the skin of my back. My whole skeleton is apparent to me as it has never been before. It's as if I don't have the fat I have. It's as if I'm stripped of more than clothes. What's left of my breasts slides near my armpit on one side and under my chin on the other. When I turn, backside out, craned neck bulging, I feel my home and my body as intricate and intricately connected contraptions, a Rube Goldberg that produces the drip of my mere and continuing life. The ropes that stretch and support me are like the wires and pipes in the walls. My cavities are rooms, my organs are furniture, my blood, transporting air, is air. Now, truly for the first time since my babyhood, there is nothing I can do. I can cry or I can not cry. As a baby I cried, but now if I know anything I know better. I can hold my breath. I can open or I can close my eyes.

I close my eyes. Here, upside down and overbalanced, the thing that happens is not what I make happen, it's what I am within the definition of suspense. First, my shoulders ache, and next they ache more. They ache in relation to how much my neck aches which aches in relation to my ankles which ache unlike each other because of how simultaneously bent and splayed I'm hung. The only other thing that happens in the time I can witness by the wall clock in the kitchen with the rooster on its face as I pass is the ticking of my mind as it tracks the shifting pulse of my body and maneuvers around the ideas lodged in its coils. My mind is a lost snake stuffed in a bowl and pressed. My mind is a snake too crushed to strike.

I open my eyes. I am turning, upside down and tangled, as if on a vertical spit, such that window after window passes in a rhythm, and then, as I let my eyes blur, I can begin to see the walls of my square house ease into curves and soon my windows make one watery strip of blue-green world. All this motion, and I am almost used to it, time passing and nothing happening outside my body's placement within everything, in fact I am almost used to this level of pain, almost content to spin within it, when peeping into the windows I see bobbing mounds of heads of hair, and one has doffed a cap, and one has pigtails like ears on her head, and another has a blow pop in her mouth, and another has a backpack that bounces up behind him as he bounces, and another must be holding an enormous toy giraffe because the giraffe's head bobs above his head and hops with him, and nods as the boy hits the ground below the sill, and bends as the boy is rising or falling each time I pass. Children are bouncing in no particular rhythm; they're like whack-a-moles at a county fair.

I unblur my eyes a little and I can see mountains creeping up behind them, green and brown, and then the children rise in slow motion and stop, framed in groups of twos and threes in the windows, as if secreted in my shrubbery, looking into my house and at my family's things, looking at me in my doorway, backdropped by the empty street. They wiggle but are almost still, as if making every effort at a dinner table.

Are these children I know? Are they from my daughter's school? Is it a field trip? Is my daughter one of them? I just can't tell—their faces and affectations, their clothing and hairdos—all aspects I recognize but aspects arbitrarily distributed to one being and then another. As individuals, not one child rings one hollow bell.

Then I remember to unblur my eyes entirely and the mountains in the background materialize into soldiers with camouflage outfits, their faces as stiff and suspicious as pioneers' in photographs, lifting the children so that they can see. The children's faces go slack, taking me in as I sparkle in my house. Some of the windows are open, with screens, and I can hear a child suck and swallow. I can hear the blow pop shift across her teeth. Then the children start squirming, because their armpits are uncomfortable and they're bored. So here and then there the soldiers put them down and I can hear shoes and voices in the shrubbery. For a few moments the soldiers talk to one another on their walkie-talkies, looking across my living room at one another, window to window, nodding and shrugging, hatching ideas, making plans. They seem to come to a decision. The giraffe's head is still in its window but I have no idea if there's anyone down there supporting it. The soldier standing framed with it does not seem to know it's there. The giraffe looks directly at me, and the soldier is in profile, with his walkie-talkie, and every burst of static has the rhythm of affirmation—roger that, ten-four—

But I'm still turning. Some of the children appear in the background, in the hilly yard of my neighbor next door. They are tossing a ball. They are jumping a jump rope. They are writing with chalk on the walkway. A soldier shifts from his window and shouts an order at them. Bark, spit, he says. One of the children comes to him, but the others ignore him. What can I do? Atrocities are imminent.

Outside another window a soldier is examining my barbecue.

Outside another a soldier is tying his boot.

Outside another a soldier continues to look at me each time I pass, because I am still turning, and turning as if the opening and closing of my eyes propels the turn, as if time itself is what turns me, as if my turning makes time move. He continues to look at me and I know everything he might do; I can see everything he might do move across his eyes in scenarios I remember from news and movies. Then he walks around the house. I can see him pass by window after window. I am following him as I turn, or my turning is pushing him along in a dance of magnets. He collects the giraffe as he passes. He hands the giraffe to the soldier who is standing with my barbecue. He's rounding the porch and I'm turning to meet him as he approaches the threshold, removing his flak helmet. His face is at my crotch. He is wiping his boots on my welcome mat.

Then I do, I cry. I try to control my breath enough so that I can do it with the duct-tape gag. It's all I can do.

My house is like the world. The furniture is islands and continents now, in sun and shadow, its inhabitants the bugs, the mice, the dust, and the knickknacks we collected on our travels. Air is water, and sky hangs, as always, above the roof, though here the roof is ozone, leaks intact. How did I get here? Sleepwalking? Sleephanging? Sleepbinding and sleepgagging? Sleepransacking of my home? Or did soldiers do this in the night?

He stops my spinning. He turns me and turns with me as if I'm a bookcase to a secret room and I can feel a shaft of sunlight settle onto my ass. He takes a poker from my fireplace and pokes me carefully so that I swing a little. Who do you think you are? Poke. What do you think you're doing? Poke. He tucks it under his arm like an umbrella and goes into the kitchen and starts opening and closing drawers. Why don't you have any pancake mix in this kitchen? (I do, but it's in the cabinet and he's still looking in drawers.) Don't you have any decent snacks?

Outside, the soldiers are directing the children to do something, to ready something, and they're scurrying about with their accessories. I am suddenly unsure if the soldiers are directing the children, or if the children are directing the soldiers, as if it's simply their toys that have grown life-size. I spot the giraffe standing near the barbecue. It's large for a toy, but it is not nearly life-size. And the soldier in my kitchen has opened his fly and let his penis flop out. This, I recognize, is nothing a grown doll could do.

Then my husband comes home. There's no sign of the car, but he comes in the back gate, stands at the patio doors, kicks his boots off, and then, as if remembering my instructions, he retrieves and sets them tidily next to the geranium pot. I have no idea why he's home so early, but the soldier has scooted back around me, taking the porch steps in one stride, setting me spinning again. He's somewhere in the yard with the rest of them, and he must have zipped up because now I cannot tell him apart from the rest of the soldiers, some of whom have found fold-out lawn chairs and are setting them up around the grill. Others are primping the coals.

My husband comes inside and makes a peanut butter sandwich. Behind my gag I am trying to regulate my breath enough to make a noise, but then he pulls a stool from the breakfast bar over to where I'm hanging and stops my spinning so we can both look the same way, out the window to the grassy side yard where they have dragged the barbecue. It's good to be still. It is so good to be still that I hardly wonder why my husband remains unalarmed. We watch as first they barbecue the giraffe and then they barbecue each other. A soldier, sitting lotus on the grill, salutes, and next it's the boy with the backpack, grinning like wax, and like wax, his face moves from comedy to tragedy mask. One and then another disappears into smoke and flames, another soldier and then the child with lollies, everyone nodding appreciatively at everyone's sacrifice.

I know there is blood, but I cannot see blood. There is a way that I want to see the blood because I feel it's my responsibility to see the blood, and it must be there, given the circumstances, but I cannot see it. I sniff but all I can smell is my own salty fluids. I focus my mind on my ears and I hear bubbles, and I hear myself swallow saliva, and beyond that I hear only what could be the ambient liquid tune of a washer or of a toilet awry.

I hear my husband chewing. Then he rests the sandwich in his lap for a moment and unties one of the ropes around my wrists and I realize that I can feel his fingers on the rope as if it is a part of my body. I think about it, and I am not making this up. The rope is part of my body. It occurs to me that when I dream I almost never have a body, let alone a face, and then it occurs to me that this phenomenon is not one exclusively of sleep. If I am as I dream, as they say, then I am a blur to myself. Unless I am looking at my reflection I never look like anything.

In this suspense, what of myself can I see? The hand my husband released has fallen out of my vision, but the bound one has shifted such that I can see my wrist as if I am checking the time, but it's ropes that I see there. They say you can tell a person's age on her hands more clearly than on her face. You can see a person's history in her hands. I'm facing the back of my hand. I know it like the back of my hand, I think, but it turns out I don't know the back of my hand at all. There's not much to my hand, now that I'm finally looking. This is not, for example, a farmer's hand. And this is a hand that has been kept clean, that has washed itself of almost everything. Skin's a little looser than it has been, the map or lake top made up by lines more pronounced than I might have guessed. On the other side of my hand, hidden on my palm, is my future.

Now I feel the rope dangling like a phantom limb. Now I remember how I came to this. I remember in slow motion that by mid-morning—in the open space after "Bye-bye sweet-ums," "Have a lovely, sugar," and that final wag from my dog's behind—in that open space the world had slipped two degrees farther in a direction it must have been shifting for a long time, like water from an eyedropper that heaps above the rim of a glass and then one more drop and it just spills. In such a way the substance of the air had suddenly thickened, becoming almost gelatinous, I remember now. I was elbow-deep in dishes and the water in the sink began to feel the same as the air, and soap bubbles felt like rubber pellets, and then I was moving through it like a deep-sea diver in all that gear, or not moving through it so much as moving with it, it guiding me as much as anything, no leading or following, just me shifting with the breath of the earth, and then these ropes growing from inside my body like extensions of my tendons as my clothes fell away, the gag rising like a scar across my face. I was moving toward the door because I wanted to get out—

I wanted to do something—

I wanted to change, and I wanted to change the world—

I opened the front door, but I couldn't move through; the planks of the porch and the wide lawn yawned before me and gravity seemed to tip and I walked on up the space where the door had been as my furniture tumbled about the room, the chandelier catching on a sofa cushion and stuffing bulging from where it tore, coffee table cracking its back over the arm of a wingback armchair. I just walked on along where the door no longer hung and my ropes coiled around me and fastened to the door frame, merged there with house; I remember the crumbling feeling of the popcorn texture of the ceiling; and I could feel the guts of the house, the pipes, the ducts, the wires, the stretching and sagging two-by-fours clinging to the drywall, and then I could feel myself stretch into warm roads coursing across town and then the country, and then I could feel myself as the jet stream and the gulf stream, planetary currents of air and water. I felt it hard, and fully. It wore me out and perhaps I slept because when I woke the world seemed as loose as ever and there I hung as if I'd been abducted by my own home.

There is simply no end to the suspense when one becomes one's own psychic landscape. Here, my unbound hand flops in the sunshine. My husband holds the dangling end of my rope in one hand, and I can feel the warmth of his hand, which is so familiar, as he resumes eating his sandwich with the other. I remember, and now I know. I am my home, and I am the world I live in. I am the ropes that bind me and the silver tape that stops my voice, hanging here, in this predicament. It did it to me, I did it to myself, I did it to it, all the same. My husband and I look out the window, head to head, although mine remains upside down, and outside, children are running about with soldiers. Some are helping each other onto the barbecue. They're all squirting one another with sauce.

LYDIA DAVIS

Five Fictions from the Middle of the Night

SWIMMING IN EGYPT

We are in Egypt. We are about to go deep-sea diving. They have erected a vast tank of water on land next to the Mediterranean Sea. We strap oxygen to our backs and descend into this tank. We go all the way to the bottom. Here, there is a cluster of blue lights shining on the entrance to a tunnel. We enter the tunnel. We swim and swim. At the far end of the tunnel, we see more lights, white ones. When we have passed through the lights, we come out of the tunnel, sud-denly, into the open sea, which drops away beneath us a full kilome-ter or more. There are fish all around and above us, and reefs on all sides. We think we are flying, over the deep. We forget, for now, that we must be careful not to get lost, but must find our way back to the mouth of the tunnel.

THE SCHOOLCHILDREN IN THE LARGE BUILDING

I live in a very large building, the size of a warehouse or an opera house. I am there alone. Now some schoolchildren arrive. I see their quick little legs coming through the front door and I ask, in some fear, "Who is it, who is it?" but they don't answer. The class is very numerous—all boys, with two teachers. They pour into the painting studio at the back of the building. The ceiling of this studio is two or even three stories high. On one wall is a huge mural of dark-complexioned faces. The schoolboys crowd in front of the painting, fascinated, pointing and talking. On the opposite wall is another mural, of green and blue flowers. Only a handful of schoolboys is looking at this one.

The class would like to spend the night here because they do not have funds for a hotel. Wouldn't their hometown raise the money for this field trip? I ask one of the teachers. No, he says sadly, with a smile, they wouldn't, because of the fact that he, the teacher, is homosexual. After saying this, he turns and gently puts his arms around the other teacher.

Later, I am in the same building with the schoolchildren, but it is no longer my home, or I am not familiar with it. I ask a boy where the bathrooms are, and he shows me one—it's a nice bathroom, with old fixtures and paneled in wood. As I sit on the toilet, the room rises—because it is also an elevator. I wonder briefly, as I flush, how the plumbing works in that case, and then assume it has been figured out.

IN THE GALLERY

A woman I know, a visual artist, is trying to hang her work for a show. Her work is a single line of text pasted on the wall, with a transparent curtain suspended in front of it.

She is at the top of a ladder and cannot get down. She is facing out instead of in. The people down below tell her to turn around, but she does not know how.

When I see her next, she is down from the ladder. She is going from one person to the next, asking for help in hanging her artwork. But no one will help her. They say she is such a difficult woman.

THE PIANO

We are about to buy a new piano. Our old upright has a crack all the way through its sounding board, and other problems. We would like the piano shop to take it and resell it, but they tell us it is too badly damaged and cannot be resold to anyone else. They say it will have to be pushed over a cliff. This is how they will do it: two truck drivers take it to a remote spot. One driver walks away down the lane with his back turned while the other shoves it over the cliff.

THE PIANO LESSON

I am with my friend Christine. I have not seen her for a long time, perhaps seventeen years. We talk about music and we agree that when we meet again she will give me a piano lesson. In preparation for the lesson, she says, I must select, and then study, one Baroque piece, one Classical, one Romantic, and one Modern. I am impressed by her seriousness and by the difficulty of the assignment. I am ready to do it. We will have the lesson in one year, she says. She will come to my house. But then, later, she says she is not sure she will be returning to this country. Maybe, instead, we will have the lesson in Italy. Or if not Italy, then, of course, Casablanca.

RIKKI DUCORNET

The Dickmare

I t all boils down to this: does she present to the Dickmare or not? She fears the lot of them, those perpetually inflated Dickmares, their uncanny magnetism matched only by their startling lack of symmetry. Yet she has been summoned. A thing as unprecedented as it is provoking.

And she has awakened with a curious rash. It circles her body like a cummerbund. A rash as florid as those coral gardens so appreciated by lovers of bijouterie. A rash having surged directly— or so she supposes—from her husband's anomalous—or so she hopes—behavior.

Once, she had thought her husband admirable. Admirable his thorny cone, his sweet horny operculum, his prowess as a swimmer, the beauty of his sudden ejections, the ease with which he righted himself when overturned. Not one to retreat into his shell, in those days his high spirits percolated throughout the yellow mud they optimistically called home.

Adolescents intellectually annihilated by lust and hopeful mysticisms would engage her husband for hours on end with thorny topics such as why Noah built the Ark without once questioning the High Clam's outburst of temper. And if the High Clam loves the fishes and the shelled fishes best (after all, they did not suffer during the forty days and nights of rain but, instead, benefited)—why were they snatched in numbers from their naps and served up Top Side boiled in beer and dressed with hot butter? And her husband instructed the small fry with cautionary tales featuring the terrible Kracken who swims on the surface of the waves like a gigantic swan downing mischievous little mollusks at will—the fear of the lie quieting both their wanderlust and their exuberance (and some were so shellacked with fear they slammed shut never to be heard from again).

The old-timers too came to her husband for advice, sleepless in expectation of those fearsome migrations they were impelled to entertain periodically for reasons beyond everyone's grasp. It seemed that everybody was in need of advice all the time anymore, and that her husband's ministry never ceased.

At first she had been proud of his popularity, or rather, had done her best not to hate the constant tide of traffic and bavardage. She would shut her eyes and cling to anything, to debris—a rotting hull, a stump of pier, a branch of *filifera*. And she would dream unfructuous dreams of the secret arms of rivers that are said to feed the sea—uncertain waters flowing from an unknowable source (because Top Side)—a source she wished to find.

Her husband's popularity came to a sudden halt right after a doleful interlude with the Cuckfield quintuplets, whom he had surprised in their daily rotations over by Sandy Bottoms. Now no one—not even the Squamosas who wear their digestive tubes in their arms—will give either of them the time of day. Once so admired, her husband has taken his problems to a Dickmare—and there is a scary rhyme the small fry trill about him:

When the moon is out
and the bivalves hop—
and cannot stop,
and cannot stop,
and a shadow steals above . . .
tell me! What is it?
What is it? My love!

—a Dickmare who orders up nacreous pills from the oyster shop, pills that resemble toothed hinges and, once swallowed, produce an egg capable of sprouting fins and swimming. These days her husband's conversation is as rare as a clam's liver. He has lost the instinct for cordiality, and his capacity for mobility is sorely compromised. He has developed two pairs of buccal palpi, and even if he had wanted to, she would not want him to kiss her. When in motion he takes no great strides, but instead stretches out his foot so slowly that she—who stands at the ready with a glass of water (these days his thirst is prodigious)—fears the tedium will kill her. But then, having set the right foot down, he withdraws the left so suddenly that, crying out, she drops the tumbler, wetting her apron. When he is mercifully out the door, another unexpectedly vigorous push with his left foot sends him headlong into his vehicle.

Is it a squid or a calamar?

When her husband returns he wishes to engage her. Occupying the recliner, he kneels on his knuckles, inching forward with one hand on each end of the apparatus. This, she fears, may lead to further disability. She can tell he has taken the other pills, the ones the size of a grain of linseed, which, like those the size of a split pea, and unlike those the size of a small haricot bean, are, at the instant of ingestion, spat out upon the floor. She stands at the ready, her small broom resting at her side.

The fine salmon pink of her husband's cheeks has darkened, and his skin exudes a peculiarly pungent odor reminiscent of dead eels. Provoked by the prescribed medicaments, within the hour she knows he will turn upon himself like a wheel in motion.

Her husband displays his lamellar and vivid portions. He wishes to excite her curiosity as, he tells her, she has excited the Dickmare's, who, having asked to see her photograph and at once been satisfied, extends an invitation to his grotto. The Dickmare suggests that she is distinguished from the schools of others of her kind, by a brilliancy of eye that, added to her moist plumpness, renders her *the most appealing analysand he could aspire to.* She is *a treasure, the single form reflected in a plurality of lesser forms, or rather, she is that plurality reflected in a singular form.*

Unclear as to what he has said, still she cannot help but be moved—as creatures such as she, so fraught with disappointments, swarm within his reach, easy prey for lesser contenders, those who do not have access, as the Dickmares do, to the tops of rocks, nor have they access to the medicines. And it is true: she is lovely, vitreous and permeable, her bottom globular. Aroused, she is luminous in the dark. So round, so smooth, so readily ablaze in her posterior part! No one, she muses, has noticed these things for a very long time. And so, after all these months watching her husband pull himself across the floor in fractions—a transaction that is always accompanied by frequent vomitings and the prodigious thirst—she weighs her chances. Risky business!

Or is it a Dick . . .

After all, the Dickmares are known to unspool and push their pistons forward with such alacrity a subconical cavity will be stunned into service before it has a chance to ignite. And she fears that rather than excite his compassion, the curious rash now tumbling to her knees like a Samoan's grass skirt will excite his scorn and, what's more, his wrath. Yet it is also true that she has just that morning shed her shell—a thing both temporary and wildly appealing. If she is at her most vulnerable, she is also at her most charming. The rash, she hopes, may well be a function of this transformation, her heightened state. Her beauty—she can see it now—has never been more poignant.

It boils down to this: might the Dickmare provide a pill less bitter than the one she has sucked ever since the Cuckfield fry gave voice to their many peculiar complaints? Might the Dickmare assuage her loneliness and her humiliation? Is she afflicted enough to dare seek out a questionable success with an Upper Mudder known to be sensuous, furious, and cruel? And she so fragile! So amply furnished with tender sockets and delicate rosettes rotundular and soft. Yes, above all *she is soft*. And so easily impressed!

It is said at Death—and once the flesh has dissolved into the limitless bodies of things so small they cannot be perceived by the naked eye—the soul is swept away by a current called Forgetfulness and carried to an edifice of foam so impalpable no one has ever seen it. She wants to be the one to see it and to inform the others as to its nature.

JULIA ELLIOTT

The Wilds

T he Wild family moved into the house behind ours. The split-level had been dead for two years; its sunken den had become a nest of slugs and millipedes, its attic a froth of bats. Eight brothers now flung their restless bodies around the property. The largest Wild, a greasy, bearded boy of seventeen, shut himself up in the den. The littlest Wild, a tangle-haired half-naked thing, rumored to be a biter, lurked around in the shrubbery. The Wilds kept cats, lizards, and ferrets. Rabbits, hamsters, turtles, and snakes. A bubble of musky ammoniac air enveloped their home like a force field, and the second you dared step through it you felt dizzy; a hundred arrows whistled around your ears. Their mother was frequently seen hauling in bags of supplies, and when she climbed from the battered exoskeleton of her station wagon, the boys would jump her like a band of hunger-crazed outlaws, snatching cookies and chips and tiny shrink-wrapped cakes. They'd scuttle up into the trees. They kept quiet up there, waiting out their mother's fits. She was a lumpy, old-fashioned lady, forever in a rumpled dress and panty hose, with a pouf of hair as golden and crunchy as a pork rind. She'd tear her hairdo into wilted clumps and shake her fists at the trees. "I'm having a nervous breakdown," she'd say, sometimes falling to her knees.

Mama said she felt sorry for Mrs. Wild. Dressed in tight jeans and heels, Mama'd invite the hunched lady to have coffee in our spotless living room. She made fun of Mrs. Wild's dresses when the poor woman left, but sometimes she was sad, and I knew she was thinking about my little brother, who'd weighed three pounds when born and looked like a frog and died in a humid tank of oxygen.

Mr. Wild always rolled in after dark, in a black Chrysler New Yorker, appearing briefly in starlight, moonlight, or streetlight, always shrouded in a suit. He worked in the secret depths of a nuclear plant, thirty miles away, a glowing futuristic fortress surrounded by high walls. The family was from way up North, somewhere between Pennsylvania and the North Pole, where the world froze into a solid block of ice for months on end and people lived half their lives indoors. But now, in the teeming Southern air, the transplanted boys were growing, faster and faster, so fast their mother had to keep two industrial freezers in the garage, one for milk, the other for meat—hot dogs, chickens, turkeys, and hams; pork chops, baloney, and liver; a thousand cuts of beef and strange bloody meats seldom eaten in our part of the world.

We were deep into summer and you could see the vines moving, winding around branches, sprouting bumps and barnacles and woody boils that would fester until they could stand it no more, then break out into red and purple. It was night and the Wild boys hooted in the shrubbery. They wore dirty cutoff jeans. They carried knives and guns and homemade bombs. I could smell their weird metallic sweat, drifting on a breeze that rustled through the honeysuckle. The Wild boys had dug tunnels under the ground. They had filled the treetops with catwalks. They whirred from tree to tree on zip lines and hopped from attic windows out into the bustling night.

I crouched in the bushes in Mama's green chiffon evening gown, wearing my crown of bird skulls. I'd collected the skulls for two years, spray-painted them gold, and glued them to a Burger King crown, along with fake emeralds and glowing shells of june bugs. Thin, long hair tickled my spine. My Barbie binoculars were crap, and I'd smashed them with a rock. I was on the lookout for Brian, the oldest Wild, who sometimes left his den to smoke. I was deeply in love with him. Every time I saw him, reclining in his plastic lawn chair, pouting in dark sunglasses, my heart twisted like a worm in the cocoon of my chest.

My father taught medieval history at the community college. I'd found an ancient love potion in one of his books. And inside a purple Crown Royal pouch, buried under an assortment of amulets, was a fancy perfume bottle full of magical fluid. Lightning bugs bobbed in the rich air. Crickets throbbed. A fat, bloody moon hung over the house of the neighborhood alcoholics.

I heard the click of the sliding glass door that led to Brian's lair. And he came out into the night, pulsing with beauty and mystery. His hair was long, wild and black. He'd shaved his beard into a devil point. And you could tell by the way he sighed and flopped around that he dreamed of better places—glamorous and distant, with a different kind of light. Because of him I'd taken up smoking. I stole butts from my father and kept them in a sock with a pink Bic, Tic Tacs, and a tiny spray can of Lysol. I fantasized about smoking with Brian: Brian leaning over to light my cigarette, our sensuous exhalations intertwining, Brian kissing my smoky mouth. My longing pulled me over the invisible boundary into the Wild's honeysuckle-choked yard. I was in the atmosphere, sniffing ferret musk and a thousand flowers, when a hand slipped over my mouth. It smelled of onions and dirt. A small, hot body pressed against my back.

"Don't make a sound," said a boy.

"We've got knives," said another. They snatched my wrists behind my back. Other boys came out into the moonlight, and Brian slipped inside the house, tossing his cigarette butt behind him.

"Stand up," a boy said.

Their chests glowed with firefly juice. They had steak knives strapped to their belts and some of them wore goggles. White cats strolled among them, sometimes sniffing their bare feet. "Move," yelled a small Wild, no older than six, a butter knife dangling from his Cub Scout belt. They pushed me toward a crooked magnolia. In the sweet, knotty dark of the tree, they'd nailed boards for climbing, and they forced me up, higher and higher, the gauze of my skirt catching on branches, until we reached their tree house, a rickety box with one window that framed the moon. Two boys squirmed around me to climb in first. They lit a stinking kerosene lantern, which sat on a milk crate. They flashed their knives at me. One of the boys prodded my butt with a stick and said, "Get in." I climbed up into the creaky orange glow of the tree house.

Five Wilds surrounded me with glares and grimaces. A cat poked its white head through the window and stared at me. Birds fluttered and fussed in the branches.

"Give Ben the signal," said the biggest boy in the room, whose name, I think, was Tim. "He knows how to deal with spies."

"Spies?" I said.

"Shut up. Don't talk. You're on our property."

One of the boys opened an old medicine cabinet that was mounted on the wall beside the window. Inside were several ordinary light switches and a doorbell. He pressed the doorbell.

"What are you?" said the little Wild, staring dreamily at my crown.

"Shut up," said Tim. "Don't speak to the prisoner. She's got to be interrogated."

Something heavy jumped in the branches then, and shook the tree house. A flash-lit mask of a wolf man appeared at the window, sputtering with evil cackles. He was copying somebody on television, though I couldn't quite place the laugh.

"What have we here?" said the wolf man. "A princess?"

Two boards beneath the window opened and the wolf man squeezed through a primitive secret door. He closed the narrow door behind him and stood before me in karate pants and a black bathrobe too big for his skinny body. He wore no shirt under the robe, and a live garter snake twirled around his pimply neck. I thought I knew which Wild he was but I couldn't quite remember the face under the mask. He sat on an overturned plastic bucket, elbows on his knees, and gazed down at me through his mask, a cheap Halloween thing with molded plastic hair. The wolf man had a silly widow's peak, a hard fat beard, and vampire fangs that looked like buck teeth.

I sat on the floor, feeling dizzy in the press of boys. They smelled of strange metals, stale biscuits, and fermented grass. Their hair was oily, and Kool-Aid stains darkened their greedy mouths.

"We'll have to search her," said the wolf man, picking a cigarette from his robe pocket. There was a small mouth-hole in the mask, and the wolf man inserted his cigarette into it. His brothers licked their lips as they watched him light it with a silver lighter. The wolf man took an awkward puff.

"Gimme one," said the little Wild, but no one paid him any attention.

"She's got something hidden under her skirt," said the wolf man, pointing with his cigarette at one of my secret pockets.

They stuck their filthy, gnarled hands into the soft film of my skirts, snatching my treasures from me: my lipsticks, my notebook, my voodoo doll of mean old drunk Mrs. Bickle. The wolf man tried to read the notebook, but he couldn't understand my special language. He emptied my purple pouch on the table and picked through my magic things.

"Quit squirming," hissed Tim, pinching my nape, looking for the nerves that would paralyze me.

The wolf man examined my amulet for night flying, a big gold medallion with a luna moth Shrinky-Dinked to the front. He opened my power locket and dumped the red powder onto the floor. I think he was smirking under the mask. His eyes gleamed, wet and meaty behind the dead plastic.

He found my love potion buried deep in the pouch, wrapped in a gauzy violet scarf, and held the soft bundle in his palm, squeezing it and cocking his head. Slowly, he unraveled it. He examined the perfume bottle in the lamplight, mouthing the word on the label: Poison. I don't think he understood that this was the name of a perfume. And the sight of this word, printed so precisely on an old-fashioned bottle filled with dark algae-green cream, as though packaged by goblins, must have unsettled him. Poison was my mother's perfume. When she dabbed it on her pulse points she made a mean face in the mirror, as though going out into the night to kill. The summer after my brother died, I saw my mother flee a noisy neighborhood party to rush into the arms of a strange man; they fell into uncut grass.

The wolf man unscrewed the cap. My love potion filled the tree house with goats and tortured lilies. He shuddered and put the cap back on and turned his wet eyes away. His brothers groaned. According to the ancient recipe, just smelling the potion was dangerous, though I'd had to make substitutes with modern ingredients from cans and boxes, and I knew this would weaken the brew.

"That smell," said the wolf man, turning to look at me. "It made me gag."

"It won't hurt you," I said. "It's not really poison."

"Make her eat it then," said the brother with the cowlick and bulldog eyes.

I tried to squirm away but the Wilds were on me, this time binding my wrists with fishing line. The wolf man knelt near me, holding the bottle in his fist. I could smell his scalp. The snake on his neck lifted its head to look at me and opened its velvety pink mouth.

Its fangs were too little to see, but I could imagine them—clear as diamonds, wet and sparkling sharp. The wolf man dabbed a green droplet on his fingertip and pushed it toward my lips.

"Lick it," he said. "If it's not poison."

I turned my face away, and the Wilds pressed around me, flashing their knives and grunting.

"Lick it, lick it, lick it," they chanted.

My tongue felt parched and gross. It slithered out and dabbed the drop. I closed my eyes to block their faces from my mind and tried not to swallow. I would hold the poison in my mouth and spit it out when they let me go. I thought of Brian, reclining in his lawn chair, but the image of the wolf man billowed up in my head. Hunched in his bathrobe, laughing his midnight-TV laugh, he staggered through the twisted branches.

I kept away from the Wilds after that and did not spy on them and grew two inches and learned how to talk to birds. My father had ordered a xeroxed copy of a book so ancient that a library in England had to keep it in a special tank. This book was full of useful information: how to communicate with animals, how to make your own cough medicine, how to keep the devil from visiting your bed at night. It also contained love potions, but when I came to these passages I skipped over them with a beating heart. School had started. I spent hours in fluorescent classrooms, breathing disinfectant and chalk and the smell of warm, young bodies shut up. Two groups of girls wanted me as a friend, and I jumped between them, keeping my independence. Ben Wild was two grades ahead of me. At school he ran with bad boys and lurked under stairwells and slipped off to McDonald's for lunch. Sometimes I saw him slinking down the hall in the silent in-school-suspension line, guarded by Mrs. Beard, a mammoth woman with a face like a sunburned fist.

Ben had a thick, pubic unibrow, and his mother couldn't keep his black curls cut. Tucked into the nest of his hair was a strange acne-scarred face with glowing green eyes and slick, pimento-red lips. Sometimes we locked eyes at school. He'd laugh at me and say, sarcastically, "There goes the fairy princess." He was always making nasty remarks to his friends. People whispered that his mother was pregnant again—with twins, triplets, quadruplets, quintuplets, sextuplets. They invented terms for outlandish broods, like *megaduplets*, and referred to the Wild boys as "the litter," "the pack," or "the swarm."

In health class we watched creepy, outdated films on lice, scabies, menstruation, scoliosis, and drug mania. I saw cartoon bugs burrowing under the soft skins of children, leaving red maps of infection. I saw pretty girls transform into twisted, tragic creatures who hobbled down school hallways in back braces. I saw hippie chicks dance ecstatically in throbbing psychedelic light, only to hurl themselves out of windows. Womanhood was bound up with disease. Ecstasy led to bashed-open skulls and the apocalyptic wail of police sirens. Parasites lurked everywhere: little bloodsuckers hopping into your hair; big perverts with candy and needles. But the disease had already touched me. My right nipple swelled. I could feel a hard lump wobbling inside when I picked at it. My mother laughed when I asked for a bra, and my deformity was visible beneath three shirts.

One day Ben Wild called me "Cyclops." The name spread through our school like lice. I vowed revenge and took to my spell books and started watching the Wild house again.

I learned that Brian had an older girlfriend from the neighborhood, a dental hygienist, which was fine with me because I didn't love him anymore. I learned that Mrs. Wild was pregnant and that she had a nervous breakdown every Wednesday evening after picking up three of her sons from midget-football practice and allowing them to gorge on ice cream. I learned that Mr. Wild sometimes lingered in his car for thirty minutes before venturing into the house. And most important, I learned that Ben wore his wolf-man mask every month on the night of the full moon.

I had several theories: Ben fantasized about being a wolf man;

Ben had told his little brothers, years ago, that he was a wolf man, and he kept up his ruse to control them with fear; Ben donned the wolf-man mask as some kind of deep, ironic joke. But no one in his family seemed afraid of the wolf-man mask. They never said much about it, simply commenting, in September, when the full moon came, that it was wolf night again. And Ben went about his activities as though everything were normal: taking out the garbage, bumming cigarettes from Brian, shooting hoops with Tim.

In October a hurricane swept through our town. Before the storm I saw Ben outside in his backyard, standing in the weird sulfurous light with wind whipping through his hair. Something flickered through me and I wanted to join him, to snuggle in the hectic, stinking warmth of the Wild pack. But Mama screamed at the back door, and I ran inside our lonely house. Daddy made us sit in the pantry, where he told stories of green knights and enchanted ladies as Mama rolled her eyes and the storm lashed at our roof. My father was getting plump. His pale, clammy skin sometimes broke out into rashes. I knew all of his stories, word by word. I knew every sarcastic phrase in my mother's repertoire, and the contents of her closet no longer fascinated me. I was sick of my parents' faces and hungry for new life. Into the dark blinking windows of my dreams, Wild boys would sometimes scramble. They'd run howling through our house, kicking over end tables and smearing mud on our wall-to-wall carpet. They'd tear doors off hinges and let night storms fly through our house.

Our power was out for four days. Houses flickered with candle-light. Children ruled the dark chaos and the Wild boys prowled the battered neighborhood with guns and knives. On the third day Tim Wild came to our back door and told us his parents were having a cookout. They had a freezer of meat that was going to go bad; the whole block was invited.

It was a warm day and autumn mange patched the ragged trees. Smells of charred meat floated through the neighborhood; a million gnats had hatched in the muggy air. It was strange to see Mr. Wild out in daylight, cooking on their rusty grill, so tall, so skinny and pale, his shiny square of hair gone bristly like the coat of a dog. He hunched over the spitting meat, grinning with long teeth. He wore glasses. His ancient jogging suit had faded to a strange purple, and sweat dripped from the stubbled point of his chin. Children whispered that he was too smart to talk, that nothing he said made sense, that he had green false teeth and a robot eye and a creepy vampire accent. His wife looked worn-out, fussing with paper napkins that kept blowing all over the yard, mustard stains blotting her massive poly-knit bosom. The boys looked exactly like Mr. Wild. Children said he'd planted his evil clones directly into her belly, and now another one was growing down in the warm, dark wet.

The Wild boys hadn't bathed since the storm and they ran around the yard with gristly bones in their fists. They had been gobbling meat all day and their mouths were slick with blood and grease. They'd darkened their faces with charcoal. They whizzed through the treetops; their heads popped up from secret holes. Immune to their mother's screams, they cackled and smacked, lunged at heaped platters, stabbed morsels of flesh on the tips of their knives. White cats jumped on the picnic table and carried whole pork chops into the trees.

There was nothing to eat but meat and white bread that turned to pure sugar when it hit your spit. There were no forks left. I fixed myself a plate and took it to Brian's lawn chair. I had a blistered wienie and a steak, black on the outside but raw and oozing inside. I had a hot dog bun infested with ice. I ate the steak with my hands, and warm blood dripped down my throat. Gnats landed on my cheeks to lick sweat with their invisible tongues. I ate more meat: crumbly, dry hamburger and fatty pork loin and chunks of bitter liver; gamy lamb and slippery lumps of veal. I gnawed at the stubborn tendons of turkey legs and savored sausage that melted like candy on my tongue. I nibbled minute greasy quail with soft skeletons and sucked tender feathers of flesh from roasted ribs. The sky flushed pink and I ate as the boiling sun sank. I ate until my paper

plate dissolved in my hands. When I finally came out of my can-
nibal trance, the moon was up, rolling like a carcass on the spit of
its axis. And Ben Wild was staring at me through the sliding glass
door that led to his brother's den. He was wearing his wolf-man
mask, as I should have expected, though I'd forgotten all about the
full moon, and he startled me with his goofy monster face.

Adults murmured near the dying grill. They were drinking beer.
My mother's sarcastic laughter drifted across the sea of withering
honeysuckle, and I knew my father had already skulked home to
bed. I peered through the door of the den and saw shapes moving in
candlelight. A boy barked. The door slid open all by itself, and I suspected that one of the Wilds had pulled it with a string. Or maybe
the little smart-asses had rigged up something more complicated.

I walked into the room and the door closed. There were animals in there, filtering the air with their strange lungs, pumping
out musk and farts. Ben sat on a small velour couch in the corner,
wearing his karate ensemble. A ferret dozed on his neck. White
cats eyed the weaselly beast as they slunk around. Three Wild boys
stalked the room with knives, obsessed with being near their older
brother. They'd made a pile of bones on Brian's dresser. Candles
flickered on the floor, bleeding wax onto ancient shag. I took a deep
breath of moldy air.

"Where's Brian?" I asked.

"With his girlfriend," said Ben, and his brothers snorted and
made kissing noises.

"We're taking over his room," said Tim. He threw his knife at a
cat and metal clattered against the dark paneled wall.

"I've got to go," I said, though it would have hurt me to leave the
room.

"Wait," said Ben. "I wanted to tell you something."

"What?"

"Get out of here, you assholes," he said.

"Make us," said Tim.

Ben stood up, and the boys ran toward a corner, where I could make out a flight of steps with a wrought iron banister. They crawled up and down the stairs, neither leaving nor staying, snickering and coughing and slapping each other. The ferret leaped from Ben's shoulder and slithered under the bed.

"I wanted to tell you I was sorry about the thing, you know," Ben whispered. "The name I called you. I didn't mean for it to get around like it did."

"Whatever," I said. My cyclopean breast burned above my mortified heart. I pulled my jean jacket tight around me. "Forget it. Don't say another word about it."

The wolf man's stupid expression didn't change, but his eyes, wet behind the plastic, fluttered over my chest.

"I was just having a bad week," he said. "You don't have any brothers or sisters, do you?"

I told him I didn't.

"You're lucky," he said. "All that privacy. Sometimes I think I'm going crazy. They never leave me alone. But when Brian goes to college next year, I'm moving down here."

"It's a cool room," I said. "You can come and go whenever you want."

"Yeah," he said. "Want a cigarette?" He pulled a pack of Marlboros from his shirt pocket. He made room for me on the couch and I sat down. The couch was too small and I could feel his body burning beside mine. I could smell the dark yellow musk of the ferret that sprawled on his neck. When I leaned in to light my cigarette, I caught the tang of wine on Ben's breath, and I wanted to drink wine too, from a silver goblet, deep in the secret tunnels the Wild boys had dug under the ground, or high in the treetops, where clouds oozed through prickly branches.

"Give me some wine," I said.

"What?" The wolf man cocked his head.

"I smell it, and I want some."

"No problem." He produced a jug from a laundry basket overflowing with dirty socks.

We sat drinking wine and smoking. White cats paced. We didn't speak, and a beautiful, sweet evil grew between us.

"How deep do your tunnels go?" I whispered.

"To hell," he said, and laughed his television laugh. "One of these days I'm going to take my little brothers down there and sell them to the devil."

On the staircase a Wild boy gasped, but the others giggled.

"I wish I had brothers—or sisters."

"Oh no." Ben shook his head. "You don't."

"I do. At night, when my parents fall asleep in their chairs, I feel so lonely I wish a spaceship would swoop down and kidnap me."

"I feel exactly the same way." Ben's voice broke. He cleared his throat. "Only worse, more desperate, with a swarm of little gnats always bothering me. And my mother . . . sometimes she calls me Brian, sometimes Tim. I know it's just a slip of the tongue, but still. And now she's going to have another one."

His eyes rolled behind the plastic and I felt the damp meat of his palm resting on my hand. Our fingers intertwined and the air pulsed around my ears. This was what it was like to hold hands with a boy. I'd never done it before. There was a film of sweat between our palms and the position I was frozen in felt uncomfortable.

The sliding glass door opened by itself, and the smell of dying charcoal drifted in from the night. The full moon hung over the Bickles' rotten roof, spilling its silver.

"Where are all the parents?" I asked, but Ben didn't answer me. He dropped my hand and let out a deep moan that made my stomach clench. He shot up from the couch and staggered around on the carpet, fingering his wolf-man mask and groaning. Ben Wild fell to his knees. He lifted his head to the moon and barked. Then an ancient, afflicted howl rocked through his body and ripped the quiet night open.

He clambered around on all fours, trotting toward me, growling and spitting, and I wanted to dissolve into the couch. He sniffed my sneakers and licked my left ankle and whimpered like a dog. I was wondering if I should run or try to pet him, when he stood up and loomed over me, the air behind him darkening as a cloud passed over the moon. He shook with demented laughter. Then the night went white, and he tore the mask from his face.

His brothers shrieked and clambered to the top of the stairs. A door slammed, and I knew that I was alone with the wolf man, with all his fury and frustration.

Ben's acne had broken into bloom. His face glowed with an eerie bluish luster, and I thought that maybe his father had brought nuclear radiation home in his clothes. Zits swarmed like fire ants on Ben's brow. Purple pimples glistened like drops of jelly on his cheeks. Fat whiteheads nestled behind the wings of his nose. Only his eyes and lips had escaped the infection.

Ben sat beside me, holding his mask in his hands. "The moon controls the tides," he said, "and brings poison boiling to the surface of my skin. But tomorrow I'll be a normal boy again. I swear."

I didn't know what to say. Some of his pimples were seeping yellow drops.

"The family curse." Ben winced. "My father had it, and his father before him. Whoever gets it always ends up having lots of sons." He rolled his eyes and forced a laugh. A complex blush lit up his zits.

He took my hand and I let him hold it. His hand looked completely normal, hot and smooth and brown, pretty enough to bite. I could feel the moon licking at my skin with its magnetic light. I wondered if it was true that the moon moved the blood of women. I wondered if mysterious clocks, ancient and new, had started to tick within me. Ben leaned toward me. I threw my head back and vamped for his kiss. I'd spent a hundred nights dressed up in gowns and makeup, kissing stuffed animals, and my lips felt fat and sweet. But the hot suction cup of his mouth hit my throat, and he bit me, digging his braces into the soft skin of my neck. When I swatted him off, he laughed like a hoodlum and scratched his bleeding chin.

"I'm a wolf man," he said sarcastically, as though that explained everything. He shrugged and lit a cigarette.

From the stinging wound on my neck, Ben's slobber trickled into my bloodstream. I waited. I felt a slight burn when the poison hit my heart. Acid rose to the back of my throat. The taste of dead animals filled my mouth. Wild hope and withering despair tainted the meat, the craziness of animals shut up. The poison was in my body now, changing me, making me stronger and meaner.

I reached for Ben's cheek and stroked a mass of greasy bumps. My fingertips drifted along his jawbone and tickled the triangular patch of downy skin under his chin. He closed his eyes like a lizard in a trance and swallowed. I pressed my lips to his neck. I tried not to laugh as I licked the tendon that ran from his collarbone toward his jaw. Ben groaned and grabbed my elbow. His ears smelled like cinnamon. When I stuck my tongue into the silky cranny beneath his left earlobe, he bucked. I could feel the pulsing of intricate muscles and secret glands. I could feel veins throbbing with fast blood. Finding the spot I'd been searching for, I gnawed it gently until I broke the skin and tasted copper. Then I bit him with my small, sharp, spit-glazed teeth.

SAMANTHA HUNT

Beast

O n page eighteen of the *National Report*, there's an article about a brother and a sister, a human-interest story telling how the brother has worked for ten years at a chicken-rendering plant by day and a security firm by night. He even sold his plasma a few times. But the clincher, what makes the story a story, is that he does all this work in order to send his twin sister to college. He must be Chinese or Amish, I think, reading the first paragraph. I flip ahead to the jump page to see if there is a picture. There is. He's just some white guy from Minnesota and I suppose I find that hard to believe. He seems like an artifact from the nineteenth century, from a plainer time when people maybe took turns churning the butter or helped one another tend their fires at night. But he's not from the nineteenth century. In the photo he's wearing sneakers and a plastic apron stained with blood. He's positioned along a conveyor belt that is dotted with the dead bodies of chickens. I wonder if it is love or something else that makes him do it.

I read the newspaper in bed at night, propping it open on my bare belly, my boobs falling off to either side as if they were already asleep. The news of the world seems to matter very little after the day is done, as if it were a breath mint or a catalog filled with clothes I wouldn't ever buy.

"Archibald Lepore never finished high school," the article says, "yet every month he sends the Student Loan Corporation, a division of Citibank, a check for $578, exactly half of his monthly take-home pay. Mr. Lepore has been working since he was sixteen years old to support his twin sister. He found a second job when they turned eighteen and she was admitted to Northwestern University without a scholarship. Mr. Lepore, from the refrigerated storeroom of PoulTech, says—"

But then it moved. Just slightly; still, I saw it.

"I think I found a tick," I tell my husband.

I put down the paper and stretch out the skin of my stomach. A tiny black dot with legs, as if a period ran away from the newspaper and is making a slow-motion, highly ineffective escape across my stomach.

"Another one?" My husband rolls over onto his side. "Let me see."

"Right here."

He moves his head in for a closer look. "That's a pimple you picked at."

"I wasn't picking at anything. I was just reading. It's a tick bite," I say. "Do you see anything?"

He spreads the skin of my stomach, looking closely. "There's a spot of blood."

"You don't see any legs?"

"I don't see anything, really."

"Deer ticks are very small."

"I know," he says. It's the third tick he's pulled off me this week.

"But I don't see anything." He keeps on looking at the spot until: "Wait. All right. Wait. I do see something."

"What?"

"They're squirming a little bit. Black."

I knew it. "Please," I say. "Pull it out."

"You're not supposed to pull them out. Then their head stays inside you." We had received an illustrated mailer from the county. Lyme Tick Awareness. The sickness is carried in their saliva, it said. Get the head out.

"Well, what am I supposed to do, then?"

He looks confused. He climbs out of bed and disappears into the bathroom for some tweezers and a cotton ball soaked in alcohol.

The cottage we live in is only one story tall and a bit run down. It's what's called a carriage house. It's on someone else's property. We are caretakers. We mow the lawn, handle the trash, look out for robbers and all that. That is how we manage to live here, a place crawling with deer and ticks, instead of in an apartment in town. At this hour, from our bedroom door, the rest of the house looks black. I can't see the living room, and beyond that, I can't see the small kitchen with two windows where I like to sit looking out onto the screened porch that looks out even farther onto the road and the mailboxes. I can't see any of that right now.

"Have you been rolling around in the grass?" he asks when he returns. He dabs at the spot and I can smell the astringent. He clamps down with the tweezers. "Ready?" he asks and yanks once, taking a bit of skin with it. "That ought to do it," he says, again applying the alcohol.

I look down at the bite. I don't know if he got the head out. His mouth is twisted, worried.

"Is it gone?" I ask.

"Yeah. You're fine."

"You're sure?"

"Yup. I'll look again in the morning."

"What if the morning is too late?"

"You're fine," he says and takes the tweezers and whatever he has tweezed back to the bathroom. The toilet flushes and I can see him walking through the living room. He wears a pair of boxers and a ribbed undershirt. When we were teenagers my husband worked in Akron's rubber plants. Now most of those plants are gone and so he found a job running the heavy machinery for, oddly enough, a heavy-machinery manufacturing center. He's still very strong. He still has the figure of a man who grew up lugging around hundred-pound tires all day. We went to high school together and married a few years after we graduated. I feel very lucky. I made a good decision by accident. In high school we all chose boyfriends blindly, like Pin the Tail on the Donkey. I thought he was handsome and that was about all I thought. So I was surprised to find, after we'd been married a few years, that my husband was someone I really did love. There were things about him that he'd kept hidden in school, secrets that made him precious to me, like kindness and wonder and a beautiful singing voice, qualities that took a couple of years to chip away at before they were revealed.

"Can you take off your clothes?" I ask him when he returns.

"I like my pajamas."

"Those aren't pajamas. They're underwear."

"Not necessarily."

He takes off his clothes anyway and then he looks at me once, as if I am a brand-new flashlight whose bulb, for some reason, has already dimmed and malfunctioned. But I'm not brand-new. We've been married for almost eleven years now.

He gets back into bed and I curl up, wrapping my body around the tick bite. I can see the picture of the chicken-rendering brother from Minnesota. He is smiling up at me from the floor, where I dropped him. I have a sister. She'd never work at a chicken plant for me. I also had a brother once but I don't think he would have done it either. Not because he wasn't kind. He was. And not because he was too busy with his own plans either. He really wasn't. He didn't have any plans or if he did he kept them very secret. My brother had trouble knowing what to make of his life. Though there were days when he'd feel inspired by a Tony Robbins infomercial or something equally stupid and he'd think, *Well, maybe I should get a job*, he never was able to hold down any sort of position except for a few short stints working at a dry cleaner's in town. He reminded me of Abraham Lincoln, tall and very skinny, but even quieter. When he graduated from high school he just sort of froze as if he were caught in the headlights, as if he were distracted by every leaf on every tree. He couldn't move forward because he couldn't, he said, see the point of it. "Don't you know where forward is headed?" he asked me one Thanksgiving. I didn't have an answer. He'd scratched his ear. He'd stood and stared out the window of our parents' house as if there might be some answer out there, some sign. I don't think he saw anything, because he sat back down and stared at the carpeting on the floor. And maybe I should have said something but I didn't know what to say. Yeah, I know where forward is headed but I try not to think about it.

We didn't find him for three days, because no one even realized he was missing for a while. He'd hanged himself from a tree, one of several that grew in a small sliver of land between my parents' house and the neighbors', out by a swing set that hadn't been touched in years. He timbered over like a sapling when my father cut him down, his body gone stiff. Afterward, my mother, a stone-faced woman, a very hard worker, kept repeating a phrase, as if it were the motto of my brother's suicide. "He was just too in love with the world." She said it to everyone even though it wasn't really true. My mother was just trying to make sense out of something that didn't make sense at all, something that there was absolutely no reason for.

"You know *The Pajama Game*?" I ask my husband, with my mouth close to the side of his chest. "The musical?"

"No."

"Yeah, you do. It's an old one. It has that song in it. 'Hernando's Hideaway.'"

"No."

"Just knock three times and whisper low that you and I were sent by Joe?"

"Oh. Yeah. Yeah."

"Well, I never understood what they were doing inside Hernando's Hideaway."

"Hmm." His eyes are closed.

"So what were they doing?" I ask.

"What?" He opens his eyes.

"Inside Hernando's Hideaway?"

"What were they doing? I don't know. Drinking, dancing, fooling around. Adult things."

"Yeah, that's it. You're right. Adult things. That's why I was scared."

"You were scared of a song?"

"Well, that song. There was something going on inside that club, something criminal."

"I don't know."

"I do."

"Then what was it?"

"Like you said. Adult things."

"What's that?"

"Well, what's the most adult thing?"

"Fucking?" he asks.

"No. Fucking's for kids. Dying is adult."

"Oh. Shhhh," he says and turns to rub my face. He puts his hand on my cheek to stop my jaw. He doesn't want to hear about how I always thought people were dying inside that song's nightclub. That the dying was the reason they kept the security so tight. My husband gets nervous now if I say anything too strange. He thinks it all has to do with my brother, that I might also end up swinging in the breeze one day. But I don't think that is contagious. I used to say strange things even before my brother died. "Shhh, baby," he says one more time before shutting off the light.

Plus, I've been having a really strange week.

"Honey?" I say once the lights are out, but he only mumbles in reply. He's trying to sleep. I hold the covers up around my chin and close my eyes, thinking it won't happen if I can just go to sleep fast enough. But I haven't been able to fall asleep quickly this week. I know it's coming so I fret and listen while my husband's breath deepens, then slows. I panic and my chest gets tight and small. My eyes go dry. Once he is asleep the night changes. I hear every sound and every sound is scary. The furnace, the frogs, the cable wire scraping against the roof. The more alone I get, the louder the world becomes. There are wild animals outside: raccoons, squirrels, skunks, possums. I listen and then I try to brace myself, holding on to the sheets. I know it's coming like a dream of a tidal wave. I get ready for it. I wait and just when I think too much time has passed, maybe it won't happen tonight, it happens, very, very quickly, so quickly that I can't scream. My hands and feet harden into small hooves, the fingers and toes swallowed up by bone, and then the most frightening part is over with, the part where I lose my opposable thumbs. Next the fur, brown-speckled with some white. This sprouting feels like a stretch or like I'm itching each individual follicle from the inside as a wiry hair pokes through a pore. My arms and legs narrow, driving all their muscles up to the flank, in a vacuum. My neck thickens and grows. I feel my tail, which gives me some comfort. I like my tail. Finally my face pulls into a tight, hard nose. My jaw extends, my tongue grows long and thick, my lips shrink before turning black and hard as leather. And then it's done. And then I'm a deer.

I still haven't told my husband. I think it will be difficult for him to understand, even more difficult than it was for me. Still, I've been trying to prepare him slowly, planning what I'll say. "Lately," I practice, "when you turn out the light, something funny happens to me."

"What?" I imagine he'll ask. Or just, "Funny? What do you mean?"

"I turn into a deer at night." I will tell him clearly like that, no hemming, no mistaking what I mean.

"A deer?" He won't believe it. I know he won't.

"A deer," I'll confirm.

"What the fuck?" he'll say, just like that. "What the fuck?" with a certain slowness.

"Calm down," I'll tell him, though he'll probably be calm already.

"What are you talking about?" he'll ask me.

❧

I am very careful, very quiet, planting my hooves on our bed. I stand over him, staring down at his body from up on my wobbly legs, straddling his belly. I sniff his neck, licking the hair of his armpit, cleaning him. I can't help it, though I don't want to wake him. I don't know what would happen if he woke up now. He keeps a .22 and a shotgun in the hall closet.

When I was growing up the land was different around here. That wasn't so long ago, thirty-five years. Mostly there were a lot of soybean farms, hog farms, and wide, wide tracts of government-owned land where every now and then you'd see men digging with bright lights late at night, looking for natural gas. Sometimes the gas diggers would wake me up. Their lights were so bright it was easy to imagine they were coming from an alien spaceship. The gas-well sites were all connected by long, straight roads on the government land. These roads went on forever, and as we drove down them, it became easy to imagine that the roads were closing up behind my parents' car, sealing us in. My brother, sister, and I would stare out the back window. It felt like entering a land of no return. It's not like that anymore. As soon as they didn't find much gas the government sold the land off to developers.

At that time, when we were young, there was a man who lived around here. Everyone said the man had fucked a deer, though I don't see how they could know that. But it was a small town so rumors were easy to spread, especially about someone who didn't talk much.

Soon people started saying even more. They said that the man fucked his own daughter also, and there might have been some truth to that. She had been taken away by Child Services and no one really knew why. They were private people. But the spookiest part of the whole story, and the reason why everyone suspected him, is that the man named the deer after his daughter, Jennifer. He'd call for the deer: "Jennifer. Jennifer." You could hear him at night. That'd be the only sound in the town. "Jennifer. Jennifer." Slowly. And the deer would come when called, as if it were a dog and not a wild creature. She'd come to him.

I've been thinking about this man a lot lately. I've been thinking about how messed-up people are by sex, by other people, because despite his failings as a human being, I could never help myself—I liked this man. He was interesting to me because he knew a lot about the woods, about nature. He knew which kinds of mushrooms you could eat and which kinds would kill you. He collected the old seed-pods of bat nuts. They looked like hard black stars. He told me that when deer are young they have no scent. That way, before the deer can walk, their mothers can hide them in the tall grass and as long as the mother goes away, no predators will find the babies, because they can't smell them. Like some divine plan. Almost. The man found Jennifer when she was just a fawn. He stumbled onto her in a field. Her mother must have been killed by a construction truck, because the fawn was about to die from hunger. She'd been waiting in the tall grass but her mother didn't return and so the man found the fawn, picked her up, carried her home, and made her a bottle of milk. He raised her in his barn after he lost his own daughter to the state. And then, when the deer was old enough, the rumor was that he treated the animal in a similar manner.

❧

Eventually I fall asleep, and when I wake in the morning, I am a woman again. I am still thinking about the deer man. My husband is just starting to move, smacking with his lips. No one ever thinks that animal fuckers might actually be in love. Maybe the man just thought, *Well, I'm no better than this deer, am I?* And I think that's a good question. I don't know what happened to the deer but the man is dead now and so I feel like I can say it here under the covers with my husband still asleep. I always thought there was something romantic about the way he named the deer after his daughter. Even if it was messed up.

❧

When I tell my husband what is happening to me at night, which I'm going to do, very soon now, he'll want to know how, and then, after that, he'll want to know why I am becoming a deer. That's the part I'm not sure I can tell him yet.

❧

"My name's Erich," he said. "With a 'ch,'" he clarified. I knew he was lying because anyone who uses too much detail is usually lying. People only use detail when they absolutely have to. Married, I thought, and I was annoyed that he would lie to me so I told him my real name. I even told him where I worked. I even told him I was married.

When my husband asked me later that night, "Did you have fun with the girls? What'd you all end up doing?" I filled his head with details just like that "ch."

I told him how we went up to Akron and went to some new, fancy club that had a bouncer at the door and a velvet rope. I told him how Sarah tripped and knocked into a cocktail waitress who was carrying a tray of three drinks, how Vicky had been getting religious lately, and I told him how Meghan had gone out on a date with Steve Perry, the singer from that old band Journey. I even told him how she said Steve Perry was nice but a little old for her. She didn't feel much attraction to him, and plus, the whole time she couldn't stop singing, "Don't stop! Believing!"

"Sounds good," my husband had said. "Steve Perry. That's cool."

In an evening filled with that many details, there wouldn't have been time for me to meet Erich, or whatever his name was, in the line for the bathroom. There wouldn't have been time for him to follow me into the ladies' room, where, with his hand up my shirt, he started biting my neck and chest like he was lost in some fever, like he was going to eat me with his lips that were so thick and filled with blood.

◦◦◦

"I'm going to call in sick to work," I tell my husband.

"You don't feel well, hon?"

"No. I'm fine. I just can't go to work today."

I walk into the living room, pick up the phone, and call my boss. It's early enough that I can just leave her a message. The machine picks up. "You've reached Sachman's Real Estate Agency. No one is here to take your call. Kindly leave your name, number, and a brief message, and one of our agents will get back to you. Thank you."

I tell her I have Lyme disease. I tell her I won't be coming in. I cough into the phone and then say good-bye. I hang up and get back in bed. The cough might have been overdoing it.

My husband is getting ready for work. He is wearing socks, boxers, a T-shirt, and a flannel. He comes into the bedroom, eating a bowl of cereal, looking for his pants and shoes. "You don't feel well?" he asks again.

"I feel fine," I tell him.

"Then why are you staying home from work?"

I stare at a blank spot above our bureau. "I hate it there."

"You do?" he asks, surprised.

"Well, I just started to yesterday."

"Oh," he says.

He shakes his head so I lie back in the bed. From under the covers I hear him open his dresser drawer. I think about how he has arms and legs that move perfectly. How he pulls ticks off me. He came from his mother and nothing is wrong with him. He went to elementary school, where probably, one day, someone wasn't nice to him. Maybe they called him "jerk." Under the covers, I hate these kids that might have said that to him, because I didn't mean to cheat on him. It was an accident, like a car crash. Except I'd tell him if I had crashed the car.

I pick up the paper from the floor, where I dropped it last night. Insurgents in Afghanistan. Murder in Darfur. Target to open a store in Manchuria. Manatees in Florida, some getting killed, some getting saved by environmentalists. And then I open to the center spread. It looks a bit like the periodic table of elements. The photos are tiny, but there, crammed onto the page, are the images of all the local soldiers who have been killed in Iraq. It's a lot of people. The dead stare out from their enlistment photos or high school senior portraits. They are arranged alphabetically. I notice how young they are. I notice how many soldiers share similar last names, as if entire families have been wiped out. But of course they're not family. They probably didn't even know one another. Anderson. Brown. Clark. Davis. DeBasi. Green. Hall. Kern. All those young people. I close the paper. None of it matters to me. I know it should but it doesn't. I have my own problems. All my head can think about is what I've done and all my body wants is to do it again.

Erich's lips tasted like a meal, a meal of a stranger's breath. I was surprised that someone new, someone I had just met in a bar, had spit that tasted a little bit familiar, a little salty, and I knew in that moment that we really all did come from the ocean once. Huge lips and watery eyes. That's about all I ever dreamed of. Erich told me, like a cut in my ear, "I'd fuck you to death," and for the past five days I've been hearing him say that over and over again. Touching the scab. "I'd fuck you to death. I'd fuck you to death." Each time it feels like getting punched in the stomach, only lower, deeper than the stomach, like I can't breathe in my legs. And then for the past five nights I've been turning into a deer.

The phone starts to ring. It is probably my sister. I lie in bed, listening to the ring.

When my sister had her second baby a couple of months ago I told her, "That's weird."

"What is?" she asked.

"You just made another death in the world."

"Fuck off," she said. I guess she thought I was referring to our brother.

"All right," I told her. "Okay." But she's been a little bit angry at me ever since. She's been a little mean, as if I were responsible for the fact that we all have to die sometime.

My husband and I both just let the phone ring. It's too early and soon enough, after five rings, it stops. I hope it wasn't the office calling me back.

I will tell him. Any minute now I'll say it. "Imagine what it's like to lose your opposable thumbs, to have them bone up into hard hooves. It was scary at first," I'll say. "How do you think deer open doors?" I'll ask him.

"I don't know. How?" He'll think I'm telling him a joke.

"They don't."

If I tell him, though, maybe he could build a special door for me. He's handy like that. A door that doesn't require opposable thumbs. Still, he'll want to know where I'm going at night. And what would I say? Out with the other deer? He wouldn't like that. All the deer around here have been forced out into the open by the new construction. They get hit by cars all the time. He won't want me to go out with the deer. So where would I go? Back to the nightclub? The bouncer would be surprised to find a deer trying to enter a club as nice as his, but he'd let me in. "It takes all kinds," he'd say, throwing open a velvet curtain on the room. Just knock three times and whisper low. The song says something about castanets and silhouettes. I'd scan the nightclub for Erich. Couples would sit around small cocktail tables, snapping their fingers in time to the rhythm of the song. A scent would hit me and I'd turn into it just like a movie star slapped across her face. Beautiful with a fever. I'd rev my hoof across the dance floor. I'd smell thick lips. I'd smell the blood of an animal the kitchen staff was preparing. I'd lick my lips, slowly, letting my pink tongue dangle out of my black mouth a little, just like some animal waiting by the side of the road for the driver who killed it to come back one more time and kill it again.

I sit up in bed now and spread out the skin of my stomach. The hole the tick made has swelled up into a bead, a pink bead of skin, like some new growth. I pick at it but it is hard and I can't get much purchase on it. I rest the tip of one finger on the spot as if my finger were a stethoscope. I try to listen to what is happening underneath and I think I hear something. There is something going on under there. A rumbling. Maybe he didn't get the head out. It's not his fault. It's hard to get the head out and he's squeamish when it comes to hurting me. Even when I ask him to.

"I wonder if I have Lyme disease," I finally say to him but this is actually a minor fear, a made-up fear, compared to what I am really thinking about: my tail, my hooves. He turns to look at me. I try again. "I mean I've been thinking a lot about deer." He has a seat beside me on the bed, raising his eyebrows. But that is not quite what I mean and so this time I try to be honest with him. I say it. "I mean I think I'm becoming a deer."

"You think you're becoming a deer?" he asks.

Erich called me at work yesterday to tell me what he wanted to do to me. He said he wanted to see me. He said he wanted to eat my roast-beef pussy. One thing very general, one thing very specific. It made it difficult for me to breathe, hearing those very specific words. No one had ever said that combination of things to me before. I was shocked by how powerful those words were. I started to think that maybe he actually wanted to kill me. Thus, the reference to beef. Thus, "I'd fuck you to death."

After he hung up I thought about Becky and Tom Sawyer in the cave, though I haven't read that book in over twenty years. I don't think Tom would ever talk that way to Becky. I couldn't actually remember what happened to them down in the cave or why they were there but I know that danger was nearby and Tom was keeping Becky safe. There were bad men in the cave, bad men who filled the cave with the stench of their badness. I bet Becky could smell it. I bet it made her think differently about Tom. Maybe she would have been interested to hear the things those bad men wanted to do to her.

This morning I can see through the living room into the kitchen. I can see the mailboxes waiting by the edge of the road. Lust makes room, the way a bomb exploding makes room, clearing things out of the way. I listen for a moment, trying to position my ear near my heart. I can't get my head very close. Ticktickticktickticktickticktick. I don't actually hear any bombs ticking. I'm just worried for my husband.

"You're becoming a deer?" he asks me again. My husband is looking out the window. He is wincing. Maybe he is thinking about something else, something that happened at the heavy-machinery plant. Maybe he is thinking about another woman, perhaps one we knew in high school who didn't have problems like this.

We sit in silence. I don't want to say anything more just yet. I want, for a moment, to let it be.

"Will you show me?" he asks and doesn't wait for an answer before telling me what to do. "Show me tonight."

That's not what I thought he'd say.

"Okay," I tell him very quietly. "I will."

"A deer," he says.

"A deer," I repeat.

"All right," he says, "all right," and then he leaves without kissing me good-bye.

"Bye," I yell.

He grabs his coat and the front door slams shut, not because he's angry but because the wood has swollen and in order to get our front door to shut, one has to slam it closed. Or maybe he is also angry and he is just disguising his slamming in the swollen door.

I stay in bed during the day, while he is at work, as if I really am sick. In the bed I feel something foreign bloom in between my husband and me, an intruder, a mold. I see my husband with eyes that don't know him, as if he quite suddenly became a man from Brazil, or grew a beard, or started speaking in a Southern accent. As if, after eleven years of marriage, he somehow had all of his secrets returned to him, made secret again.

✧

We don't talk about it at dinner or even after dinner, when we're watching TV or brushing our teeth. Instead he tells me a story about a guy at work who's been running a credit card scam and got caught. "You never would have suspected this guy," he says. "Older fella, balding and stooped. He didn't seem smart enough. He didn't seem like he cared enough about being rich to become a criminal."

I climb in bed to read the paper but I can't much concentrate on the words there. The nervousness inside me is messing with my thoughts, getting ready to blow. The newspaper says something about the Peking Opera, something about a volcano in Indonesia, something about a government cover-up, but it's all the same to me.

My husband has stopped talking. He takes off his clothes without my even asking him to and stands in front of me, pulling on one ear like there is an honesty tonight, a bright rawness I've never seen before. He is beautiful to look at. I slide the newspaper to the floor and he shuts off the light. We don't say good night to one another. I'm too nervous. We don't say anything and the air is rigid between us in the dark. I wait, blinking my eyes, seeing nothing. I worry. There's no guarantee that anything will happen. Just because something has happened doesn't mean it will continue to happen, and then he will think I'm crazy and then he will call some girl we knew in high school, one who doesn't have problems like this. One who doesn't have a dead brother. I listen for him to fall asleep, for his breath to change, but it doesn't. Instead he clears his throat. I hear him stay awake, imagining his eyes blinking open against the dark like mine. I wait and wait, listening. America at night, a couple of cars, some wind, a plane overhead, a blue jay or a crow—one of the birds with an ugly voice is upset about something outside. I wait and listen until I can't wait any longer. The blanket is up around the back of my neck. My eyes shut as a woman and I am asleep before it happens.

When I wake it is still night. I can tell because there is a small knot of unknown fear in my lungs and a soupy proximity to every memory I've ever had. Something is rousing me, something wants for attention. A poke, a sharpness dragged across the fur of my back. I seize up the muscles in my neck. The barrel of a gun.

Though the room is dark I can see in the light of the alarm clock's blue digital numbers, 12:32. I can see my hooves. I am too scared to move, too scared to turn around. The newspaper lies on the floor. The brother in Minnesota is probably still at his security job after having worked all day at the chicken plant. I think of him. I wonder if his sister is home asleep or if she is out at the bar with her college friends. It seems important to know which just at that moment. It seems important to understand whether or not it is worth it to sacrifice yourself for someone else.

I feel the poke again. It is sharp. There is no mistaking it and so I release my breath, resigned. I get all four legs underneath me. They tremble as I turn, prepared for what I might deserve. I decide, in that moment, that it's worth it even if I don't really mean that.

The digital clock changes to 12:33. There is no gun.

He has his front hoof raised. A buck, almost twice my size, with nearly eight points of antlers, is waiting, his leg raised as if looking for the answer to some question I didn't hear asked. The light of the clock reflects dully in the curve of his worn antlers. My front knees loosen and shake, so that I stumble. My head dips away from him. There is a deer in my bedroom, one besides me, that is, and I am terrified, more terrified than I would be by all the guns in the world. I know what a gun means. I haven't got any idea what a deer does.

I lift my eyes to him. He winces again when we meet. He lowers his hoof down to the rug and, turning his back on me, walks from the bedroom. It is then that I pick up his scent. His mother gave birth to him. High school. A tire plant. Akron. Heavy machinery. The dinner I made him just hours ago. Mine.

I follow him into our living room. "How?" I want to ask him but we are both deer now and deer cannot speak. His neck is bent and he is maneuvering between his antlers, working on something. He has the front doorknob in his mouth, in his jaws. He twists his head, opening the door as if he's done this a hundred times before. He is demonstrating to me how it is done. The door sticks with the humidity but he shoves it open with his neck. I can see he's really good at opening the door with his mouth, practiced. The night rushes in and he stands back from it, looking up at me. I can't be sure what he is saying. Either, "Get out," or "Come on." His deer eyes are dark and hard to read. But he is waiting for me to do something. I nudge the screen door with my nose. I walk out in front of him, scared to leave, wondering if he will follow.

Outside, the night is beautiful. Stars and cold. A navy blue sky. The grass underfoot breaks into a spicy smell, oregano and dirt. Why should anyone be afraid of night? But then there is motion around me like standing in a flooded river, and I'm terrified. I am afraid of this night. I stumble back, trying to figure out what I'm looking at, to let the world come into focus. Fur and flanks and pointy hips and rib cages pass slowly before me. Sharp ears that nervously twitch forward and back. Everywhere the warmth of blood. Dark brown eyes lined with white fur, quivering backs that shake an itch. Silence. The road, the yard, the whole county it seems, is filled with deer, a calm stampede of them. An ocean of brown fur moving both together and separately, the way a caterpillar's back will resist and accept the ground at the same time. Some deer going up the road, some going down. They thread each other. Not one of the deer says a word. It's quiet. Each looks exactly the same, a flood of the ordinary. I am humiliated by their numbers, by the way they clump themselves together desperately, like insects.

I turn to go back inside our house but he is standing on the front step. He stomps his foot. He doesn't want us to go back inside. He curls his spine and lurches quickly, urging me forward as if that is where we both belong, as if that is where we've both always been. I know exactly where forward is headed. I look out at the deer again, trying to pick out just one from the mass. This is very hard to do. They are guarding what's individual by disguising it with what's not. Try to see one leaf in a forest. It's hard.

My husband steps forward, in front of me. He too is staring at the deer now, the way a person might stare at the sea without thought, without time. I catch a scent. What do the deer mean? That is a good question. That is the best question. I think the answer is somewhere nearby. I can smell it. I could almost say what the answer is but I am a deer now and deer can't talk.

My husband steps forward again and I follow him right up to the edge of the deer. His antlers have nearly eight points. I tell myself I'll remember. I'll find him. I step forward and then I step forward again, closer to the deer. I feel the warmth of that many animals. I feel their plainness rising up to swallow me. I step forward into the stream of beasts.

MIRANDA JULY

Oranges

I.

Are you the favorite person of anybody?
What?
Are you anyone's favorite person?
Oh.
I can give you more time to think about it.
No, no, that's okay.
Some very prominent people are not anyone's favorite, it doesn't
necessarily mean—
I am.
You are?
Yes. My ex-girlfriend's. Christina.

Great! Thank you! Can I ask you how sure you are of this: very certain, confident, you think so, not so sure, or could be?

I'm very certain.

That's the highest.

Oh, it is? What was the second highest?

Confident.

Oh.

The one below that is you think so.

Yeah. That one.

You think so?

Yeah.

Okay, this has been really helpful.

I'm glad.

Send anyone down here if you think they might want to do the survey.

I will.

Thanks again.

Okay, bye.

Bye.

II.

Are you the favorite person of anybody?

What?

Are you anyone's favorite person?

Okay, I'm not interested.

It's just a survey.

Yeah, I don't vote.

It's not political—

Yeah, I understand, I'm not interested in that sort of stuff.

What sort of stuff?

Free love and all that.
What? That's not what it's about!
Okay, I know, I'm sure it's a good thing, I just don't want to be
involved.
Okay, that's fair.
Okay, bye.
Bye.

III.

Are you the favorite person of anybody?
What?
Are you anyone's favorite person?
Oh. No.
Are you sure?
Yeah, definitely.
Great! Thank you! Can I ask you how sure you are of this: very cer-
tain, confident, you think so, not so sure, or could be?
I'm very certain.
That's the highest.
I know.
Hey, do you want an orange?
What?
An orange—my wife asked me to get rid of some of these oranges.
We have three trees and they just keep producing.
So it's free?
Totally free. You'd be doing us a favor.
Can I have two?
Sure.
My girlfriend might like one.
Take three.

Are you sure?
Yeah!
Terrific! These are great oranges, thanks!
Thank you.
Thanks again!
Okay, bye!
Bye.

IV.

Are you the favorite person of anybody?
What?
Are you anyone's favorite person?
I don't know but can I ask you a question?
What?
If I keep walking down this way will I get to the beach?
The beach? No. The beach is on the other side of town.
But isn't it in this direction?
Well sure, it's west, but it's like thirty miles or something.
Thanks.
You're not going to walk there, are you?
Yeah.
It's too far.
It's okay, I've got a lot of time.
Shit, you really do.
Yeah.
I'd get bored and then after that I'd get lonely.
I'll be fine.
Really?
Yeah.
It might even be nice, right? Kind of peaceful?

Yep.

Sounds nice. I wish I could do that.

You're welcome to come with me.

Yeah?

Sure.

Naw. I have to stay and do this.

Suit yourself.

Yeah, this is pretty important. This survey. Did I already ask you?

What?

Are you the favorite person of anybody?

Yeah, you did.

Right, sorry.

Well, see you later.

Yeah, see you.

V.

Are you the favorite person of anybody?

Oh, no thank you, I already did the survey.

What?

I did it back there, with another guy.

Oh shit.

Maybe you should go to another area, farther away.

Yeah, shit, though. You were going to be my last person for the day.

Oh.

Yeah, see, that's the thing, if you would've been able to answer I could've gone home now.

Oh.

Yeah, there's this show I really wanted to watch on TV.

What show?

America's Next Top Model.

Oh yeah, that's kind of like the survey.

What?

You know, it's like America's Next Top Favorite Person of Everybody.

Oh, I see where this is headed.

What?

You think I work for *America's Next Top Model.*

No I don't.

Yeah, you think I'm out recruiting models for the next season.

No, not at all, I was just free-associating.

Exactly, you were trying to associate yourself with the show, through me.

No I wasn't.

Well, I've got news for you: One, I *could* be working for super-model Tyra Banks, I could very well be, because this is LA and it's a free country. But I'm not. And secondly, you aren't pretty enough to be a model.

I know that.

Well, that's good, because you could waste your life trying to get into modeling instead of doing something useful with yourself.

Like what?

Well, like anything, like, you know, I don't know, anything.

Like walking?

No, not walking, that's not useful.

Oh.

You could, like, be a doctor or something. I don't know.

Or a veterinarian.

Yeah, that's a good example.

But I'll never do that, I don't have the discipline.

Me either, I can barely do *this.*

Yeah, me too. I can barely keep up with everything as it is.

Yeah, even without medical school and all that.

Yeah, I can't even go to the gym.

The gym? I can barely even move.

Me too, I can't move at all usually.

I'm like a brick or a stone.

Or a piece of food.

Food?

Like a piece of food that someone dropped on the ground and not even the dogs want to eat it.

Yeah, not even the bugs or worms will eat me.

Not even germs.

Germs won't even touch me.

I'm the same way.

Yeah? Are you the favorite person of anybody? I'm not, are you?

I'd like to think so.

Even though you're like a piece of dropped food?

Sure, why not? Maybe I have a secret admirer.

How sure are you of this?

I'm not so sure.

But why not hope?

Right, hoping's free.

You take care.

You too.

Bye.

Bye.

KELLY LINK

Light

TWO MEN, ONE RAISED BY WOLVES

The man at the bar on the stool beside her: bent like a hook over some item. A book, not a drink. A children's book; dog-eared. When he noticed her stare, he grinned and said, "Got a light?" It was a Friday night, and the Splinter was full of men saying things. Some guy off in a booth was saying, for example, "Well, sure, you can be raised by wolves and lead a normal life but—"

Lindsey said, "I don't smoke."

The man straightened up. He said, "Not that kind of light. I mean a *light*. Do you have a *light*?"

"I don't understand," she said. And then because he was not bad-looking, she said, "Sorry."

"Stupid bitch," he said. "Never mind." The watercolor illustration in his book showed a boy and a girl standing in front of a dragon the size of a Volkswagen bus. The man had a pen. He'd drawn word bubbles coming out of the children's mouths, and now he was writing in words. The children were saying—

The man snapped the book shut; it was a library book.

"Excuse me," she said, "but I'm a children's librarian. Can I ask why you're defacing that book?"

"I don't know, *can* you? *Maybe* you can and *maybe* you can't, but why ask me?" the man said. Turning his back to her, he hunched over the book again.

Which was really too much. She opened her shoulder bag and took out her travel sewing kit. She palmed the needle and then jabbed the man in his left buttock. Very fast. Her hand was back in her lap and she was signaling the bartender for another drink when the man howled and sat up. Now everyone was looking at him. He slid off his stool and hurried away, glancing back at her once in outrage.

There was a drop of blood on the needle. She wiped it on a bar napkin.

At a table behind her three women were talking about a new pocket universe. A new diet. A coworker's new baby: a girl, born with no shadow. This was bad, although, thank God, not as bad as it could have been, a woman—someone called her Caroline—was saying.

A long, lubricated conversation followed about over-the-counter shadows—prosthetics, available in most drugstores, not expensive and reasonably durable. Everyone was in agreement that it was almost impossible to distinguish a prosthetic shadow from a real one.

Caroline and her friends began to talk of babies born with two shadows. Children with two shadows did not grow up happy. They didn't get on well with other children. You could cut a pair of shadows apart with a pair of crooked scissors, but it wasn't a permanent solution. By the end of the day the second shadow always grew back, twice as long. If you didn't bother to cut back the second shadow, then eventually you had twins, one of whom was only slightly realer than the other.

Lindsey had grown up in a stucco house in a scab-raw development in Dade County. Opposite the house had been a bruised and trampled nothing. A wilderness that grew, was razed, then grew back again. Banyan trees dripping with spiky epiphytes; tunnels of coral reef barely covered by blackish, sandy dirt that Lindsey—and her twin, Alan, not quite real enough, yet, to play with other children—lowered herself into, to emerge skinned, bloody, triumphant. Developers' bulldozers made football field–size depressions that filled with water when it rained and produced thousands and thousands of fingernail-size tan toads. Lindsey kept them in jars. She caught blue crabs, Cuban lizards, yellow-pink tobacco grasshoppers the size of toy trucks. They spat when you caged them in your hand. Geckos with their papery clockwork insides, ticktock barks; anoles whose throats pulsed out like bloody fans; king snakes coral snakes *red and yellow kill a fellow, red and black friendly Jack* corn snakes. When Lindsey was ten, a lightning strike ignited a fire under the coral reef. For a week smoke ghosted up. They kept the sprinklers on but the grass cooked brown. Alan caught five snakes, lost three of them in the house while he was watching Saturday-morning cartoons.

Lindsey had had a happy childhood. The women in the bar didn't know what they were talking about.

It was almost a shame when the man who had theories about being raised by wolves came over and threw his drink in the face of the woman named Caroline. There was a commotion. Lindsey and the man who had theories about being raised by wolves went for a walk on the beach. He was charming, but she felt his theories were only that: charming. When she said this, he became less charming. Nevertheless, she invited him home.

"Nice place," he said. "I like all the whatsits."

"Most of it belongs to my brother," Lindsey said.

"Your *brother*. Does he live with you?"

"God, no," Lindsey said. "He's . . . wherever he is."

"I had a sister. Died when I was two," the man said. "Wolves make really shitty parents."

"Ha," she said, experimentally.

"Ha," he said. And then, "Look at that," as he was undressing her. Their four shadows fell across the bed, sticky and wilted as if from lovemaking that hadn't even begun. At the sight of their languorously intertwined shadows, the wolf man became charming again. "Look at these sweet little tits," he said over and over again as though she might not ever have noticed how sweet and little her tits were. He exclaimed at the sight of every part of her; afterward, she slept poorly, apprehensive that he might steal away, taking along one of the body parts or pieces that he seemed to admire so much.

In the morning, she woke and found herself stuck beneath the body of the wolf man as if she had been trapped beneath a collapsed and derelict building. When she began to wriggle her way out from under him, he woke and complained of a fucking terrible hangover. He called her "Joanie" several times, asked to borrow a pair of scissors, and spent a long time in her bathroom with the door locked while she read the paper. "Smuggling ring apprehended by___. Government overthrown in___. Family of twelve last seen in vicinity of___. Start of hurricane season___." The wolf man came out of the bathroom, dressed hurriedly, and left.

She found a spongy black heap, the amputated shadow of his dead twin, and three soaked, pungent towels, on the bathroom floor; there were stubby black bits of beard in the sink. The blades of her nail scissors were tarry and blunted.

She threw away the reeking towels. She mopped up the shadow, folding it into a large Ziploc bag, carried the bag into the kitchen, and put the shadow down the disposal. She ran the water for a long time.

Then she went outside and sat on her patio and watched the iguanas eat the flowers off her hibiscus. It was 6:00 a.m. and already quite warm.

NO VODKA, ONE EGG

Sponges hold water. Water holds light. Lindsey was hollow all the way through when she wasn't full of alcohol. The water in the canal was glazed with light, which wouldn't hold still. It was vile. She had the beginnings of one of her headaches. Light beat down on her head and her second shadow began to move, rippling in waves like the light-shot water in the canal. She went inside. The egg in the refrigerator door had a spot of blood when she cracked it into the pan. She liked vodka in her orange juice, but there was no orange juice and no vodka in the freezer, only a smallish iguana.

The Keys were overrun with iguanas. They ate her hibiscus; every once in a while she caught one of the smaller ones with the pool net and stuck it in her freezer for a few days. This was supposedly a humane way of dealing with iguanas. You could even eat them, although she did not. She was a vegetarian.

She put out food for the bigger iguanas. They liked ripe fruit. She liked to watch them eat. She knew that she was not being consistent or fair in her dealings, but there it was.

MEN UNLUCKY AT CARDS

Lindsey's job was not a particularly complicated one. There was an office, and behind the office was a warehouse full of sleeping people. There was an agency in DC that paid her company to take responsibility for the sleepers. Every year, hikers and cavers and construction workers found a few dozen more. No one knew how to wake them up. No one knew what they meant, what they did, where they came from.

There were always at least two security guards on duty at the warehouse. They were mostly, in Lindsey's opinion, lecherous assholes. She spent the day going through invoices, and then went home again. The wolf man wasn't at the Splinter and the bartender threw everyone out at 2:00 a.m.; she went back to the warehouse on a hunch, four hours into the night shift.

～⚬～

Bickle and Lowes had hauled out five sleepers, three women and two men. They'd put Miami Hydra baseball caps on the male sleepers and stripped the women, propped them up in chairs around a foldout table. Someone had arranged the hands of one of the male sleepers down between the legs of one of the women. Cards had been dealt out. Maybe it was just a game of strip poker and the two women had been unlucky. It was hard to play your cards well when you were asleep.

Larry Bickle stood behind one of the women, his cheek against her hair. He seemed to be giving her advice about how to play her cards. He wasn't holding his drink carefully enough, and the woman's neat lap brimmed with beer.

Lindsey watched for a few minutes. Bickle and Lowes had gotten to the sloppy, expansive stage of drunkenness that, sober, she resented most. False happiness.

When Lowes saw Lindsey he stood up so fast his chair tipped over. "Hey now," he said. "It's different from how it looks."

Both guards had little, conical, paper party hats on their heads.

A third man, no one Lindsey recognized, came wandering down the middle aisle like he'd been shopping at Wal-Mart. He wore boxer shorts and a party hat. "Who's this?" he said, leering at Lindsey.

Larry Bickle's hand was on his gun. What was he going to do? Shoot her? She said, "I've already called the police."

"Oh, fuck me," Bickle said. He said some other things.

"You called the police?" Edgar Lowes said.

"They'll be here in about ten minutes," Lindsey said. "If I were you, I'd leave right now. Just go. It isn't as if I can stop you."

"What is that bitch saying?" Bickle said unhappily. He was really quite drunk. His hand was still on his gun.

She took out her own gun, a Beretta. She pointed it in the direction of Bickle and Lowes. "Put your gun belts on the ground and take off your uniforms too. Leave your keys and your ID cards. You too, whoever you are. Hand over your ID and I won't press charges."

"You've got little cats on your gun," Edgar Lowes said.

"Hello Kitty stickers," she said. "I count coup." Although she'd only ever shot one person.

The men took off their clothes but not the party hats. Edgar Lowes had a purple scar down his chest. He saw Lindsey looking and said, "Triple bypass. I need this job for the health insurance."

"Too bad," Lindsey said. She followed them out into the parking lot. The third man didn't seem to care that he was naked. He didn't even have his hands cupped around his balls, the way Bickle and Lowes did. He said to Lindsey, "They've done this a couple of times. Heard about it from a friend. Tonight was my birthday party."

"Happy birthday," she said. She watched the three men get into their cars and drive away. Then she went back into the warehouse and folded up the uniforms, emptied the guns, cleaned up the sleepers, used the dolly to get the sleepers back to their boxes. There was a bottle of cognac and plenty of beer. She drank steadily. A song came to her, and she sang it. *Tall and tan and young and drunken and—* She knew she was getting the words wrong. *A midnight pyre. Like a bird on fire. I have tried in my way to be you.*

It was almost 5:00 a.m. The floor came up at her in waves, and she would have liked to lie down on it.

The sleeper in Box 113 was Harrisburg Pennsylvania, a young boy. The sleepers were named after their place of origin. Other countries did it differently. Harrisburg Pennsylvania had long eyelashes and a bruise on his cheek that had never faded. The skin of a sleeper was always just a little cooler than you expected. You could get used to anything. She set the alarm in her cell phone to wake her up before the shift change.

In the morning, Harrisburg Pennsylvania was still asleep and Lindsey was still drunk. She'd drooled a little on his arm.

❧

All she said to her supervisor, the general office manager, was that she'd fired Bickle and Lowes. Mr. Charles gave her a long-suffering look, said, "You look a bit rough."

"I'll go home early," she said.

She would have liked to replace Bickle and Lowes with women, but in the end she hired an older man with excellent job references and a graduate student, Jason, who said he planned to spend his evenings working on his dissertation. (He was a philosophy student, and she asked what philosopher his dissertation was on. If he'd said "Nietzsche" she might have terminated the interview. But he said "John Locke.")

She'd already requested additional grant money to pay for security cameras, but when it was turned down she went ahead and bought the cameras anyway. She had a bad feeling about the two men who worked the Sunday-to-Wednesday day shift.

AS CHILDREN, THEY WERE INSEPARABLE

On Tuesday, there was a phone call from Alan. He was yelling something in LinLan before she could even say hello.

"*Berma lisgo airport. Tus fah me?*"

"Alan?"

He said, "I'm at the airport, Lin-Lin, just wondering if I can come and stay with you for a bit. Not too long. Just need to keep my head down for a while. You won't even know I'm there."

"Back up," she said. "Where are you?"

"The airport," he said, clearly annoyed. "Where the planes are."

"I thought you were in Tibet," she said.

"Well," Alan said. "That didn't quite work out. I've decided to move on."

"What did you do?" she said. "Alan?"

"Lin-Lin, please," he said. "I'll explain everything tonight. I'll make dinner. House key still under the broken planter?"

"*Fisfis meh*," she said. "Fine."

❧

The last time she'd seen Alan in the flesh was two years ago, just after Elliot had left for good. Her husband.

They'd both been more than a little drunk and Alan was always nicer when he was drunk. He gave her a hug and said, "Come on, Lindsey. You can tell me. It's a bit of a relief, isn't it?"

❧

The sky was low and swollen. Lindsey loved this, the sudden green afternoon darkness as rain came down in heavy drumming torrents so loud she could hardly hear the radio station in her car, the calm, jokey pronouncements of the local weather witch. The vice president was under investigation; evidence suggested a series of secret dealings with malign spirits. A woman had given birth to a dozen rabbits. A local gas station had been robbed by invisible men. Some religious cult had thrown all the infidels out of a popular pocket universe. Nothing new, in other words. The sky was always falling. U.S. 1 was bumper-to-bumper all the way to Plantation Key.

Alan sat out on the patio behind her house, a bottle of wine under his chair, the wineglass in his hand half full of rain, half full of wine. "Lindsey!" he said. "Want a drink?" He didn't get up.

She said, "Alan? It's raining."

"It's warm," he said and blinked fat balls of rain out of his eyelashes. "It was cold where I was."

"I thought you were going to make dinner," she said.

Alan stood up and made a show of wringing out his shirt and his peasant-style cotton pants. The rain collapsed steadily on their heads.

"There's nothing in your kitchen. I would have made margaritas, but all you had was the salt."

"Let's go inside," Lindsey said. "Do you have any dry clothes? In your luggage? Where's your luggage, Alan?"

He gave her a sly look. "You know. In there."

She knew. "You put your stuff in Elliot's room." It had been her room too, but she hadn't slept there in almost a year. She only slept there when she was alone.

Alan said, "All the things he left are still there. Like he might still be in there too, somewhere down in the sheets, all folded up like a secret note. Very creepy, Lin-Lin."

Alan was only thirty-eight. The same age as Lindsey, of course, unless you were counting from the point where he was finally real enough to eat his own birthday cake. She thought he looked every year of their age. Older.

"Go get changed," she said. "I'll order takeout."

"What's in the grocery bags?" he said.

She slapped his hand away. "Nothing for you," she said.

CLOSE ENCOUNTERS OF THE ABSURD KIND

She'd met Elliot at an open mike in a pocket universe near Coral Gables. A benefit at a gay bar for some charity. Men everywhere, but most of them not interested in her. Elliot was over seven feet tall; his hair was canary yellow and his skin was greenish. Lindsey had noticed the way that Alan looked at him when they first came in. Alan had been in this universe before.

Elliot sang the song about the monster from Ipanema. He couldn't carry a tune, but he made Lindsey laugh so hard that whiskey came out of her nose. He came over and sat at the bar. He said,

"You're Alan's twin." He had only four fingers on each hand. His skin looked smooth and rough at the same time.

She said, "I'm the original. He's the copy. Wherever he is. Passed out in the bathroom, probably."

Elliot said, "Should I go get him or should we leave him here?"

"Where are we going?" she said.

"To bed," he said. His hair was feathers, not hair. His pupils were oddly shaped.

"What would we do there?" she said, and he just looked at her. Sometimes these things worked and sometimes they didn't. That was the fun of it.

She thought about it. "Okay. On the condition that you promise me that you've never fooled around with Alan. Ever."

"Your universe or mine?" he said.

Elliot wasn't the first thing Lindsey had brought back from a pocket universe. She'd gone on vacation once and brought back the pit of a green fruit that fizzed like sherbet when you bit into it and gave you dreams about staircases, ladders, rockets, things that went up and up, although nothing had come up when she planted it, although almost everything grew in Florida.

Her mother had gone on vacation in a pocket universe when she was first pregnant with Lindsey. Now people knew better. Doctors cautioned pregnant women against such trips.

For the last few years Alan had had a job with a tour group that ran trips out of Singapore. He spoke German, Spanish, Japanese, Mandarin Chinese, passable Tibetan, various pocket-universe trade languages. The tours took charter flights into Tibet and then trekked up into some of the more tourist-friendly pocket universes. Tibet was riddled with pocket universes.

"You lost them?" Lindsey said.

"Not all of them," Alan said. His hair was still wet with rain. He needed a haircut. "Just one van. I thought I told the driver Sakya but I may have said Gyantse. They showed up eventually, just two days behind schedule. It's not as if they were children. Everyone in Gyantse speaks English. When they caught up with us I was charming and full of remorse and we were all pals again."

She waited for the rest of the story. Somehow it made her feel better, knowing that Alan had the same effect on everyone.

"But then there was a mix-up at customs back at Changi. They found a reliquary in this old bastard's luggage. Some ridiculous little god in a dried-up seedpod. Some other things. The old bastard swore up and down that none of it was his. That I'd snuck up to his room and put them into his luggage. That I'd seduced him. The agency got involved and the story about Gyantse came out. So that was that."

"Alan," she said.

"I was hoping I could stay here for a few weeks."

"You'll stay out of my hair," she said.

"Of course," he said. "Can I borrow a toothbrush?"

MORE LIKE DISNEY WORLD THAN DISNEY WORLD

Their parents were retired, living in an older, established pocket universe that was apparently much more like Florida than Florida had ever been. No mosquitoes, no indigenous species larger than a lapdog, except for birdlike creatures whose songs made you want to cry and whose flesh tasted like veal. Fruit trees that no one had to cultivate. Grass so downy and tender and fragrant that no one slept indoors. Lakes so big and so shallow that you could spend all day walking across them. It wasn't a large universe, and nowadays there was a long waiting list of men and women waiting to retire to it. Lindsey and Alan's parents had invested all of their savings into a one-room cabana with a view of one of the smaller lakes. "Lotus-eating," they called it. It sounded boring to Lindsey, but her mother no longer e-mailed to ask if Lindsey was seeing anyone. If she were ever going to remarry and produce children. Grandchildren were no longer required. Grandchildren would have obliged Lindsey and Alan's parents to leave their paradise in order to visit once in a while. Come back all that long way to Florida. "That nasty place where we used to live," Lindsey's mother said. Alan had a theory that their parents were not telling them everything. "They've become nudists," he insisted. "Or swingers. Or both. Mom always had exhibitionist tendencies. Always leaving the bathroom door open. No wonder I'm gay. No wonder you're not."

Lindsey lay awake in her bed and listened to Alan make tea in the kitchen. Alan hanging up his clothes in Elliot's closet. Alan turning the television on and off. At two in the morning, he came and stood outside her bedroom door. He said, softly, "Lindsey? Are you awake?"

She didn't answer and he went away again.

In the morning he was asleep on the sofa. A DVD was playing; the sound was off. Somehow he'd found Elliot's stash of imported pocket-universe porn, the secret stash she'd spent weeks looking for and never found. Trust Alan to turn it up. But she was childishly pleased to see he hadn't found the gin she'd hidden in the sofa.

When she came home from work he was out on the patio again, trying, uselessly, to catch her favorite iguana. "Be careful of the tail," she said.

"Monster came up and bit my toe," he said.

"That's Elliot. I've been feeding him," she said. "Probably thinks you're invading his territory."

"Elliot?" he said and laughed. "That's sick."

"He's big and green," she said. "You don't see the resemblance?" Her iguana disappeared into the network of banyan trees that dipped over the canal. The banyans were full of iguanas, leaves rustling greenly with their green and secret meetings. "The only difference is he comes back."

✧

The next morning Alan drove her to work and went off with the car. In the afternoon Mr. Charles came into her office. "Bad news," he said. "Jack Harris in Pittsburgh went ahead and sent us two dozen sleepers. The new kid, Jason, signed for them down at the warehouse. Didn't think to call us first."

"You're kidding," she said.

"'Fraid not," he said. "I'm going to call Jack Harris. Ask what the hell he thought he was doing. I made it clear the other day that we weren't approved with regards to capacity. He'll just have to take them back again."

"Has the driver already gone?" she said.

"Yep. Maybe you could run over to the warehouse and take a look at the paperwork. Figure out what to do with this group in the meantime."

There were twenty-two new sleepers, eighteen males and four females. Jason already had them on dollies.

"Where were they before Pittsburgh?" she asked.

Jason handed over the dockets. "All over the place. Four of them turned up on property belonging to some guy in South Dakota. Says the government ought to compensate him for the loss of his crop."

"What happened to his crop?" she said.

"He set fire to it. They were underneath a big old dead tree out in his fields. Fortunately for everybody his son was there too. While the father was pouring gasoline on everything, the son dragged the sleepers into the bed of the truck, got them out of there. Called the hotline."

"Lucky," she said. "What the hell was the father thinking?"

"People your age—" Jason said and stopped. Started again. "Older people seem to get these weird ideas sometimes. They want everything to be the way it was. Before."

"I'm not that old," she said.

"I didn't mean that," he said. Got pink. "I just mean, you know . . ."

She touched her hair. "Maybe you didn't notice, but I have two shadows. So I'm part of the weirdness. People like me are the people that people get ideas about. Why are you on the day shift?"

"Jermaine's wife is out of town so he has to take care of the kids. What do we do with the sleepers now?"

"Leave them on the dollies," she said. "It's not like it matters to them."

She tried calling Alan's cell phone at five thirty, but got no answer. She checked e-mail and played solitaire. She hated solitaire. Enjoyed shuffling through the cards she should have played. Playing cards when she shouldn't have. Why should she pretend to want to win when there wasn't anything to win?

At seven thirty she looked out and saw her car in the parking lot. When she went down to the warehouse Alan was flirting with Jason while the other guard, Hurley, ate his dinner.

"Hey, Lin-Lin," Alan said. "Come see this. Come here."

"What the hell are you doing?" Lindsey said. "Where have you been?"

"Grocery shopping," he said. "Come here, Lindsey. Come see."

Jason made a don't-blame-me face. She'd have to take him aside at some point. Warn him about Alan. Philosophy didn't prepare you for people like Alan.

"Look at her," Alan said.

She looked down at a sleeper. A woman dressed in a way that suggested she had probably been someone important once, maybe hundreds of years ago, somewhere, probably, that wasn't anything like here. Versailles Kentucky. "I've seen sleepers before."

"No. You don't *see*," Alan said. "Of course you don't. Hey, Lin-Lin, this kind of haircut would look good on you."

He fluffed Versailles Kentucky's hair.

"Alan," she said. A warning.

"Look," he said. "Just look. Look at her. She looks just like you. She's *you*."

"You're crazy," she said.

"Am I?" Alan appealed to Jason. "You thought so too."

Jason hung his head. He mumbled something. Said, "I said that maybe there was a similarity."

Alan reached down into the container and grabbed the sleeper's bare foot, lifted the leg straight up.

"Alan!" Lindsey said. She pried his hand loose. The prints of his fingers came up on Versailles Kentucky's leg in red and white. "What are you doing?"

"It's fine," Alan said. "I just wanted to see if she has a birthmark like yours. Lindsey has a birthmark behind her knee," he said to Jason. "Looks like a battleship."

Even Hurley was staring now.

The sleeper didn't look a thing like Lindsey. No birthmark. Funny, though. The more she thought about it the more Lindsey thought maybe she looked like Alan.

NOT HERSELF TODAY

She turned her head a little to the side. Put on all the lights in the bathroom and stuck her face up close to the mirror again. Stepped back. The longer she looked the less she looked like anyone she knew.

Alan was right. She needed a haircut.

The kitchen stank of rum; Alan had the blender out. "Let me guess," he said. "You met someone nice in there." He held out a glass. "I thought we could have a nice, quiet night in. Watch the Weather Channel. Do charades. You can knit. I'll wind your yarn for you."

"I don't knit."

"No," he said. His voice was kind. Loving. "You tangle. You knot. You muddle."

"You needle," she said. "What is it that you want? Why are you here? To pick a fight?"

"*Per bol tuh*, Lin-Lin?" Alan said. "What do *you* want?" She sipped ferociously. She knew what she wanted. "Why are *you* here?"

"This is my home," she said. "I have everything I want. A job at a company with real growth potential. A boss who likes me. A bar just around the corner, full of men who want to buy me drinks. A yard full of iguanas. And a spare shadow in case one should accidentally fall off."

"This isn't your house," Alan said. "Elliot bought it. Elliot filled it up with his junk. And all the nice stuff is mine. You haven't changed a thing since he took off."

"I have more iguanas now," she said. She took her rumrunner into the living room. Alan already had the Weather Channel on. Behind the perky blond weather witch, in violent primary colors, a tropical depression hovered off the coast of Cuba.

Alan came and stood behind the couch. He put his drink down and began to rub her neck.

"Pretty, isn't it?" she said. "That storm."

"Remember when we were kids? That hurricane?"

"Yeah," she said. "I probably ought to go haul the storm shutters out of the storage unit."

"That kid at your warehouse," he said. His eyes were closed.

"Jason?"

"He seems like a nice kid."

"*Kid* being the key word. He's a philosophy student, Lan-Lan. Come on. You can do better."

"Do better? I'm thinking out loud about a guy with a fine ass,

Lindsey. Not buying a house. Or contemplating a career change. Oops, I guess I am officially doing that. Perhaps I'll become a do-gooder. A do-better."

"Just don't make my life harder, okay? Alan?"

"He has green eyes. Jason. Really, really green. Green as that color there. Right at the eye. That swirl," Alan said, draining his third rumrunner.

"I hadn't noticed his eyes," Lindsey said.

"That's because he isn't your type. You don't like nice guys." He was over at the stereo now. "Can I put this on?"

"If you want to. There's a song on there, I think it's the third song. Yeah. This one. Elliot loved this song. He'd put it on and start slithering all over the furniture."

"Oh yeah. He was a god on the dance floor. But look at me. I'm not too bad either."

"He was more flexible around the hips. I think he had a bendier spine. He could turn his head almost all the way around."

"Come on, Lindsey, you're not dancing. Come on and dance."

"I don't want to."

"Don't be such a pain in the ass."

"I have a pain inside," she said. And then wondered what she meant. "It's such a pain in the ass."

"Come on. Just dance. Okay?"

"Okay," she said. "I'm okay. See? I'm dancing."

Jason came over for dinner. Alan wore one of Elliot's shirts. Lindsey made a perfect cheese soufflé, and she said nothing when Jason assumed that Alan had made it.

She listened to Alan's stories about various pocket universes as if she had never heard them before. Most were owned by the Chinese government and, as well as the more famous tourist universes, there were ones where the Chinese sent dissidents. Very few pocket universes were larger than, say, Maryland. Some had been abandoned a long time ago. Some were inhabited. Some weren't friendly. Some pocket universes contained their own pocket universes. You could go a long ways in and never come out again. You could start your own country out there and do whatever you liked, and yet most of the people Lindsey knew, herself included, had never done anything more venturesome than go for a week to someplace where the food and the air and the landscape seemed like something out of a book you'd read as a child; a brochure; a dream.

There were sex-themed pocket universes, of course. Tax shelters and places to dispose of all kinds of things: trash, junked cars, murder victims. People went to casinos inside pocket universes more like Vegas than Vegas. More like Hawaii than Hawaii. You must be this tall to enter. This rich. Just this foolish. Because who knew what might happen? Pocket universes might wink out again, suddenly, all at once. There were best-selling books explaining how that might happen.

Alan began to reminisce about his adolescence in a way that suggested it had not really been all that long ago.

"Venetian Pools," he said to Jason. "I haven't been there in a couple of years. Since I was a kid, really. All those grottoes that you could wander off into with someone. Go make out and get such an enormous hard-on you had to jump in the water so nobody noticed and the water was so fucking cold! Can you still get baked ziti at the restaurant? Do you remember that, Lindsey? Sitting out by the pool in your bikini and eating baked ziti? I heard you can't swim now. Because of the mermaids."

The mermaids were an invasive species, like the iguanas. People had brought them back from one of the Disney pocket universes, as pets, and now they were everywhere, small but numerous in a way that appealed to children and bird-watchers. They liked to show off and although they didn't seem much smarter than, say, a talking dog, and maybe not even as smart, since they didn't speak, only sang and whistled and made rude gestures, they were too popular with the tourists at Venetian Pools to be gotten rid of.

Jason said he'd been with his sister's kids. "I heard they used to drain the pools every night in summer. But they can't do that now, because of the mermaids. So the water isn't as clear as it used to be. They can't even set up filters, because the mermaids just tear them out again. Like beavers, I guess. They've constructed this elaborate system of dams and retaining walls and structures out of the coral, these elaborate pens to hold fish. Venetian Pools sells fish so you can toss them in for the mermaids to round up. The kids were into that."

"They sing, right?" Lindsey asked. "We get them in the canal sometimes, the saltwater ones. They're a lot bigger. They sing."

"Yeah," Jason said. "Lots of singing. Really eerie stuff. Makes you feel like shit. They pipe elevator music over the loudspeakers to drown it out, but even the kids felt bad after a while. I had to buy all this stuff in the gift shop to cheer them up."

Lindsey pondered the problem of Jason, the favorite uncle who could be talked into buying things. He was too young for Alan. When you thought about it, who wasn't too young for Alan?

Alan said, "Didn't you have plans, Lindsey?"

"Did I?" Lindsey said. Then relented. "Actually, I was thinking about heading down to the Splinter. Maybe I'll see you guys down there later?"

"That old hole," Alan said. He wasn't looking at her. He was sending out those old invisible death rays in Jason's direction; Lindsey could practically feel the air getting thicker. It was like humidity, only skankier. "I used to go there to hook up with cute straight guys in the bathroom while Lindsey was passing out her phone number over by the pool tables. You know what they say about girls with two shadows, don't you, Jason?"

Jason said, "Maybe I should head home." But Lindsey could tell by the way he was looking at Alan that he had no idea what he was saying. He wasn't even really listening to what Alan said. He was just responding to the vibe that Alan put out. That *come hither come hither come a little more hither* siren song.

"Don't go," Alan said. "Stay a little longer. Lindsey has plans, and

I'm lonely. Stay a little longer and I'll play you some of the highlights from Lindsey's ex-husband's collection of pocket-universe gay porn."

"Alan," Lindsey said. Second warning. She knew he was keeping count.

"Sorry," Alan said. He put his hand on Jason's leg. "*Husband's* collection of gay porn. She and Elliot, wherever he is, are still married. I had the biggest hard-on for Elliot. He always said Lindsey was all he wanted. But it's never about what you want, is it? It's about what you need. Right?"

"Right," Jason said.

⁓❧⁓

How did Alan do it? Why did everyone except for Lindsey fall for it? Except, she realized, pedaling her bike down to the Splinter, she did fall for it. She still fell for it. It was her house, and who had been thrown out of it? Who had been insulted, dismissed, and told to leave? Her. That's who.

Cars went by, riding their horns. Damn Alan anyway.

She didn't bother to chain up the bike; she probably wouldn't be riding it home. She went into the Splinter and sat down beside a man with an aggressively sharp cologne.

"You look nice," she said. "Buy me a drink and I'll be nice too."

THERE ARE EASIER WAYS OF TRYING TO KILL YOURSELF

The man tried to kiss her. She couldn't find her keys, but that didn't matter. The door was unlocked. Jason's car still in the driveway. No surprise there.

"I have two shadows," she said. It was all shadows. They were shadows too.

"I don't care," the man said. He really was very nice.

"No," she said. "I mean my brother's home. We have to be quiet.

Okay if we don't turn on the lights? Where are you from?"

"Georgia," the man said. "I work construction. Came down here for the hurricane."

"The hurricane?" she said. "I thought it was headed for the Gulf of Mexico. This way. Watch out for the counter."

"Now it's coming back this way. Won't hit for another couple of days. You into kinky stuff? You can tie me up," the man said.

"Better knot," she said. "Get it? I'm not into knots. Can never get them untied, even sober. This guy had to have his foot amputated. No circulation. True story. Friend told me."

"Guess I've been lucky so far," the man said. He didn't sound too disappointed, either way. "This house has been through some hurricanes, I bet."

"One or two," she said. "Water comes right in over the tile floor. Messy. Then it goes out again."

She tried to remember his name. Couldn't. It didn't matter. She felt terrific. That had been the thing about being married. The monogamy. Even drunk, she'd always known who was in bed with her. Elliot had been different, all right, but he had always been the same kind of different. Never a different kind of different. Didn't like kissing. Didn't like sleeping in the same bed. Didn't like being serious. Didn't like it when Lindsey was sad. Didn't like living in a house. Didn't like the way the water in the canal felt. Didn't like this, didn't like that. Didn't like the Keys. Didn't like the way people looked at him. Didn't stay. Elliot, Elliot, Elliot.

"My name's Alberto," the man said.

"Sorry," she said. She and Elliot had always had fun in bed.

"He had a funny-looking penis," she said.

"Excuse me?" Alberto said.

"Do you want something to drink?" she said.

"Actually, do you have a bathroom?"

"Down the hall," she said. "First door."

But he came back in a minute. He turned on the lights and stood there.

"Like what you see?" she said.

His arms were shiny and wet. There was blood on his arms. "I need a tourniquet," he said. "Some kind of tourniquet."

"What did you do?" she said. Almost sober. Putting her robe on. "Is it Alan?"

But it was Jason. Blood all over the bathtub and the pretty half-tiled wall. He'd slashed both his wrists open with a potato peeler. The potato peeler was still there in his hand.

"Is he okay?" she said. "Alan! Where the fuck are you? Fuck!"

Alberto wrapped one of her good hand towels around one of Jason's wrists. "Hold this." He stuck another towel around the other wrist and then wrapped duct tape around that. "I called 911," he said. "He's breathing. Who is this guy? Your brother?"

"My employee," she said. "I don't believe this. What's with the duct tape?"

"Go get me a blanket," he said. "Need to keep him warm. My ex-wife did this once."

She skidded down the hall. Slammed open the door to Elliot's room. Turned on the lights and grabbed the comforter off the bed.

"*Vas poh!* Your new boyfriend's in the bathroom," she said. "Cut his wrists with my potato peeler. Wake up, Lan-Lan! This is *your* mess."

"*Fisfis wah*, Lin-Lin," Alan said, so she pushed him off the bed.

"What did you do, Alan?" she said. "Did you mess with him?"

He was wearing a pair of Elliot's pajama bottoms. "You're not being funny," he said.

"I'm not kidding," she said. "I'm drunk. There's a man named Alberto in the bathroom. Jason tried to kill himself. Or something."

"Oh fuck," he said. Tried to sit up. "I was nice to him, Lindsey! Okay? It was real nice. We fucked and then we smoked some stuff and then we were kissing and I fell asleep."

She held out her hand, pulled him up off the floor. "What kind of stuff? Come on."

"Something I picked up somewhere," he said. She wasn't really listening. "Good stuff. Organic. Blessed by monks. They give it to the gods. I took some off a shrine. Everybody does it. You just leave a bowl of milk or something instead. There's no fucking way it made him crazy."

The bathroom was crowded with everyone inside it. No way to avoid standing in Jason's blood. "Oh fuck," Alan said.

"My brother, Alan," Lindsey said. "Here's a comforter for Jason. Alan, this is Alberto. Jason, can you hear me?" His eyes were open now.

Alberto said to Alan, "It's better than it looks. He didn't really slice up his wrists. More like he peeled them. Dug into one vein pretty good, but I think I've slowed down the bleeding."

Alan shoved Lindsey out of the way and threw up in the sink.

"Alan," Jason said. There were sirens.

"No," Lindsey said. "It's me. Lindsey. Your boss. My bathtub, Jason. Your blood all over my bathtub. My potato peeler! Mine! What were you thinking?"

"There was an iguana in your freezer," Jason said.

Alberto said, "Why the potato peeler?"

"I was just so happy," Jason said. He was covered in blood. "I've never been so happy in all my life. I didn't want to stop feeling that way. You know?"

"No," Lindsey said.

"Are you going to fire me?" Jason said.

"What do you think?" Lindsey said.

"I'll sue for sexual harassment if you do," Jason said. "I'll say you fired me because I'm gay. Because I slept with your brother."

Alan threw up in the sink again.

"How do you feel now?" Alberto said. "You feel okay?"

"I just feel so happy," Jason said. He began to cry.

NOT MUCH OF A BEDSIDE MANNER

Alan went with Jason in the ambulance. The wind was stronger, pushing the trees around like a bully. Lindsey would have to put the storm shutters up.

For some reason Alberto was still there. He said, "I'd really like a beer. What've you got?"

Lindsey could have gone for something a little stronger. Everything smelled of blood. "Nothing," she said. "I'm a recovering alcoholic."

"Not all that recovered," he said.

"I'm sorry," Lindsey said. "You're a really nice guy. But I wish you would go away. I'd like to be alone."

He held out his bloody arms. "Could I take a shower first?"

"Could you just go?" Lindsey said.

"I understand," he said. "It's been a rough night. A terrible thing has happened. Let me help. I'll stay and help you clean up."

Lindsey said nothing.

"I see," he said. There was blood on his mouth too. Like he'd been drinking blood. He had good shoulders. Nice eyes. She kept looking at his mouth. The duct tape was back in a pocket of his cargo pants. He seemed to have a lot of stuff in his pockets. "You don't like me after all?"

"I don't like nice guys," Lindsey said.

༄

There were support groups for people whose shadow grew into a twin. There were support groups for women whose husbands left them. There were support groups for alcoholics. Probably there were support groups for people who hated support groups, but Lindsey didn't believe in support groups.

༄

By the time Alan got back from the hospital it was Saturday night; she'd finished the gin and started in on the tequila. She was almost wishing that Alberto had stayed. She thought about asking how Jason was, but it seemed pointless. Either he was okay or he wasn't.

She wasn't okay. Alan got her down the hall and onto her bed and then climbed into bed too. Pulled the blanket over both of them.

"Go away," she said.

"I'm freezing," he said. "That fucking hospital. That air-conditioning. Just let me lie here."

"Go away," she said again. "*Fisfis wah.*"

When she woke up, she was still saying it. "Go away, go away, go away." He wasn't in her bed. Instead there was a dead iguana, the little one from the freezer, on the pillow beside her face.

Alan was gone. The bathtub stank of blood and the rain slammed down on the roof like nails on glass. Little pellets of ice on the grass outside. Now the radio said the hurricane was on course to make land somewhere between Fort Lauderdale and Saint Augustine sometime Wednesday afternoon. There were no plans to evacuate the Keys. Plenty of wind and rain and nastiness due for the Miami area, but no real damage. She couldn't think why she'd asked Alberto to leave. The storm shutters still needed to go up. He had seemed like a guy who would do that.

If Alan had been there, he could have opened a can and made her soup. Brought her ginger ale in a glass. Finally, she turned the television on in the living room, loud enough that she could hear it from her bedroom. That way she wouldn't be listening for Alan. She could pretend that he was home, sitting out in the living room, watching some old monster movie and painting his fingernails black, the way he had done in high school. Kids with conjoined shadows were supposed to be into all that Goth makeup, all that music, so Alan was into it. When Alan had found out that twins were supposed to have secret twin languages, he'd done that too, invented a language, LinLan, and made her memorize it. Made her talk it at the dinner table. *Ifzon meh nadora plezbig* meant *Guess what I did? Bandy Tim Wong legkwa fisfis, meh* meant *Went all the way with Tim Wong.* (Tim Wong fucked me, in the vernacular.)

People with two shadows were *supposed* to be trouble. They were supposed to lead friends and lovers astray, bring confusion to their enemies, bring down disaster wherever they went. (She never went anywhere.) Alan had always been a conformist at heart. Whereas she had a house and a job and once she'd even been married. If anyone was keeping track, Lindsey thought it should be clear who was ahead.

∝◎∽

Monday morning Mr. Charles still hadn't managed to get rid of the sleepers from Pittsburgh. Jack Harris could shuffle paper like nobody's business.

"I'll call him," Lindsey offered. "You know I love a good fight."

"Good luck," Mr. Charles said. "He says he won't take them back until after the hurricane goes through. But rules say they have to be out of here twenty-four hours before the hurricane hits. We're caught between a rock—"

"And an asshole," she said. "Let me take care of it."

She was in the warehouse, on hold with someone who worked for Harris, when Jason showed up.

"What's up with that?" Valentina was saying. "Your arms."

"Fell through a plate-glass door," Jason said.

"That's not good," Valentina said.

"Lost almost three pints of blood. Just think about that. Three pints. Hey, Lindsey."

"Valentina," Lindsey said. "Take the phone for a moment. Don't worry. It's on hold. Just yell if anyone picks up. Jason, can I talk to you over there for a moment?"

"Sure thing," Jason said.

He winced when she grabbed him above the elbow. She didn't loosen her grip until they were a couple of aisles away. "Give me one good reason why I shouldn't fire you. Besides the sexual harassment thing. Because I would enjoy that. Hearing you try to make that case in court."

Jason said, "Alan's moved in with me. Said you threw him out."

Was any of this a surprise? Yes and no. She said, "So if I fire you, he'll have to get a job."

"That depends," Jason said. "Are you firing me or not?"

"*Fisfis buh.* Go ask Alan what that means."

"Hey, Lindsey. Lindsey, hey. Someone named Jack Harris is on the phone," Valentina said, getting too close for this conversation to go any further.

"I don't know why you want this job," Lindsey said.

"The benefits," Jason said. "You should see the bill from the emergency room."

"Or why you want my brother."

"Ms. Driver? He says it's urgent."

"Tell him one second," Lindsey said. To Jason: "All right. You can keep your job on one condition."

"Which is?" He didn't sound nearly as suspicious as he ought to have sounded. Still early days with Alan.

"You get the man on the phone to take back those six sleepers. Today."

"How the fuck do I do that?" Jason said.

"I don't care. But they had better not be here when I show up tomorrow morning. If they're here, you had better not be. Okay?" She poked him in the arm above the bandage. "Next time borrow something sharper than a potato peeler. I've got a whole block full of good German knives."

"Lindsey," Valentina said, "this Harris guy says he can call you back tomorrow if now isn't a good time."

"Jason is going to take the call," Lindsey said.

EVERYTHING MUST GO

Her favorite liquor store put everything on sale whenever a hurricane was due. Just their way of making a bad day a little more bearable. She stocked up on everything but only had a glass of wine with dinner.

Made a salad and ate it out on the patio. The air had that electric, green shimmy to it she associated with hurricanes. The water was as still as milk, but deflating her dock was a bitch nevertheless. She stowed it in the garage. When she came out, a pod of saltwater mermaids was going out to sea. Who could have ever confused a manatee with a mermaid? They turned and looked at her. Dove down, although she could still see them ribboning there, down along the frondy bottom.

The last time a hurricane had come through, her dock had sailed out of the garage and ended up two canals over.

She threw the leftover salad on the grass for the iguanas. The sun went down without a fuss.

Alan didn't come back, so she packed up his clothes for him. Washed the dirty clothes first. Listened to the rain start. She put his backpack out on the dining room table with a note. *Good luck with the philosopher king.*

In the morning before work she went out in the rain, which was light but steady, and put up the storm shutters. Her neighbors were doing the same. Cut herself on the back of the hand while she was working on the next to last one. Bled everywhere. Jason's car pulled up while she was still cursing, and Alan got out. He went into the house and got her a Band-Aid. They put up the last two shutters without talking.

Finally Alan said, "It was my fault. He doesn't usually do drugs at all."

"He's not a bad kid," she said. "*So* not your type."

"I'm sorry," he said. "Not about that. You know. I guess I mean about everything."

They went back into the house and he saw his suitcase. "Well," he said.

"*Filhatz warfoon meh,*" she said. "*Bilbil tuh.*"

"*Nent bruk,*" he said. No kidding.

He didn't stay for breakfast. She didn't feel any less or more real after he left.

❧

The twenty-two sleepers were out of the warehouse and Jason had a completed stack of paperwork for her. Lots of signatures. Lots of duplicates and triplicates and fucklipates, as Valentina liked to say.

"Not bad," Lindsey said. "Did Jack Harris offer you a job?"

"He offered to come hand me my ass," Jason said. "I said he'd have to get in line. Nasty weather. Are you staying out there?"

"Where would I go?" she said. "There's a big party at the Splinter tonight. It's not like I have to come in to work tomorrow."

"I thought they were evacuating the Keys," he said.

"It's voluntary," she said. "They don't care if we stay or go. I've been through hurricanes. When Alan and I were kids, we spent one camped in a bathtub under a mattress. We read comics with a flashlight all night long. The noise is the worst thing. Good luck with Alan, by the way."

"I've never lived with anybody before." So maybe he knew just enough to know he had no idea what he had gotten himself into. "I've never fallen for anybody like this."

"There isn't anybody like Alan," she said. "He has the power to cloud and confuse the minds of men."

"What's your superpower?" Jason said.

"He clouds and confuses," she said. "I confuse and then cloud. The order makes a big difference."

She told Mr. Charles the good news about Jack Harris; they had a cup of coffee together to celebrate, then locked the warehouse down. Mr. Charles had to pick up his kids at school. Hurricanes were holidays. You didn't get snow days in Florida.

On the way home all the traffic was going the other way. The wind made the stoplights swing and flip like paper lanterns. She had that feeling she'd had at Christmas, as a child. As if someone was bringing her a present. Something shiny and loud and sharp and messy. She'd always loved bad weather. She'd loved weather witches in their smart, black suits. Their divination kits, their dramatic seizures, their prophecies that were never entirely accurate but always rhymed smartly. When she was little she'd wanted more than anything to grow up and be a weather witch, although why that once had been true she now had no idea.

She rode her bike down to the Splinter. Had a couple of whiskey sours and then decided that she was too excited about the hurricane to get properly drunk. She didn't want to be drunk. And there wasn't a man in the bar she wanted to bring home. The best part of hurricane sex was the hurricane, not the sex, so why bother?

The sky was green as a bruise and the rain was practically horizontal. There were no cars at all on the way home. She went down the middle of the road and ran over an iguana almost four feet long, nose to tail. Stiff as a board, but its sides went out and in like little bellows. The rain got them like that sometimes. They got stupid and slow in the cold. The rest of the time they were stupid and fast.

She wrapped her jacket around the iguana, making sure that the tail was immobilized. You could break a man's arm if you had a tail like that. She carried it under her arm, walking her bike, all the way back to her house and decided it would be a good idea to put it in her bathtub. She went out into her yard with a flashlight. Checked the storm shutters to make sure they were properly fastened and discovered three more iguanas. Two smaller ones and one real monster. She brought them all inside.

By 6:00 p.m. it was pitch-dark. The hurricane was still two miles out at sea. Picking up water to drop on the heads of people who didn't want any more water. She dozed off at midnight and woke up when the power went off.

The air in the room was so full of water she had to gasp for breath. The iguanas were shadows stretched along the floor of the living room. The black shapes of the liquor boxes were every

Christmas present she'd ever wanted.

Everything outside was clanking or buzzing or yanking or shrieking. She felt her way into the kitchen and got out the box with her candles and flashlight and emergency radio. The shutters banged away like battle.

"Swung down," the announcer was saying. "How about that— and this is just the edge, folks. Stay indoors and hunker down if you haven't already left town. This is only a Category 2, but you betcha it'll feel a lot bigger down here on the Keys. It's 3:00 a.m. and we're going to have at least three more hours of this before the eye passes over us. This is one big baby girl, and she's taking her time. The good ones always do."

Lindsey could hardly get the candles lit; the matches were that soggy, her hands greasy with sweat. When she went to the bathroom, the iguana looked as battered and beat, in the light from her candle, as some old suitcase.

Her bedroom had too many windows for her to stay there. She got her pillow and her quilt and a fresh T-shirt. A fresh pair of underwear.

When she went to check Elliot's room there was a body on the bed. She dropped the candle. Tipped wax onto her bare foot. "Elliot?" she said. But when she got the candle lit again it wasn't Elliot, of course, and it wasn't Alan either. It was the sleeper. Versailles Kentucky. The one who looked like Alan or maybe Lindsey, depending on who was doing the looking.

She dropped the candle again. It was exactly the sort of joke Alan liked. Not a joke at all, that is. She had a pretty good idea where the other sleepers were—in Jason's apartment, not back in Pittsburgh. And if anyone found out, it would be her job too. No government pension for Lindsey. No comfy early retirement.

Her hand still wasn't steady and she was running low on matches. When she held up the candle, wax dripped onto Versailles Kentucky's neck. But if it were that easy to wake a sleeper, Lindsey would already know about it.

In the meantime, the bed was against an exterior wall and there were all the windows. Lindsey dragged Versailles Kentucky off the bed.

She couldn't get a good grip. Versailles Kentucky was heavy. She flopped. Her head snapped back, hair snagging on the floor. Lindsey squatted, took hold of the sleeper by her upper arms, pulled her down the dark hall, trying to keep her head off the ground. This must be what it must be like to have murdered someone. She would kill Alan. Think of this as practice, she thought. Body disposal. Dry run. *Wet* run.

She dragged Versailles Kentucky through the door of the bathroom and leaned the limp body over the tub's lip. Grabbed the iguana. Put it on the bathroom floor. Arranged Versailles Kentucky in the tub, first one leg and then the other, folding her down on top of herself.

Next she got the air mattress out of the garage; the noise was worse out there. She filled the mattress halfway and squeezed it through the bathroom door. Put more air in. Tented it over the tub. Went and found the flashlight, got a bottle of gin out of the freezer. It was still cold, thank God. She swaddled the iguana in a towel that was stiff with Jason's blood. Put it into the tub again. Sleeper and iguana. Madonna and her very ugly baby.

Everything was clatter and wail. Lindsey heard a shutter, somewhere, go sailing off to somewhere else. The floor of the living room was wet in the circle of her flashlight when she went to collect the other iguanas. Either the rain beginning to force its way in under the front door and the sliding glass doors, or else it was the canal. The three iguanas went into the tub too. "Women and iguanas first," she said, and swigged her gin. But nobody heard her over the noise of the wind.

She sat hunched on the lid of her toilet and drank until the wind was almost something she could pretend to ignore. Like a band in a bar that doesn't know how loud it's playing. Eventually she fell asleep, still sitting on the toilet, and only woke up when the bottle broke when she dropped it. The iguanas rustled around in the tub. The wind was gone. It was the eye of the storm or else she'd missed the eye entirely, and the rest of the hurricane as well.

Light came faintly through the shuttered window. The batteries of her emergency radio were dead, but her cell phone still showed a signal. Three messages from Alan and six messages from a number that she guessed was Jason's. Maybe Alan wanted to apologize for something.

She went outside to see what had become of the world. Except that what had become of the world was that she was no longer in it.

The street in front of her house was no longer the street in front of her house. It had become someplace else entirely. There were no other houses. As if the storm had carried them all away. She stood in a meadow full of wildflowers. There were mountains in the far distance, cloudy and blue. The air was very crisp.

Her cell phone showed no signal. When she looked back at her house, she was looking back into her own world. The hurricane was still there, smeared out onto the horizon like poison. The canal was full of the ocean. The Splinter was probably splinters. Her front door still stood open.

She went back inside and filled an old backpack with bottles of gin. Threw in candles, her matchbox, some cans of soup. Her gun. Padded it all out with underwear and a sweater or two. The white stuff on those mountains was probably snow.

If she put her ear against the sliding glass doors that went out to the canal, she was listening to the eye, that long moment of emptiness where the worst is still to come. Versailles Kentucky was still asleep in the bathtub with the iguanas, who were not. There were red marks on Versailles Kentucky's arms and legs where the iguanas had scratched her. Nothing fatal. Lindsey got a brown eyeliner pencil out of the drawer under the sink and lifted up the sleeper's leg. Drew a birthmark in the shape of a battleship. The water in the air would make it smear, but so what. If Alan could have his joke, she would have hers too.

She lowered the cool leg. On an impulse, she picked up the smallest iguana, still wrapped in its towel.

When she went out her front door again with her backpack and her bike and the iguana, the meadow with its red and yellow flowers was still there and the sun was coming up behind the mountains, although this was not the direction that the sun usually came up in and Lindsey was glad. She bore the sun a grudge because it did not stand still; it gave her no advantage except in that moment when it passed directly overhead and she had no shadow. Not even one. Everything that had once belonged to her alone was back inside Lindsey where it should have been.

There was something, maybe a mile or two away, that might have been an outcropping of rock. The iguana fit inside the basket on her handlebars and the backpack was not uncomfortably heavy. No sign of any people, anywhere, although if she were determined enough, and if her bicycle didn't get a puncture, surely she'd come across whatever the local equivalent of a bar was, eventually. If there wasn't a bar now, then she could always hang around a little while longer, see who came up with that bright idea first.

LYDIA MILLET

Snow White, Rose Red

I met the girls and instantly liked the girls. Of course I liked the girls. A girl is better than a feast.

This was before the arrest, before the indictment and the media stories.

The girls were sisters, as you may know, and lived, during the summer, in one of those upstate mansions built by the robber barons who made their fortunes off railroads and steel and unfair business practices. It was in the Lower Peaks of the Adirondacks—the southern part with glassy lakes and green slopes and white-spotted fawns. The girls, who were innocent in the glut of their wealth because they'd never known anything else, called their summer house "the cottage" to distinguish it from "the apartment," which was a ten-thousand-square-foot penthouse on Fifth Avenue near Washington Square Park.

Their father was in real estate, but no one ever saw him. Correction: from time to time we caught sight of him briefly, the girls and I, getting in or out of a long, gleaming car. Once, from the woods, I spotted him walking down to the dock in a pale-gray suit, his phone held to his ear.

He looked like a groom doll on a wedding cake. I wanted to tear his legs off.

At twilight, on the grounds of the massive yet log-cabin-style robber-baron mansion, dozens of deer stood around, their graceful necks lowered, eating the grass. There's an abundance of deer up there, due to the hunters who've killed off all the animals that were supposed to be preying on them. So the deer.

And the girls, equally graceful with their light, carrying laughter and long limbs, spun glow-in-the-dark Hula-hoops or played croquet with ancient peeling mallets as the purple dusk fell. The older one had honey-colored hair and blue eyes; the younger had brown hair and her eyes were a shade of amber. They hardly looked like sisters, but they were. The blonde was called Nieve, Spanish for snow, and the brunette was Rosa, but she went by Rose. Their mother—a former ballerina from Madrid who was both anorexic and mentally slow—had named them but often she forgot their names.

We only met because I came out of the woods one night. I came out of the woods and walked right across the rolling lawn, scattering the Bambis. The sun was setting over the lake and a slight breeze rippled the water.

I admit the girls appeared frightened. What Rosa told me later was this: those first few seconds, they actually mistook me for a bear.

They'd never seen a homeless guy before—they were that sheltered, even though they lived in downtown Manhattan; trust me, it can be done—and though I wasn't technically homeless I had that same dirty, hirsute aspect. I'm not a small man but tall and barrel-chested, and that June evening I wore filthy clothes and a long beard and needed badly to bathe in the lake.

I had a home in the forest, or a temporary shelter, anyway; but to girls that pampered and young there's no perceptible difference between an aging hippie and a transient.

So they were frightened at first, but I held up my hands as I walked up to the porch. The cottage had a wide wraparound porch, stone-floored, with swings, chairs, rugs, and potted plants. The girls retreated partway up the stairs and stood there uncertainly on the steps in their simple cotton frocks, clutching a Frisbee and a skipping rope. I held up my hands like a man who was surrendering.

I was lucky the help wasn't around and the mother, as usual, had gone to bed early. If anyone else had been there—the cook, for one, who was a domineering type—they probably would have run me off.

I'd had too much to drink, of course. It was my pastime then— the summer before my divorce, a strange and isolated time. I was camped out in an old airplane hangar on one of the smaller lakes and now and then I hitchhiked into town, bought booze and groceries, and prayed not to run into my estranged wife. We'd had our own, more modest summer place nearby.

What I'd done was, I'd disappeared. I didn't want my wife to know where I had gone. It was the only trick I had left: hiding and vanishing. I got some meager satisfaction from an idea I had of her not knowing whether I lived or died—her wondering if maybe, defying all her expectations, I'd left my dull old self behind and flown off to a distant and unknown country.

Those girls were good. Plenty of rich girls aren't, we all know that. But those two girls were innocent. I don't know how they turned out that way, with the mother who wasn't all there and the father who wasn't there at all. That goodness came from them like milk from a rock.

Snow, as I came to call her, because I couldn't be bothered to pronounce her real name, mostly liked books, and sat in the shade of the porch on afternoons, reading. Her sister was more social and spent her time talking to everyone. She rode her bicycle to an old folks' home most days and helped the people there.

As I stood on the lawn looking up at them, I noticed something I hadn't seen from a distance: the girls' skin glowed. Both of them had this luminous kind of skin.

That clear, young skin is part of what makes girls look so edible.

I asked them not to be afraid. I told them my name, and after a few moments they seemed to relax, and told me theirs. They had a dog, an old Irish setter who lay around and barely raised his tail even for flies. I sat down on the steps and petted the dog, after a while.

So we were friends. Of course, I wouldn't have had a chance if the girls hadn't been left on their own so much. Now and then a friend their own age came up from the city to visit and I didn't intrude upon them then.

But those visits were rare. Often at dawn or dusk, when the deer and the girls were out, I was the only company they had. I kept a low profile and did not throw the Frisbee back and forth with them, in case someone could see us from the house. Usually we stood together and we talked, a little out of sight. Once or twice they sat on the end of the dock and trailed their feet through the water, and I swam, only my head above the darkening surface.

From the high bedroom windows of the cottage's second floor, that wouldn't have looked like anything.

The girls were kind to me. They let me use the canoes in the boathouse, even encouraged me, and some mornings I would row out into a hidden bay and sit and drift, trying idly to fish in the shade of a red pine. There were some old rods in the boathouse, and since I had none of my own I used to borrow them.

Snow would leave me sandwiches or sometimes bring a bowl of ice cream onto the porch. Rose offered small hotel bottles of shampoo and told me to use them.

These girls were both honest. Once Snow said to me, "You smell not too good. Did you know?"

I told her that I washed my clothes whenever I could, in the coin laundry in town or the lake. I also tried to swim and use soap on myself, but now and then I lost track and missed a day or two.

"I wish you wouldn't," said Snow wistfully.

My back hurt from sleeping on the cement floor of the hangar and I ended up asking the sisters for aspirin. For several days my back and neck had been sore, and the pills took the worst edge off the pain but that was all. Then Rose said I should sleep in the cottage, which had more bedrooms than could easily be counted. There was a certain servants' part of the house, they said, which had its own entrance, and none of the help used it. I could sneak in at night and sleep in the comfortable bed, which had down pillows and high-thread-count sheets.

I protested at first; I had some fear I'd run into one of the other members of the household. But it was silent when I snuck in there at night, after the girls had gone to bed. It was so quiet that it almost seemed to me they lived there by themselves, and food and water were furnished to them by invisible hands.

The bed was a nice change from concrete floors, so nice I almost questioned my recent course in life—hunkering down in the hangar, unshaved and unwashed, hiding from my soon-to-be-ex-wife. But then I came full circle; the hiding couldn't be so wrong, for it had brought me here, to this great mansion with its soft sheets and gentle girls.

After that I often slipped in by the servants' narrow stairs and slept in my private room, tucked up under the roof. I set my wrist-watch alarm and crept out at the crack of dawn. The cottage doors were never locked during the summer months; the family was always there, the family or the staff. I watched them from the shadows whenever I could. The Mexican groundskeeper rode around on his lawn tractor uselessly, mowing nothing, happy to sit aloft. The live-in maid smoked cigarettes near the garden shed and sometimes slipped away to have sex with the groundskeeper in the bushes.

One day the mother had a brief flash of life and donned her sparkling tennis whites. She ran outside and hit a few balls feebly with Rose on the clay tennis court. Meanwhile Snow, on the sidelines, took snapshots for the family album.

It was a rare occasion, to see the mother outside in the sun, acting alive like that.

But only fifteen minutes passed before the mother went inside again, apparently angry or depressed. She threw her racquet down and blurted something that I couldn't quite make out. I saw the girls' faces as they watched her go. Their faces were both sad and calm; the girls were resigned to this beautiful, semi-retarded mother with her spidery limbs and odd tantrums.

Perhaps she was never a ballerina, I thought to myself. There aren't too many retarded ballerinas in this world, is my perception of the thing, although there certainly are a few who, like the mother, starve themselves.

That evening, around dusk, the girls came swimming with me in the lake; Rose lathered my hair up with shampoo. It was one of the only times I felt the sisters' touch. They weren't too prone to physical contact. They hadn't grown up with affection, and also, I was an older, often bad-smelling man, quite unattractive to them. No doubt they were afraid that any touching would be mistaken for an invitation.

But on this occasion, beyond the end of the dock, Rose ducked my head under, laughing, and when I came up spluttering and trying to catch my breath Snow pushed my head under again, and both of them were playfully drowning me.

We were happy.

Then Rose said, "What would he look like with no beard?"

Snow looked at me, too, considering, and then climbed up onto the dock, toweled off, and ran into the house. She came back in a minute with shaving equipment. She even had scissors—clearly no razor, by itself, would be up to the task—and an old hand mirror of heavy silver.

Snow cut off the part of the beard that hung. Then they watched while I sat in the shallows and, with Rose holding up the mirror, shaved off the stubble that was left.

"He's not that bad," she said, when I was done.

I dipped my face under and came up again, wiping the water away from my eyes, the flecks of girl-scented shaving foam floating.

"He looks like that actor," said Snow, cocking her head. "You know, that big French one with the crooked nose."

"You look like that actor," concurred Rose, nodding.

"He's sort of ugly," said Snow. "And you have to like him."

"Exactly," said Rose. "Ugly, like you."

"But also likable," said her older sister.

"Girls," I said ruefully, "you're going to have to find a way to tell the truth a little less often."

"Why?" asked Snow.

"Well, for one thing, it hurts people's feelings."

"We're sorry," said Rose. "We didn't mean to."

"I know," I said. "I know. And B, if you get in this habit of telling men the truth, you'll never find true love and get married."

"I won't get married anyway," said Rose.

"I won't either," said Snow.

"How do you know?" I asked.

"It seems really stupid," said Snow.

"Like cutting off your leg," said Rose.

"Every marriage is different," I said.

"Get out," said Snow.

"Well, you're supposed to be married," said Rose. "But now your wife likes someone else better."

"So soon you won't be, anymore."

"More or less accurate," I conceded.

"Then why are you defending it?" asked Snow.

"Once you were practically normal," added Rose. "But now you carry a roll of toilet paper around in a greasy disgusting backpack," and she shuddered visibly.

"We're just saying," said Snow, almost apologetic.

It was then that we heard a rare sound—at least, rare to us in the tranquility of those summer evenings: car tires crunching on gravel in front of the house.

"No way," breathed Snow.

"Daddy," said Rose.

"It's the third time this whole summer," said Snow.

"The first time lasted for an hour," Rose told me.

"The second was on my birthday," said Snow.

"He stayed fifteen minutes."

"He brought me a gift certificate."

I tensed up, worried I'd get caught with them. My clothes were heaped on the bank, except for the boxer shorts I wore. There was a clean line of sight, if he came around the corner. But I had other clothes in the hangar so all I had to do was swim away—swim across to the part of the shore that was hidden from the house by trees, and from there retreat to my hangar.

"I should go," I said.

"Don't worry. We'll totally distract him," said Rose.

They climbed up onto the dock, legs dripping. Towels swirled up around their shoulders, feet left wet prints on the dry wood before they slipped into flip-flops. Then the girls were headed up the grassy slope—not running, not eager. Just dutiful.

I felt a rush of thankfulness that I'd never had children to disappoint. Though I wished the girls were my own daughters; even I would have shone in comparison with the gray doll.

I didn't have his wealth. But still.

I sank down in the water and spied on them, the waterline beneath my nose. I kept my mouth clamped shut.

The suit was undertaker-black this time and I could just make out a silver-colored headset. He talked into the headset as the girls went up the hill to meet him. Rose stepped toward him awkwardly, as though she wanted to embrace, but he held up his hand and shook his head and kept talking, turning around as he paced.

She stepped back.

It occurred to me then that they would be better off if he died, but it was an academic, impersonal thought. It had nothing to do with me.

A second later, it also occurred to me that, if someone tore the groom in half, the girls would still have his money but not his cold and persistent disregard.

It was painful, on the other hand, the loss of a father. Even a negligent father. And with the semi-retarded mother on the brink of death surprisingly often—due to the repeated self-starving activities, which made her subject to sudden hospital visits—the poor girls might be farmed out to relatives. Separated.

So as quickly as I had it, I gave up the idea of murdering him. You know: murder goes through your head sometimes, and then goes out again. It's normal, in my opinion.

Anyway, the thought had no bearing on subsequent events.

After a while the father stopped talking into his headset mouthpiece. By that time the girls had already given up and drifted into the house without, as far as I could tell, even a smile of greeting from him. Some fragments of his one-sided conversation floated down to me—a few words in the twilight, "value-added," "deal structure," and possibly "red herring."

Then he, too, disappeared.

What happened later that night was simple, as I would testify.

Around one in the morning, as I lay trying to sleep on the hangar floor, my back started to hurt. It hurt a lot, mainly because there was nothing between me and the cracked cement but a threadbare sleeping bag I'd filched from a Goodwill bin in Albany. During the vanishing act I hadn't wanted to reveal myself by using my joint-account ATM card. And I had no painkillers left from the prescription stash the girls had given me. So finally, driven by discomfort, I crept out onto the dirt road, pain shooting through my back, grasping my heavy, antique flashlight.

There was a dim glow in the ground-floor windows of the mansion where lamps had been left on, but through those windows I could see no one was reading by their light. The family was sleeping. So I went around behind the house and up the servants' stairs, taking off my shoes and walking in my sock feet. I found my room as usual and went to sleep myself, so relieved by the comfort of the bed that I forgot my back.

But presently I was woken up. There was a loud, terrible noise. Bleary, I didn't recognize it at first. I thought it was a cat, in pain or trying to mate. Then I understood it was human—human and female. I sat right up, jolted with fear for those sweet girls. I had to do something, so I grabbed my flashlight and ran out into the corridor.

I didn't know the house at all, only the route to my secret cubby. So I was stumbling down narrow halls like I was in a maze, basically running blind, this way and that, trying to follow the screaming. It stopped for a short time and I faltered—partly in confusion, partly out of a growing conviction that the sound wasn't coming from either of the girls. It was too feral and too hoarse. But then it started up again and I ran, tearing up and down halls in a panic, because I couldn't be sure.

Eventually I came out into a wider hall where lights were ablaze; a long carpet down the middle, and there was the mother. She wore nothing at all and was so emaciated that her jutting ribs resembled zebra stripes. I couldn't help but notice she was shaved completely bare beneath. And there was the father, in seersucker pajamas, who seemed to be choking or suffocating her. They were thrashing around, and she must have been the one screaming, though now his fingers were over her mouth. He had the upper hand, clearly, being a man and not mentally or physically impaired. A fear seized me—though behind that fear I was relieved that Snow and Rose were not the targets of this violent assault—and without thinking I threw myself into the fray.

The flashlight was the only weapon I had, and as I said, it was heavy.

Before I knew it the groom doll lay upon the ground, the left side of his head stove in.

Once we understood the gravity of the situation, we threw ourselves into reviving him. I knelt beside him and performed CPR, which I'd learned as a lifeguard in the seventies; Rose, in her frilly teddy-bear nightgown, ran to the telephone and called 911; Snow sat, her face solemn, and held one of her father's limp white hands, which I noticed was almost effeminate in the perfection of its manicure. Only the starving mother, still naked, hung back, sitting with her knobby knees raised to her chin against the far wall's wainscoting, beneath the pompous portrait of a wattled ancestor.

As you may already be aware, if you're the type to follow crime-beat or society news stories, the father did not die. In fact—and this is little-known—he came out of the hospital substantially improved. It was as though he'd had a personality alteration, the sort that might follow a frontal lobotomy, for instance. He was more pleasant, after he recovered. He had more time for his wife and his children.

I even heard from my lawyer that he sought professional help for the mother. Not for the retardation, I don't think—there isn't much they do for that—but for the eating disorder.

And me, I never heard from the girls again. Not personally. But they must be better off now, too.

Because the father, who'd already made enough money to keep the family in fine linens and silverware for life, was no longer interested in business. That part of his character had simply been removed, either by the impact of the flashlight or the subsequent brain bleed. It wasn't that, as my lawyer assures me, his cognitive capacity was reduced, per se. He still performed adequately in standard aptitude tests.

No, it seemed to be more a matter of a changed disposition.

Myself, I didn't fare so well. It adds up against you when you're indigent at the time of felony commission, abusing alcohol, etc., even if the crime was committed in defense of a vulnerable party. And there was the trespass issue—although the girls, I have to say, did not desert me in my hour of need. They told the police I'd had their full permission to sleep in the house that night. Sadly, due to their ages—eleven and twelve—that testimony did not go far to clear me of the trespass charge.

I sometimes dwell on my last moments with those girls. It's true we sat upon an old carpet, discolored by the father's spreading blood, between dark-painted walls adorned with grim, even judgmental-looking paintings of the girls' dead relatives. It's true our clothing was splattered and gruesome, and the unconscious father was stretched out between us, casting a pall.

But I gazed up and around, when I'd done all the CPR I could—it was a kind of coma, I guess, though it wouldn't last long once they got him to the emergency room—and saw the semi-retarded mother. Even a ballerina, I remember thinking, did not deserve to be asphyxiated, and I was still glad I'd come to her aid. Now she was staring at me with eyes as big as saucers, murmuring something in her native tongue. She spoke the dialect of Spanish where everyone has a lisp. I saw Snow, whose lovely face, lit from within, bore the light, drying tracks of tears, and the vibrant Rose, nervous and biting her nails beside a Tiffany table lamp effulgent with orange-pink roses.

And I was overcome with a curious feeling of belonging and satisfaction, as though I'd eaten a full meal and was preparing now for a long winter sleep. With the father lying inert between us in his blue-and-white seersucker, I felt we were all where we were meant to be, all posed in a tableau whose composition had been perfectly chosen a very long time ago. Whatever came afterward, I recall thinking, this was a warm cave full of soft, harmless things.

Hot, Fast, and Sad

I am boiling inside a kettle with five other people. Our limbs are bound, our intestines and mouths stuffed with herbs and garlic, but we can still speak. We smell great despite the pain.

The guy next to me looks like Elvis because of his fluffy, vaguely pubic black hair. It could be the humidity.

Across the kettle a man is trying to cry, but his tears keep evaporating before they can roll down his cheeks. For a moment, I have the romantic thought that maybe we are actually boiling in tears, hundreds of thousands of them, the sweetest true tears of infants and children, and not a yellowy, chicken-ish broth.

I am the only woman in the kettle, which strikes me as odd. I'm voluptuous and curvy; I can quite understand why someone would want to gobble me up. The men do not look so delicious. One, a very old man across the kettle, keeps drifting in and out of a semiconscious state. His head droops down toward the broth, then suddenly, just as the top of his nose touches one of the surface bubbles, he snaps upright and utters a name. "Geoffrey" is the first. The second, "Laura." We think he is saying the names of his children; we even continue to humor him after he gets to the fifteenth (perhaps he's moved on to grandchildren?), but as he yells his fortieth name it's clear that he is not poignant but nuts.

"He *isn't* crazy," the crying man sobs. "These are the last few moments of our lives. Shouldn't we all be calling out the names of everyone we've ever met? Ever known? Ever loved?"

"Uh-huh," agrees Elvis.

But the man on the other side of the kettle is not so fond of this idea. Teardrop tattoos on his upper cheek indicate victories in multiple prison-kills. Ironically, he is tied up right next to the crying man. "I like quiet," the tattooed man says.

The man next to me, he isn't really my type. His features are feminine in a way that makes him look boyish like Peter Pan. But he's smiling at me through the spices and trimmings shoved into his mouth; despite them he manages a nice, soft look.

Since we're about to be eaten, I lower my standards and choose to be bold.

"I love you," I say. It's coming from a good pretend place. I just want to pack as much into these last few moments as I can.

Yet when I watch the impact my words have on his face, the effect is very real. Maybe, I figure, since we are all cooking toward the finish line, things are fast-forwarding. Maybe what I've just said can actually be true.

And then it is. Seconds pass and love for him grows suddenly, like ice crystals or sea monkeys, all over my body.

We stare at one another and he scoots toward me as much as our fetters will allow, enough that our fingertips can touch. "I love you too," he says. "If we weren't tied up, I'd give you the softest kiss you've ever felt in your life, right on your steamy lips."

From the corner of my eye, I notice that the tattooed man, who up until this point hasn't been very chatty, is suddenly showing multiple upper teeth. His lips pull back wide in order to verbalize the list of things *he* would do to me, were we not tied up. They are not romantic or legal.

"You're a monster," my lover says to him. "The rest of us shouldn't have to boil in your juices."

"Uh-huh," says Elvis.

"We're dying just like this criminal," weeps the crying man. "It isn't fair."

Suddenly the old man raises his head. A drop of yellow broth falls from the tip of his nose. "Kelly," he rasps, then his eyes roll back and his head falls down. I smile.

"That's my name!" Glee fills me, though I don't know why. "He just spoke my name," I tell my new lover, whose fingertips squeeze my own.

"Kelly." My lover whispers my name into the hot mist.

"What if it's some kind of death list?" the crying man snivels. "What if that old codger has been here for ages, been in pots with hundreds of people who've all been eaten, but he always gets left because he's so old. It would drive a person crazy. It might make him repeat over and over again the names of people he's watched die in a halfhearted attempt to bring them back." After pondering this, the crying man lets out a long, shrill sob that is chirp-like. It reminds me of a parakeet I had when I was young. I try to remember its name.

"Thomas," the old man says.

"That's *my* name," my lover says and laughs, bouncing a little in the water. "He just said our names back-to-back. The power of our love, it planted them in his head!"

The tattooed man makes a gagging noise.

For fun, I ask everyone to please mouth his name, just to see if the old man will say it next. I encourage them to hurry up and do it while the old man's head is flaccid beneath a layer of broth.

"James," whimpers the crying man.

"Fred," sings Elvis.

"Fuck off," mutters the tattooed man.

Thomas and I watch the old man with anticipation. Finally his old head surfaces, and he gums the broth dripping down his cheeks before saying, "Cinderella."

"See," my lover coos. "Our names before; it was magic."

I want this moment to stay. I want it to multiply on and on with the unnatural growth of things just before death, speeding off the pure fat of life's last moments. I want the feeling of our brushing fingertips to breed like cancerous cells.

When the steel door opens, even the old man sits up and blinks his wet lashes. A chef walks in sharpening a long knife against a stone. "Who first?" he barks. We're all silent, though I think I hear the old man whisper, "Shirley."

"All right then." The chef points his knife at me and moves it a little like he's writing his name in the air. "I'll take you, since you're the meatiest."

I give my lover a farewell glance but suddenly his screams fill the room. "No!" he cries, thrashing madly and fishlike. "Take me in her place. Please, I beg you, make her the very last one."

"Yes," says the chef, but first he twirls his knife at me a little more like he's casting a spell, just so I know who's in charge.

Two men wearing long oven gloves come over and cut my lover's ropes. He stretches his lips out to kiss me, but is too soon pulled away and carried from the room like a ladder—one man at his shoulders, the other at his feet. "Please," he begs, "one kiss," but the two men aren't as permissive as the cook and they possibly do not speak English.

"That was so beautiful," says the crying man, sobbing. "Such love."

Despite my grief, I try to live in the moment. "Do you sing?" I ask Elvis-Fred.

"There's a moon out tonight," he croons. The garlic cloves really muffle his vibrato.

When the chef and his goons reenter, the tattooed man speaks up. "Take me," he says, "I hate these people."

So they take him. As he's pulled from the water, we see that he also has a tattoo on his arm that reads, "MOM." This makes Crying-James cry even harder. I should've called my mother more," he laments. "Told her I love her and appreciated her cooking."

"This one's for Mom," says Elvis-Fred. He begins singing again. "You are the sunshine of my life."

Crying-James's sobs are uncontrollable. His emotion touches me. The ripples in the broth move from his torso over to mine, lapping at my stomach like a soft current. "It will be okay, James," I assure him. I want to extend my foot across our little bullion pond and wipe his tears with one of my brothy toes, but my legs are bound together at the ankles.

When the door opens, four men, increasingly sour from the first to the fourth, enter with the chef. "I need two," he orders. The men grab Elvis-Fred and Crying-James, who continue singing and weeping, respectively, as they are carried away.

Alone with the old man it's very quiet, and I realize how loud the boiling has become. He lifts his head and says, "Tanya."

I knew a Tanya once. From a ballet class in high school. I imagine being taken from the kettle and laid onto a silver platter next to a giant cake, and on top of that cake Tanya is posed in a graceful pirouette.

When they lift the old man from the broth, I'm surprised to see he is missing a leg. I wonder if he arrived with it missing, or if they'd already eaten his leg and then put him back. Without the others, the boiling bubbles feel far more scalding than before. I am bad at science and uncertain if before we had all somehow shared the heat but now I alone bear its brunt. It seems so. I miss my lover, and my willingness to suffer perhaps makes the broth feel hotter as well.

As the footsteps come, I wonder if there will be anything after death. Perhaps Thomas will be waiting for me on the other side and our new and budding love will be allowed to blossom from the beyond. Then, although morbid, I try to prepare myself for what it will feel like when they cut me up. "There are worse ways to die," I tell myself, "than being boiled, then sliced with a knife." But it takes me a while to think of one.

Finally I imagine being carried out the door to a table where all five of my kettle mates are waiting, forks and knives in their hands, skins still pink from the boiling broth. I imagine Thomas saying he has dibs on my heart, and the others laughing; Elvis singing "Good Night, Sweetheart," as my carving starts and I lose consciousness to the sounds of battling forks and knives. This daydream dampens the horror of my fate like a bowl placed over a candle. *You can bear anything*, I tell myself, *if you know you're not alone*, and cold air stings my boiling skin as the men lift me into their arms. Their fingers are strong with knowledge; I'm only going where others have already been.

GINA OCHSNER

Song of the Selkie

aving swallowed too many bones, the sea has a bad case of indigestion. This sound of dyspepsia shatters the nerves and Erlen Steves knows that is why no one wants to live at the lighthouse. It doesn't help matters that three men died during its construction. When the mail boat ferries him to the docks, this fact is just one of the many things Erlen knows to keep quiet about in the presence of the local coasties.

Which suits him fine. He is not in the business of making noise, but of making light. In water and at sea, life revolves around his light. And each evening before starting his watch, Erlen recites the Light Keeper's Prayer. A longish prayer—Erlen does not have it up by heart. Which is why the prayer is typed, framed, hanging at the landing at the base of the light tower. Erlen does not bother with the beginning, but the end holds salt: . . . *grant, oh Thou Blessed Savior,*

that Thou would join us as we cross the last bar and struggle for the far-
ther shore, the lee shore of the land where the sun never goes down, and
where there is no darkness for He who is the light of the world will be the
light thereof.

No one would accuse Erlen of being overly religious, but he isn't
the type to stand in the way of it either. A prayer can't hurt here
on the rock, he thinks when he climbs the steep sixty-foot spiral
staircase to the service room, where the light is kept. The light, a
first-order Fresnel, stands nearly twelve feet tall and six feet wide.
The lenses are composed of glass segments arranged in rings and
stacked in concentric circles.

When his father kept the light it used to take the young boy—and
then later the young man—Erlen all of a day to clean the nearly one
thousand pieces of glass. This left only a little free time to comb the
rocks for pieces of the sea: sand-smoothed pebbles, razor clam
shells, the spiraled dog whelks that house miniature tornadoes
inside their fragile casings. The shells held to his ear, the young
man Erlen marveled that out of such dryness could issue the musical sound of water. And that the high tide could carry such items of
fragility and strength (once—whole green and blue glass floats all
the way from Japan) seemed a mystery intended for him to solve.
Imagine his surprise when he found one day not a shell, but a
woman, nude and shivering, washed up on the breakers. What
could he do but take her and that bedraggled fur coat tucked under
her arm into the lighthouse? What could he do but fall in love with
and marry her? What could he do but get her with children—twins
no less? And what could he do, being book-bound and a little forget-
ful, but lose her?

"I'm not surprised," Inspector Wilson said when Erlen had
delivered the news: Mrs. Erlen Steves, wearing nothing but that tattered fur coat minus the collar and a portion of the left sleeve, had
jumped from the rocks. "This lighthouse has a history of driving its
keepers mad." Inspector Wilson circled a finger around his ear, and
then tugged on the jacket of his Coast Guard uniform.

Erlen searched his memory of all the logbooks he'd read. "I didn't know that."

"Well, you know it now," Inspector Wilson said, casting a long look at the girls, already toddlers, tethered to a laundry line—in accordance with the light keeper's safety manual.

◦◦◦

"A selkie loves water," Astrid says.

"—A selkie loves land," says her sister, Clarinda.

"—A selkie walks on two feet . . . "

"—whenever she can."

Jump-rope geniuses, Astrid and Clarinda sing out tandem rope rhymes and never miss a beat. At the Mt. Angel boarding school they are unusual girls—always have been, Mother Iviron thinks—and not just because they are twins. Skin pale, jaws strong, mouths flat, the girls have eyes a color of blue so reluctant they border on gray. The only way Reverend Mother Iviron can tell them apart is the way Astrid pushes out her lower jaw in the presence of uninvited pity, while Clarinda tears up and turns red.

They are united utterly, so that what one girl starts the other girl finishes: rhymes, riddles, math problems. A phrase in the mouth of one twin finds its completion in the mouth of the other. If Astrid feels the bite of a nail, Clarinda cries out as it punctures the sole of her shoe. When Astrid slaps the girl who calls her "creepy times two," it is Clarinda who makes penance with a spate of *Hail Marys*, repetition being the heaven of duplicate things.

> *Hail Mary, full of grace, the Lord is with thee.*
> *Blessed art thou among women, and the fruit of thy tomb, Jesus.*

Fruit of the tomb? Mother Iviron, beyond girlhood puns, doesn't think twice when she makes the girls wear the hair shirts. Old-fashioned, oh yes. But to tell the truth, they don't seem to mind it too much.

Equally suspicious to Mother Iviron is the way the girls prepare for bed. They slide their cots together and before climbing in, they line up their shoes, turning the points toward each other as if the shoes might continue an ongoing conversation.

> *"When a selkie drags you under . . . "*
> *"—she'll split your skin asunder."*

When she hears this kind of talk, Mother Iviron stretches a hurting smile across her face. Far be it from her to stifle the imagination. And certainly tragic stories of the sea bear instructional value. But when the girls turn eleven and substitute sea chanteys for prayers, Mother Iviron sends them home to their father with her regrets.

∽◉◟

The lighthouse stands sixty feet high, tall as a castle. The painted rings of black and white turn the light tower into layered cake, spun sugar. The staircase curves in a tight spiral, the corkscrewed architecture of a lightning whelk. In the lantern room, the girls crack open a window and take turns playing Rapunzel. All the lighthouse needs now is a resident witch.

The girls shout into the wind: *Come find us!* In the meantime they keep busy. The work: polishing brass and cleaning glass, doing all to bend and multiply light in its refractions and reflections. Special care must be given to the first-order Fresnel and its catadioptric lens assembly. The bull's-eye lens rotates and magnifies the light as it swings. From a distance of twenty-six miles away the light appears as a flash over the water. At least, this is what their father's manual of operation says. But to the girls wearing their green safety goggles, the lenses look like a gigantic, transparent beehive. The rotating bulb behind the bull's-eye is the queen bee. Astrid and Clarinda, the custodians of the glass, are the confused, dim-witted drones.

For the longest time they thought the light was meant to lure the ships nearer—yes, right up to the rocks. Never did they imagine the light was meant to turn away every vessel except the mail boat or Inspector Wilson's tender, which can arrive in evenings without any warning and set their father scrambling. Astrid and Clarinda aren't quite sure what to make of Mr. Wilson, the Coast Guard's Aid to Navigation Inspector. When he comes with his high-powered nose lowered, Mr. Wilson always examines the kitchen first, tallying its contents and cleanliness down to every drawer and cupboard, each piece of cutlery. Astrid thinks he looks like a bloodhound on the scent of something turned sour. Clarinda thinks he looks like God wearing a dark uniform and white gloves. Only God would smile more often, Clarinda decides as she pockets two knives, a fork, and a spoon—just to throw the count off.

Bewildered. Erlen Steves is bewildered. Nobody told him how to raise girls. His many books about sea creatures, legend, and lore have been no help at all. And nothing in the engineering texts or the lighthouse operation manuals explains how to ease the loss of a wife and a mother.

All of which is to say, Erlen hasn't fully recovered. He knows this. Lulled by the changing moods of the water, its murmur and roar, it's hard not to think water, think salt, think tears. He knows it's unseemly to grieve for so long, but his sorrow is amplified, doubled, on account of the girls. He is not sad for himself: he lost a wife he suspects he was never meant to have. But for the girls to lose their mother while still so young—it splits his heart in half every time he looks at them.

He tries to be strong. He kisses them each on the forehead. Astrid's skin is always a little cool to the touch, Clarinda's always a little warm, feverish even, and then he climbs the sixty feet to sit with the light. The night watch he spends alone in the service room, cleaning the glass, polishing the bull's-eye lamp, which turns and turns as regularly and steadily as the beating of a heart. That anything so large or so small as a bulb could whirl with such constancy brings a comfort to him here in the lighthouse, where he knows nothing, not even water, should be taken for granted—neither the things the water carries away nor what the water might bring.

By day Sister Rosetta teaches the K–6 boarders at the Mt. Angel Parochial School. By night she writes a religious mystery novel and edits the *Convent Cloister Herald,* circulation thirty-eight. Thirty-seven after Sister Margaretta, God bless her, died peacefully in her sleep.

She's got a talent, that one, the other sisters say. A real way with the words, the way they never lockstep fail on her. And the way she can phrase a question: "Does Jesus still bear the wounds in his side and hands and feet now that he is ascended to the right hand of the Father?" A question so direct it unsettles the older sisters, Mother Iviron in particular, whose eyebrows stitch together at the scent of such mysteries. Such unanswerable questions ring with the hollow interior of the rhetorical. They make Mother Iviron's joints ache and her teeth throb. Sister Rosetta, blissfully unaware of what her words do to Mother Iviron, pokes around for the soft entrails, for the heart of faith, keeps poking with these questions in her nighttime dreaming.

Her dreams! Sister Rosetta's dreams could fill an ocean. Will she ever stop? "Honestly," Mother Iviron says. The way Sister Rosetta's frolicking queries keep the first-year postulants up at night, roiling the calm, rarified air within the stone walls of the convent—it's enough to drive them to distraction. *Why did Jesus heal some and not others?* Sister Rosetta asks in a dream, and the postulants and novitiates rise and bob in the gathering waters of Sister Rosetta's viscous questions.

It wouldn't be so bad, except Sister Rosetta is always the first to stir, waking with a shout and leaving the rest awash in her unnavigable dreams. Some of the postulants have signed up for swimming lessons. Others wear life jackets under their seersucker bedclothes and clamp plugs over their noses.

After too many nights left stranded in Sister Rosetta's dreams, Mother Iviron makes phone calls, drafts letters. In record speed, Sister Rosetta's résumé makes the rounds.

A man fell in love with a woman.
But the woman was in love with the sea.

Their father's voice winds down the staircase from the service room, that furnace of green and light and heat grown thick with their father's singing. He is shaping his grief, casting sorrow line by line, limb by limb, into the figure of a woman they cannot remember. In the place of her body, Astrid and Clarinda have these weepy words they know they were never meant to hear, but have long ago committed to memory. The same words that pushed Sister Iviron's determined smile askew, words that make the girls thirsty to know things. So many questions Astrid and Clarinda would love to ask their mother. So much about sky, skin, water, they would like to know. But their mother swam out to sea one day and forgot to return. "It was very strange—she being a champion swimmer," their father sometimes says.

When they cannot bear to hear their father sing, they climb the steps, put on the safety goggles, and tug on his sleeves. They pull him down to the kitchen for dinner, for midnight snacks, for a breakfast which is always the same fare: Spam on crackers or macaroni with canned tomato sauce.

"Tell us a story."

"A sad, strange story."

"A strange, scary story."

Erlen tries. He collects and collates the strangest stories he can find. To date he has amassed two notebooks full of sea lore and legendry. As they eat their macaroni and Spam, he tells of lighthouse ghosts and large boats split to splinters on rocks like these, and small, mischievous sea creatures. He tells them about a mermaid who almost married a prince. But the prince married another and the mermaid came to him one night as he lay sleeping and killed him with a poisoned kiss upon the lips.

"That's not so sad," Astrid says.

"And it's not so strange," Clarinda adds. She holds a row of macaroni noodles between her teeth and makes strange music through her homemade harmonica.

"Then maybe you've heard about the selkies, who look astonishingly like seals. In their whiskers they carry magic. If they fall in love with a human—and they do this more often than you might think—then they will unzip their fur, tuck it into a bundle, and hide it somewhere safe. Later, when they are tired of their human body, tired of human love, they simply pull their fur back on and swim out to sea."

The girls shudder. The pupils of their eyes dilate, then shrink to pinpoints, as if their eyes themselves are breathing. Erlen likes to tell this story because it's the only story the girls sit still for. But certain parts of the story he doesn't tell. A wayward selkie who has children with a human must come back for the children when they become women—otherwise those children will remain trapped forever in their human bodies. But this involves the changing of bodies and desires, and this isn't something Erlen likes to think about. He doesn't like change. To Erlen's reckoning, his girls will always be girls just as the lighthouse will always be their stronghold, their safety.

But one night he finds the girls in the lantern room, their long hair braided into knots and flung out the window as a ladder, their bodies leaning dangerously over the sill, and he realizes in a blink how thoroughly he doesn't understand them—how foolish he's been to hand them so many fictions to inhabit. He hauls them back in, too hard. His fingers leave a mark on Astrid's arm. But it's Clarinda who gasps and narrows her eyes. And he knows everything he will do to make it up from this point forward will be exactly the wrong thing.

In the waking world water is danger, water will drown them. The girls do not know how to swim. Though long since off their lighthouse leads, they still cling to each other behind the rail, afraid of the seventh wave, the sneaker that might pull them over and out. At night they push their beds together. Two commas, if they lie on their beds, touch toes to toes, head to head, their bodies form a circuitous loop. Choosing one heart to live in, one body of dreaming to inhabit, they drift in no time into each other's dreams. Barefoot they clamber over shore rock and into the shallows where the limpets and starfish move so slowly it's as if in dreams; time sheds its hold over things born in water. Deeper they wade until they feel underfoot the velvet and buzz of the corals.

Farther out, the rock and sand shelf plunge and the water swallows them. It burns a little to take it in through the nose. But they've been practicing every night in their dreams and breathing under water comes more easily than it used to. Overhead the sun blooms purple, blooms blue, a kelp bulb floating across their untroubled liquid ceiling. When they wake to a waterless sun, the light carries edges and angles, slicing their room. Gone are the dreams, the very memory of the fact that they had indeed been dreaming. The only clues: salt rimming their eyelids and crusted under their fingernails, their nightgowns wet and wadded into a pile at the foot of their beds.

The girls are good readers, having scoured the lighthouse logs for any mention of their mother. And they've even memorized the Light Keeper's Prayer in its entirety—no easy feat. But theirs is a lopsided education, and when the girls ask how to divide twins by twos—a problem of fractions if ever he's heard one—Erlen writes to Mr. Wilson, requesting a visiting schoolteacher and nanny.

In no time he receives a typed letter on heavy linen paper. It is from Mt. Angel Convent. A suitable candidate will be sent over immediately. Erlen scratches his head, sniffs the lily-white stationery in sheer amazement. He cannot recall actually mailing his request. The notion that God and Mr. Wilson might work in tandem, and quicker than the Tuesday mail boat, only adds to his bafflement. For there is Mr. Wilson's tender, nosing alongside the landing. All this on a Monday!

With a bellow from the foghorn, the boat heaves to, and down Erlen goes, *clink, clink, clink,* his boots over the steps. The girls, eyes gray as stone, stand on the landing and clutch the rail. But it's the new teacher Erlen's worried about, bobbing and pitching in Inspector Wilson's tender. Erlen ties off the boat and studies her. He can see she's a stranger to water: her face is as pale as her starched collar and veil, and she's got a fine sheen of sweat above her upper lip. It's the look of an inlander just about to feed the crabs. *Go ahead,* he'd like to tell her, *retching is the best way to beat the nausea.* Instead he says nothing. When he grabs for her hands, soft and pudgy like a child's, they melt to fit his. Erlen lifts her from the boat and his breath stutter-steps. He realizes he has forgotten what a woman's hands feel like.

Sister Rosetta, a little queasy in Mr. Wilson's tender, takes his advice, pushes her glasses a little higher up on her nose, and locks her gaze on the unmoving lighthouse. She spots the two girls standing at the railing. Hard telling where one girl begins and the other ends and Sister Rosetta understands why she's been sent: to care for them in the singular, to care for them in the plural. For it's clear in a glance that this land does not love these girls—stick-thin, chalky-faced, their long brown hair whipped to tails. Sister Rosetta sees a picture of twinned longing so raw and pure she has to look away.

Mr. Steves, the girls' father, reaches out and pulls her from the boat. His hand is rough against her skin and though his grip is completely appropriate, she feels flustered, can't help thinking that this is perhaps the first and last time she will be touched by a man, any man.

The boat leaves with another blast. Mr. Steves strides ahead to the lighthouse with her suitcases. Sister Rosetta angles her head and studies the girls, whose fingers have turned white under the pressure of their grip.

"Are you all right?" she asks them.

"Seven," says the girl on the left.

"Cry seven tears at high tide and a selkie will cry with you," explains the girl on the right.

"Seven," Sister Rosetta says, "is God's number."

"Why?"

Sister Rosetta nudges her glasses higher onto her nose again. "Because on the seventh wave, what God has taken He gives back."

"Our mother was swept away on the seventh wave. It was very strange—"

"—she being a near-champion swimmer."

"I'm sorry. I didn't know that," says Sister Rosetta, blinking fiercely behind her glasses.

"Well, you know it now," says the girl on the left, her jaw thrust out.

The girl on the right: nose red and snuffling, chin all atremble. It's going to be a job, Sister Rosetta knows, but the girls turn sweet, leading her by the hand up, up, up the winding stairs, throwing open the door to each room so that she can see for herself: the storage room, kitchen, sleeping quarters and bathroom, library, and, at the very top, the service room. Sister Rosetta doesn't know about the green-tinted safety goggles and looks directly into the heart of the light, into brilliance so fierce it's like looking at God in glory, a light meant to guide but that viewed too closely would certainly blind.

Days pass, each one a crow-shaped stain falling from the shore pines. The wind kicks up, breaks brittle days into halves, throws Erlen's nose out of kilter. The lighthouse smells of metal, of wet pennies. It was his wife's smell: pure and elemental, edged and biting like salt. One afternoon Erlen leaves the lantern room, his nose roving in all directions, tracking the scent of skin and wet fur. His nose leads him to the library, where the wind has snapped a windowpane. Sister Rosetta is there, a flurry of pages from the primer swirling around her. She stands on tiptoe reaching for the paper that curls out and away from her. She looks like a figurine in a snow globe. The sight of her, not at all a bad-looking woman, provokes his heart to skip. At that precise moment Erlen becomes a religious man, thanking God for this wind, for stirring things up.

The wind, Sister Rosetta, too, is thankful for. It howls through the lighthouse, inside her ears. But then Sister Rosetta, textbooks and papers in hand, stumbles. Her veil, cowl, and wimple fall, baring her shaved head. Where are her feet? she wonders, as the floor rises to meet her. And then Erlen is there, catching her. It's a surprise, the sureness of his grip. For even she doesn't quite remember where her elbows or knees are beneath the voluminous folds of the wool habit, and yet he knows exactly how to right her: an arm hooked around her rib, another anchoring her elbow.

Don't ever let go. That's what Sister Rosetta is thinking. What she says instead: "Is there something you were wanting?" She is trying so hard to sound utterly unflappable, though she can feel herself blushing, yes, down to the roots of her shorn hair.

Erlen retrieves her glasses, hands over her limp headpiece. He is careful with her vestments, averts his gaze even as he helps her with the veil, the hem of which has come unraveled. But his nose can't quit. Erlen's arms go stiff, his elbows lock. He considers Sister Rosetta, points his nose at her neck. She's not the source of that scent he's tracking, he realizes.

"Give the girls a bath," Erlen whispers, his nose twitching, "with extra soap."

Sister Rosetta's religious mystery novel is not going well. The hardest question—*Does God really know what He is doing?*—hasn't provoked a quick answer. Not in her writing, not in her life. Equally uncooperative are the twins, who do not want to shave their legs and underarms, who do not want to bathe at all. The three of them sit on the rim of the enormous metal tub and look at the water.

"Skin replaces itself," Astrid leads off.

"—cell by cell," Clarinda adds.

"—every thirty days . . . "

"—but hair replaces itself more slowly."

"Besides, we like being hairy—"

"—the hair keeps us warmer at night."

A smile starts on the left side of Astrid's face and travels from girl to girl. Sister Rosetta shrugs. The truth is, underneath her habit she is a little hairy too.

"I'll go first," Sister Rosetta says, hanging her habit and veil on a hook. She soaps herself and shows them how to run a razor the length of a leg, around the tricky points of the ankle. Her flesh hangs from her body in doughy folds. Sister Rosetta wonders if they know how unmoored she feels inside her own skin, this awkward, transparent sleeve. Can they even guess how badly she wants to turn the razor and make a longitudinal incision, stem to stern, and step free of this body that weighs on her, shames her?

But the girls aren't even watching her. Astrid bends to the tub, trails a finger in the water. "Our mother liked baths."

"Took them on full moon nights like this one," Clarinda adds, nodding at the window where the moon is a buoy in the dark sky.

"She's coming back for us." Astrid steps out of her pants. "She's going to teach us how to swim." The girls climb into the tub and no sooner have they settled in the water than they begin to bleed. Simultaneously, of course: two scarlet threads unspool from between their thighs. The girls are unnaturally calm, looking at Sister Rosetta with their wide eyes.

Sister Rosetta helps them out, towels them off, shows them what a strange contraption the belt and hook is, what good for girls becoming women such modern-day conveniences are. Afterward, Sister Rosetta carries the bathwater, pink and smelling of iron, in large pots down to the landing. Like carrying a comb to the sea, it's a risky thing to do but Sister Rosetta pours the contents of the pots over the railing anyway.

That night as Sister Rosetta climbs into bed, she considers the lighthouse lens turning silently. She thinks about Erlen with his hand at the light, true and shining. In no time at all, she is asleep, awash in a dream where she stands knee-deep in the surf and unlocks a suitcase full of keyhole limpets, chitons, lightning whelks, and several specimens of spindled murex. *How wide are heaven's gates, how deep?* Sister Rosetta wonders. She is stringing a rosary made of these musings, each question another chiton or whelk, the surfaces asymmetrical in pattern and design. Meanwhile, the good nuns at the abbey, uncostumed and unrestrained, turn their gazes to the expanse of Sister Rosetta's borderless dreaming. They link arms and kick their heels together with glee as they rush for the water. Wearied of the rosaries worn down between their fingers and thumbs, they are only too glad to wade in deep, exchange their smooth beads for the sharp points of Sister Rosetta's queries.

❧

Sister Rosetta's snoring keeps Astrid and Clarinda from sleep. Boredom and insomnia provoke their curiosity. Though the ground floor storage room is strictly off-limits, with Sister Rosetta asleep and their father up in the lantern room, there's no one to stop them.

The storage room is black as tar. It's an interesting proposition, such darkness held in the belly of the lighthouse. For fun they do not light matches or shine flashlights. Instead they drop to hands and knees and crawl across the floor, ending up in a far corner, where they find fur: one long strip and a smaller crescent-shaped patch. They tuck the scraps under their arms and race up to their room, where they survey the scraps atop the bedspread.

The fur is shiny silver like a seal's. They know without speaking it aloud, the fur is from their mother's coat. Instinctively, Astrid drapes the long swatch of fur over her shoulder, where it adheres to her skin, stretching from tip of shoulder to point of hip. Clarinda fastens the collar of fur around her neck and the girls know: there isn't a shoehorn big enough, a crowbar strong enough, to pry these strips loose now.

❧

Later that night the moon slips off its lead and a storm rolls in hard and fast. The wind whistles harsh lullabies that send the girls into unsettled sleep. Only their thin and flimsy human skin separates all that water outside from the water inside their bodies. They could drown—this has been the point of their father's stories, they know. But Sister Rosetta has taught them fractions and they now understand that they are two-thirds water, maybe more. They will float like the fish that swallowed the moon. They will rise buoyant and swim. All their lives it seems they've been practicing—in dreams, of course.

They know Sister Rosetta understands this. They know this

because that very night they wade into each other's dreams: the girls into Sister Rosetta's dreams and Sister Rosetta into the combined dreaming of the girls. In their dreams nobody wears clothes, and so they swim naked—Sister Rosetta and Astrid and Clarinda—their fears and their terrible longings and their many questions bobbing beside them. And they show each other what they never could during day: Astrid's strip of fur that now girdles her waist and Clarinda's collar of fur, which has already spread as a cape across her shoulders. The girls are sloughing their cracked and flimsy skins and Sister Rosetta runs her fingers over their beautiful patchwork bodies in utter amazement.

And then Sister Rosetta reveals her raw heart, ready for something more than wind and salt. Something more than the threads of her veil binding her up or her many lesson plans. And the girls, with their eyes grown so gray now they are nearly black, see Sister Rosetta's heart and know exactly what they are seeing.

"You take care of him," they implore in the singular and Sister Rosetta bolts upright in bed.

Midnight. The fur has spread, covering the girls from neck to knee. They turn their skins under and roll them down, as women do when stepping out of a pair of nylons. They tuck their skins under their arms and wind their way carefully down the stairs. Astrid trails a hand along the stone to steady them, while Clarinda bites her lip. With each step Clarinda thinks *right*, thinks *left*. Thinks *down*.

"Don't—" Astrid whispers.

"—be afraid," Clarinda replies. It's what their mother said, the day she swan-dived from the rock for the water. Now they know, now they remember. How to swim? That will come. But it's the land they must leave, once and for all, leave it for the water that will lift and carry them. *Water*, Clarinda thinks as she pushes the sky aside with her hands.

"C'mon," Astrid urges. "Hurry now." At the landing Clarinda hesitates. "Don't—" Astrid says.

"—be afraid," Clarinda replies.

Don't be afraid.

When Astrid lifts her left foot over the ledge, Clarinda steps off with her right.

ഛൟ

Erlen smells the girls. He leaps to his feet. *Slap, slap, slap,* down the stone steps. Above him the light turns behind the glass. You would think for all this light he might see something. But he doesn't, can't, the light shining miles and miles beyond him. By the time he gets to the landing, the girls are gone.

"Come back!" he shouts, knowing full well they can't hear him, having slipped beneath the water with their slick and oily bodies. Two transparent skins drape over the railing; two unzipped, girl-shaped casings drip the color of fog.

Erlen, beyond bewilderment, fingers the skins. Next to him is Sister Rosetta, her lips moving silently. *Guide them,* she prays. Her prayers stand tiptoe to press against the invisible beating heart of God. *Guide us all.* She understands, looking at Erlen, looking at the skins he folds into halves, into quarters, that none of them has ever been quite right for this world, casting about in skins they aren't quite suited for.

Erlen turns to Sister Rosetta. "They're not coming back, are they?"

Sister Rosetta peers out over the water. "No." She is crying hot, oily tears. She will miss those girls with their luminous eyes and stories. But she is not really worried. It's Erlen she's thinking of now. No, it's herself and Erlen—together—she's thinking of. She rests her palms flat and hard against her heart, her heart so full she thinks it will burst from the pressure. Sister Rosetta smiles, can't help thinking this is another mystery, this hurt wrecking her, this full measure of sky she's swallowed, pressed and running over. So full in her lungs she might drown on it.

Is it love? she wonders, considering Erlen leaning at the railing. Is this how love finds us even when we're sure it won't, finds us anyway, splits us wide open? It's an unforeseen plot complication and she's not sure what to do but offer thanks: thank you, parable. Thank you, rhyme. Thank you, unanswerable questions.

♋

Erlen presses his hips against the railing. His daughters are gone, he can feel it as certainly as he feels his heart tumbling. Gone but not lost, he feels that too. In the hills the dogs bark and bark, beyond reason, beyond logic, barking for the sheer joy of repetition. To see, perhaps, if the moon might wag its tail.

Erlen turns to Sister Rosetta. Her face glows beneath the moonlight. Her woolen habit is beneath Erlen's hand. Sister Rosetta is beneath the habit. From rib to rib his heart is a melon falling rung by rung down a long ladder.

"Sister Rosetta—"

"Rose," she says, slipping her hand in his. The wind whips her veil and cowl off her head. She doesn't have time to think: *Catch it.* It tumbles past the breakers, caught now and carried beyond the surf, where it disappears into darkness.

STACEY RICHTER

The Doll Awakens

Thee had once been a time when to exist and to be cherished were one and the same thing. Miss Pretty had been adored almost from the moment she was manufactured—her hair had been silky and fresh-spun and her dress had been starched and clean, and she was trucked from the factory in her own pink box, wrapped in gold paper and slobbered over by Tina, all in a seamless roll of time. Then years passed and a litany of bad things happened until finally she was shoved into a box and left to rot, in a trailer without climate control, with several pieces of her original outfit gone AWOL, and no one cared. It was obvious after all these years that no one cared. Miss Pretty stared at the lid of the cardboard box for longer than it seemed possible to stare. She would have liked to sleep but sleep was impossible—the counterweights tugged on her eyelids but they wouldn't slide shut, they were fused open, and so she gazed at the cardboard and at the occasional, disgusting silverfish carousing across its surface. Her destiny waited on the other side; she could feel it out there, but she couldn't reach it. Sometimes she'd push on the box, or give it a gnaw, but she lacked the energy to go on and she'd lost the source of it.

And then, one day, when she had released the last strand of hope, when it seemed that she was destined to remain forever pickled in the juices of her own memories, she was picked up. She felt the buoyant lightness of being carried, that bouncing weightlessness. Dust streamed across her. Just like that, the lid of the box was whisked away. She was ready for the nightclub, the flashbulbs, the popping of champagne corks, but instead Miss Pretty found herself staring at a white snout made of paper. The snout was attached to a woman's face. Above it were two dark and squinty eyes. It was not a young face, not a believer's face. It wasn't the kind of face she'd want to sing to.

"Do you have to save everything?" the face said, turning and shouting over a shoulder.

Miss Pretty stared; she had no choice. It wasn't a snout, she realized. It was a woman wearing a dust mask.

"Hey," a man's voice echoed through space, "you never know what might come in handy." The man lumbered into view. Of course she recognized him. All those pieces: the shirtless belly, the ponytail—no longer red, but gray and mostly gone on top—the face like putty arranged with a spatula. It was Gordon, her nemesis, an older, fatter, balder version.

"Why can't I ever have a normal boyfriend? Normal people part with objects. They chuck out trash."

"Come on, Beverly. She's cute. Carol Ann's kid used to drag her everywhere."

"Oh. Now I see. *Carol Ann.*"

Gordon put his hands on her and lifted her from the box. A deep loathing passed across Miss Pretty's surface. She felt a jolt whip along her hair plugs. The torpor lifted a little and she felt a small zip, though she still would have preferred to sleep.

They sat her on a high shelf. She gazed down upon a tableau that was strikingly similar to the déclassé scenes she'd witnessed before, in that other smelly house, in that other hot place. There was Gordon, looking more than ever like an engorged lawn leprechaun. Beside him was his new woman, Beverly, shrill and hectoring, breathing in labored gasps. Beverly had eventually taken off her mask but her face retained a bulbous, snouted appearance anyway. They were inside a tiny trailer with a kitchenette and fold-down benches. The walls were lined with shelves crammed full of glass beakers and bags of powder and glass vials that glowed red when the burner was turned on. The hum of a generator permeated the air. Below her, the two sifted powders into solutions, like sorcerers. Miss Pretty watched bubbles rising in test tubes, milky fluids poured through filters of cat litter, cakes being milled into powder in an old, hand-cranked ice crusher. It was the same world, over and over, that's what she had been reborn into. There was no glamour, no compensation. They hardly paid any attention to her at all.

Only every now and then, Gordon would look up at her, briefly. Then, a bit more often.

On the first day Miss Pretty was out of the box, the two continued with what they kept referring to as "a little chemistry action" for several hours. Gordon worked in a soiled T-shirt and plaid shorts, pointing out the ingenuity and grace of his methods to his companion, occasionally humming. One of his hands was knobby and deformed and had only two fingers on it, the thumb and ring finger. He held it slightly away from his body, as though it were unaffiliated with him. The woman assisted him, yawning when he expounded on his superior abilities as a chemist. She wore a yellow bikini. Or she wore a loose white shirt over the bikini. Or she wore a black sweater over the bikini. She was thin for the most part but blobby, muscle-less, and her rear end ballooned out from her narrow waist. Now and then she complained about the toxic fumes and put the mask back on, then said it was choking her and that it was Gordon's responsibility to design a better ventilation system. Miss Pretty found her hideous.

After a while, Beverly began to wheeze, touching her chest while she breathed. Then she announced that "peak cancer hours" were open for business and that she was going for a little break action. She rubbed oil all over her body and left the trailer, a shaft of light entering like a laser when she opened the door. She carried a folded aluminum chair under her arm.

Gordon continued working, glancing at Miss Pretty now and then, first at half-hour intervals, then every five or ten minutes. He couldn't stop molesting her with his eyes. They traveled up and down her petite body, from plastic shoe to nylon hair.

He said, "Stop staring at me, you little witch."

And then, a while later, he said, "I'm not afraid of you, you tiny fucker."

She knew him. He had always been a coward.

She liked to think of herself as beautiful—she had the kind of cool, abstract beauty of Norwegian royalty, an ice queen who betrays almost nothing on the surface. She still pictured herself as she had once been: perfect, Mint in Box. But the years and the heat had taken their toll on her complexion, some kind of molded plastic that might outlast a planet's worth of organic material but not without cracking somewhat in the interim. As she came to terms with the fact that her freckles had faded, Miss Pretty began to feel more worldly, exotic. She was left with a faint brown wash over her button nose, like sun-bleached calico, a fetching effect. No wonder he kept looking at her. As she watched Gordon work with his chemical paraphernalia, a tune entered her mind, velvet and slow. She hummed it to herself.

"Why do you keep looking up there?" asked the woman. She'd set up the aluminum chair inside the trailer and sat in it, stinking like a piña colada.

"Baby doll."

"Come again?"

"Baby doll's freaking me out."

The woman wrinkled her lips. "You need to let me know when you're going to be testing the product, okay? Could you do me that courtesy? I do not need to be out in the middle of nowhere with a hallucinating person."

"I haven't *tested*," Gordon said. "That baby doll's face is demented."

Miss Pretty scoffed. She was *not* a baby doll. This was a well-known fact. She stood on her own two feet; she did not loll on her back as baby dolls lolled. She was a *companion* doll, manufactured to look like a complete little girl in and of herself, eighteen inches high from molded foot to pigtailed head. Well, the pigtails had transformed into something more like dreadlocks at this point but she could live with that if she had to. A certain amount of wear was acceptable, as long as she could recover her panties and her shoe. Completeness was more important than condition.

Down below, she noticed, the woman had switched into a little-girl voice. "Do you love me?"

Gordon looked away. "I don't like the *L* word."

"Then say it the way I told you."

"I can't remember."

"Abby says any man who can't say it is a pig."

"Okay," said Gordon, "I adore you."

"What was that?"

"I adore you."

"Oh great." She rolled her eyes. "I *adore* you too."

At night, Gordon and Beverly pulled cots down off the wall and swaddled themselves in sleeping bags. After a brief fight over security vs. ventilation they threw open the doors and Miss Pretty watched lizards and scorpions crawl into the trailer as the night deepened. They didn't touch each other, except for once when

Gordon left his cot and tried to crawl in with the woman. She mumbled at him to get off her, and burrowed deeper into her bag. Gordon sat on the edge of his cot for a long time, chewing tobacco and spitting it into a soup can between his feet. After a while he shuffled over to Miss Pretty and shone a flashlight on her face. He was wearing a sleeveless T-shirt made of a very light material that seemed to float on top of his chest hair. He whispered, "I remember you, you little gnome. You wee, fucking midget."

She watched a scorpion scuttle toward his ankle, its tail bursting with venom.

Neither of them seemed to change their clothes, or wash, though the woman's skin had begun to turn a deep, glossy brown. She held out her limbs and admired them and encouraged Gordon to do the same. Gordon nodded and stared away blankly. He'd begun to chew tobacco constantly. If he wasn't doing that, he ate candy bars and tossed the wrappers into the greasy paper bag they used as a trash can. The woman *requested* that he get back to work—her hair lank and falling into her dust mask. They didn't have all the time in the world, she warned, for him to *gaze* around this godforsaken trailer—fucking *gaze*—while it took her an hour and a half to drive to the nearest town for a hamburger. She hadn't gone to Wellesley for this shit.

The next time the woman left the trailer, he moved the chair next to the shelf and climbed up on it. He leaned his head in close to Miss Pretty until she was marinated in his vile, sour breath. He whispered: "I don't remember your name, but you were her ally. You were against me then, and you're against me now. I remember you," he said, tapping his forehead to emphasize the concept of memory.

He was such a jerk. Of course he had forgotten her name, but Miss Pretty hadn't forgotten him. It was her genius to remember everything.

She remembered the toupee he wore for a week while Tina's drug-addled mother called him a goddamn used-car salesman and a gentleman's valet and a lounge lizard and a fucking embarrassment.

She remembered him punching his fist through the wall while Tina's mother swayed on her feet and whispered, "Just ignore him."

She remembered how he touched a cigarette to the back of Tina's hand, then said, "Oops."

She remembered everything he wanted to forget.

The man and woman unfolded a table in the middle of the trailer. They divided the tabletop into four sections with strips of cardboard anchored with masking tape. They used this as a device for sorting capsules according to the color and texture of their contents.

"I have a feeling this is my most profound batch yet," Gordon said, shaking a bag of capsules. "This stuff is going to show those poor suckers the face of God."

"I just want something to keep me thin," Beverly said, and stared at him for a while.

Then, as if something had clicked, Gordon said: "What are you talking about? You look great."

Miss Pretty tried to ignore them. She hated the shelf. She preferred to be the center of attention, prized for her beauty and charisma. When she swept into a room, heads were supposed to swivel. The music found a sultry groove—yeah, that's an alto sax, buddy. Husbands dropped their hands below the table and screwed off their wedding rings. Women felt suddenly deficient, ashamed of their sequins and pearls, because nothing could shine as brightly, no one could be as effortless and gorgeous, as Miss Pretty in her prime. The cinnamon hair, the dainty face, world-weary and lined—they didn't call it age in her case, they called it "vintage," a far sweeter concept. She was it. She was the doll. When she sang she would hold her body very still, like Peggy Lee, but she had something Peggy Lee never did—an iron confidence, a ruthless pride. She would be no one's doormat, no one's little victim. Never ever.

So much energy had crept into her limbs. She felt them buzzing like a beehive. She was awake now. She remembered so much.

She remembered a girl, her girl, being pulled out of school in the middle of the morning and put into the back of a car. Then Tina was driven away from all her little friends so that Miss Pretty was her only friend in the whole world. In those days she'd slept and awakened and slept again. Every time her eyes opened, Tina was there, staring back.

She remembered being dropped into a sandbox and abandoned with one shoe shucked off, buried with a spoon. Ants swarmed under her dress, into the hollow of her mouth, but Miss Pretty endured it, because she knew Tina would always come back for her. She knew Tina didn't have anyone else.

When they had finished sorting the pills, the woman again rubbed oil on her limbs and exited the trailer. Gordon planted himself on a chair below Miss Pretty. He stared at her and she stared back. "It's not my fault," he complained. "I didn't do anything."

Miss Pretty gazed at him, unperturbed. She had begun composing a song in her head, a sensual ballad:

Wouldn't take much
To topple you in
To a high, rushing river
Where you'd flail,
But couldn't swim

You think I won't do it
But I will . . . but I will
Maim and hurt you
(Though you struggle)
And dismember
And kill

In the chair below her, Gordon scratched his armpit and muttered, "I saw that. I saw you move."

Finally it seemed that the chemistry action was coming to an end. The man and woman gathered up the empty bags and the plastic containers that had held powdered chemicals, and liquids, as well as the boxes and bags that they were packed in, and dragged them out of the trailer. A while after that, Miss Pretty smelled the sharp, acrid smell of peculiar substances burning, and later she identified the terrifying odor of scorched plastic. Gordon combed his hair back with a wet comb; the woman put on a tight, expensive dress that toggled her appearance from that of a dissipated, over-tan bag lady to a bored socialite just back from the spa. They spoke to each other politely, on their best behavior, as light slanted through the trailer's high, dirty windows. They began to pack the capsules into various objects that seemed to have been modified to serve as containers. There was a hollow radio lined with felt. There was a six-pack of cola with bottoms that screwed off, leaving only a hairline seam. There was a down jacket with a series of small, ingenious pockets sewn into the puffiest sections. Miss Pretty watched from her perch as the pills were packed away, all but a handful or two.

Beverly was smiling. "Let's go to one of those islands where natives feed you pineapple on silver forks."

Gordon glanced up at Miss Pretty. "What do you want to do there? Work on your tan?"

Miss Pretty gazed down at the people made of meat. Gordon couldn't keep his eyes off her. He gave her that casual squint. Yeah, buddy, *cherchez la femme*. He obviously had a crush on her. So she was relaxed, in control; she wasn't anticipating any trouble when Gordon pulled up the chair and grabbed her. He swept her off the shelf. He used the claw to hook up her dress—her blue dress with the nautical collar that had been reduced to a stained and shredded remnant over the years, but was still sort of cute in a ragamuffin way—and he jerked it over her head so her bottom half was completely bare.

He went in via the wedge-shaped opening in her belly, where he'd forced his way through at knifepoint once before. Little Tina had patched the area with masking tape that had decayed with age, but enough stickiness remained to encourage the formation of a membrane of hair and lint. Gordon plowed through that and cracked the entrance wider with spreading motions of the claw. He held her open and shoved a baggie full of capsules into her as though she were his private receptacle, a thing to be handled whatever way he saw fit.

No one's little victim. Never again.

Gordon laughed and said, "See? I told you she'd come in handy."

He handed the doll to the woman, who had again donned her dust mask. She snickered and whipped the dress back down with a flick of her wrist. Inside Miss Pretty's body the capsules settled, along with the terrible injustice of being inert and silent and tampered with and used. For a few seconds rage seethed inside her like bubbles in a beaker. And then, without thought or reflection of any kind, Miss Pretty did what she'd been born to do. She crooked her little head downward and bit a hunk of flesh the size of a crab apple out of Beverly's arm.

Beverly howled and sank to the floor. She stayed there gasping, gripping her arm while a puddle of blood spread around her like a skirt.

Gordon started to laugh. "I knew it!" he said. "I knew I saw her move!"

KAREN RUSSELL

The Seagull Army Descends on Strong Beach

he gulls landed in Athertown on July 10, 1979. Clouds of them, in numbers unseen since the ornithologists began keeping records of such things. Scientists all over the country hypothesized about climate change and migratory routes. At first sullen Nal barely noticed them. Lost in his thoughts, he dribbled his basketball up the boardwalk, right past the hundreds of gulls on Strong Beach, gulls grouped so thickly that from a distance they looked like snowbanks. Their bodies capped the dunes. If Nal had looked up, he would have seen a thunderhead of seagulls in the well of the sky, rolling seaward. Instead, he ducked under the dirty turquoise umbrella of the Beach Grub cart and spent his last dollar on a hamburger; while he struggled to open a packet of yellow mustard, one giant gull swooped in and snatched the patty from its bun with a surgical jerk. Nal took two bites of bread and lettuce before he realized what had happened. The gull taunted him, wings akimbo, on the Beach Grub umbrella, glugging down his burger. Nal went on chewing the greasy bread, concluding that this was pretty much par for his recent course.

All summer long, since his mother's termination, Nal had begun to sense that his life had jumped the rails—and then right at his nadir, he'd agreed to an "avant" haircut performed by Cousin Steve. Cousin Steve was participating in a correspondence course with a beauty school in Nevada, America, and to pass his Radical Metamorphosis II course, he decided to dye Nal's head a vivid blue and then razor the front into tentacle-like bangs. "Radical," Nal said dryly as Steve removed the foil. Cousin Steve then had to airmail a snapshot of Nal's ravaged head to the United States desert, $17.49 in postage, so that he could get his diploma. In the photograph, Nal looks like he is going stoically to his death in the grip of a small blue octopus.

Samson Wilson, Nal's brother, took his turn in Cousin Steve's improvised barber chair—a wrecked church pew that Steve had carted into his apartment from off the street. Cousin Steve used Samson as a guinea pig for "Creative Clippers." He gave Samson a standard buzz cut to start, but that looked so good that he kept going with the razor. Pretty soon Samson had a gleaming cue-ball head. He'd cracked jokes about the biblical significance of this, and Nal had secretly hoped that his brother's power over women would in fact be diminished. But to Nal's dismay, the ladies of Athertown flocked to Samson in greater multitudes than before. Girls trailed him down the boardwalk, clucking stupidly about the new waxy sheen to his head. Samson was seventeen and had what Nal could only describe as a bovine charm: he was hale and beefy, with a big laugh and the deep serenity of a grazing creature. Nal loved him too, of course—it was impossible not to—but he was baffled by Sam's ease with women, his ease in the world.

That summer Nal was fourteen and looking for excuses to have extreme feelings about himself. He and Samson played a lot of basketball on summer nights and weekends. Nal would replay every second of their games until he was so sick of his own inner sportscaster that he wanted to puke. He actually had puked once—last September he had walked calmly out of the JV tryouts and retched in the frangipani. The voice in his head logged every on-court disaster, every stolen ball and missed shot, the unique fuck-ups and muscular failures that he had privately termed "Nal-fouls." Samson had been on the varsity team since his freshman year, and he wasn't interested in these instant replays—he wanted the game to move forward. Nal and his brother would play for hours, and when he got tired of losing, Nal would stand in the shade of a eucalyptus grove and dribble in place.

"It's just a pickup game, Nal," Samson told him.

"Quit eavesdropping on me!" Nal shouted, running the ball down the blacktop. "I'm talking to myself."

Then he'd take off sprinting down the road, but no matter how punishing the distance he ran—he once dribbled the ball all the way down to the ruined industrial marina at Pier 12, where the sea rippled like melted aluminum—Nal felt he couldn't get away from himself. He sank hoops and it was always Nal sinking them; he missed, and he was Nal missing. He felt incapable of spontaneous action: before he could do anything, a tiny homunculus had to generate a flowchart in his brain. If p, then q; if z, then back to a. This homunculus could gnaw a pencil down to a nub, deliberating. All day, he could hear the homunculus clacking in his brain like a secretary from a 1940s movie: Nal shouldn't! Nal can't! Nal won't! and then hitting the bell of the return key. He pictured the homunculus as a tiny, blankly handsome man in a green sweater, very agreeably going about his task of wringing the life from Nal's life.

He wanted to get to a place where he wasn't thinking about every movement at every second; where he wasn't even really Nal any longer but just weight sinking into feet, feet leaving the pavement, fingers fanning forcelessly through air, the *swish!* of a made basket and the net birthing the ball. He couldn't remember the last time he had acted without reservation on a single desire. Samson seemed to do it all the time. Once, when Nal returned home from his miles-long run with the ball, sweating and furious, they had talked about his aspiration for vacancy—the way he wanted to be empty and free. He'd explained it to Samson in a breathless rush, expecting to be misunderstood.

"Sure," Samson said. "I know what you're talking about."

"You do?"

"From surfing. Oh, it's wild, brother." Why did Samson have to know him so well? "The feeling of being part of the same wave that's lifting you. It's like you're coasting outside of time, outside your own skin."

Nal felt himself redden. Sometimes he wished his brother would simply say, "No, Nal, what the hell do you mean?" Samson had a knack for this kind of insight: he was like a grinning fisherman who could wrench a secret from the depths of your chest and dangle it in front of you, revealing it to be nothing but a common, mud-colored fish.

"You know what else can get you there, Nal, since you're such a shitty athlete?" Samson grinned and cocked his thumb and his pinky, tipped them back. "Boozing. Or smoking. Last night I was out with Vanessa and we were maybe three pitchers in when the feeling happened. All night I was in love with everybody."

So Samson was now dating Vanessa Grigalunas? Nal had been infatuated with her for three years and had been so certain, for so long, that they were meant to be together, he was genuinely con-fused by this development, as if the iron of his destiny had gone soft and pliant as candle wax. Vanessa was in Nal's grade, a fellow survivor of freshman year. He had sat behind her in Japanese class and it was only in that language—where he was a novice and felt he had license to stammer like a fool—that he could talk to her. "K-k-k," he'd say. Vanessa would smile politely as he revved his stubborn engine syllable, until he was finally able to sputter out a

"Konnichiwa."

Nal had never breathed a word about his love for Vanessa to any-one. And then in early June, out of the clear blue, Samson began raving about her. "Vanessa Grigalunas? But . . . why her?" Nal asked, thinking of all the hundreds of reasons that he'd by now col-lected. It didn't seem possible that the desire to date Vanessa could have co-evolved in Samson. Vanessa wasn't his type at all; Samson usually dated beach floozies, twentysomethings with hair like dry spaghetti, these women he'd put up with because they bought him liquor and pot, who sat on his lap in Gerlando's, Athertown's only cloth-napkin restaurant, and cawed laughter. Vanessa's hair shone like a lake. Vanessa read books and moved through the world as if she were afraid that her footsteps might wake it.

"I can't stop thinking about her," Samson grinned, running a paw over his bald head. "It's crazy, like I caught a Vanessa bug or something."

Nal nodded miserably—now he couldn't stop thinking about the two of them together. He sketched out interview questions in his black composition notebook that he hoped to one day ask her:

1. What is it that you like about my brother? List three things (not physical).

2. What made you want to sleep with my brother? What was your thought in the actual moment when you decided? Was it a conscious choice, like, Yes, I will do this! Or was it more like col-lapsing onto a sofa?

3. Under what circumstances can you imagine sleeping with me? Global apocalypse? National pandemic? Strep throat shuts down the high school? What if we were to do it immediately after I'd received a lethal bite from a rattlesnake so you could feel confi-dent that I would die soon and tell no one? Can you just quantify for me, in terms of beer, what it would take?

It made Nal sadder still that even Vanessa's mom, Mrs. Griga-lunas—a woman who had no sons of her own and who treated all teenage boys like smaller versions of her husband—even kindly, delusional Mrs. Grigalunas recognized Nal as a deterrent to love. One Saturday night Samson informed him that the *three* of them would be going on a date to Strong Beach together; they needed Nal's presence to reassure Mrs. Grigalunas that nothing dangerous or fun would happen.

"Yes, you two can go to the beach," she told Vanessa, "but bring that Nal along with you. He's such a nice boy."

What were all these seagulls doing out flying at night? Usually Nal came out here to Strong Beach solo, dribbling his ball past these dunes in a fog of fantasies about Vanessa—anatomically vague, excruciatingly arousing fantasies, wherein she spontaneously lost her top. But now that he was here with Vanessa and Sam he finally noticed them. They were kelp gulls, big ones. He was shocked to see how many of the birds now occupied Strong Beach. Where'd they all come from? He hoped they'd leave soon, anyway. He was trying to finish a poem. White globs of gull shit kept falling from the sky, a cascade that Nal found inimical to his writing process. The poem that Nal was working on had nothing to do with his feelings—poetry, he'd decided, was to honor remote and immortal subjects, like the moon. "Lambent Planet, Madre Moon" was the working title of this one, and he'd already jotted down three sestets. *Green nuclei of fireflies*, Nal wrote. *The red commas of two fires.* A putrid, stinky blob fell from above and put out his word. "Shoo, you shit balloons!" he yelled as the gulls rained on.

There were no fireflies on the beach that night, but there were plenty of spider fleas, their abdomens pulsing with low-grade toxins. The air was tangy and cold. Between two lumps of sand about a hundred yards behind him, Vanessa and Nal's brother, Samson, were . . . Nal couldn't stand to think about it. In five minutes' time they had given up on keeping their activities a secret from him, or anybody. Vanessa's low moan was rising behind him, rich and feral and nothing like her classroom whisper.

Nal felt a little sick.

What on earth was the moon like? he wondered, squinting. What did the moon most resemble to him? Nal wiped at his dry eyes and dug into the paper. One of the seagulls had settled on an auburn coil of seaweed a few feet away from his bare foot. He tried to ignore it, but the gull was making a big production out of eviscerating a cigarette. It drew out red flakes of tobacco with its pincerlike bill and ate them. Perfect, Nal thought. Here I am trying to eulogize Mother Nature and this is the tableau she presents me with.

Behind him, Samson growled Vanessa's name. Don't look back, you asshole! he thought. Good advice, from Orpheus to Lot. But Nal couldn't help himself. He lacked the power to look away, but he never worked up the annihilating courage to look directly at them either; instead, he angled his body and let his eyes slide to the left. This was like taking dainty sips of poison. Samson's broad back had almost completely covered Vanessa—only her legs were visible over the dune, her pink feet twitching as if she were impatient for sleep. "Oh!" said Vanessa, over and over again. "Oh!" She sounded happy, astonished.

Nal was a virgin. He kicked at a wet clump of sand until it exploded. He went on a rampage, doing whirling jujitsu kicks into a settlement of abandoned sand castles along the beach for a full minute before he paused, panting, to recover himself. The tide rushed icy fingers of water up the beach and covered Nal's foot.

"Ahh!" Nal cried into one of the troughs of silence between Samson and Vanessa's moans. He had wandered to the water's edge, six or seven dunes away from them. His own voice was drowned out by the ocean. The salt water sleuthed out cuts on his legs that he had forgotten about or failed to feel until now, and he almost enjoyed the burning, which felt to him like a violent reanimation. His heartbeat hadn't slowed yet. He looked around for something else to kick but only one turret remained on the beach, a bucket-shaped stump in the middle of damp heaps. The giant seagull was standing beside it. Up close the gull seemed as large as a house cat. Its white face was luminous, its wings ink-dipped; its beak was fixed in that perennial shit-eating grin of all shearwaters and frigate birds.

"What are you grinning at?" Nal muttered. As if in response, the gull spread its wings and opened its shadow over the miniature ruins of the castle—too huge, Nal thought, and vaguely humanoid in shape—and then it flew off, laboring heavily against the wind. In the soft moonlight this created the disturbing illusion that the bird had hitched itself to Nal's shadow and was pulling his darkness from him.

Nal wasn't supposed to be in town that summer. He had been accepted to LMASS, the Lake Marion Achievement Summer Seminars: a six-week precollege program for the top 3 percent of the country's high school students. It was a big deal—seniors who completed all four summers of the program were automatically admitted to Lake Marion College with a full scholarship package. "Cream Rises" was the camp's motto; their mascot was an oblong custard-looking thing, the spumy top layer of which Nal guessed was meant to represent the gifted. In March a yellow T-shirt with this logo had arrived in the mail, bundled in with his acceptance letter. Nal tried to imagine a hundred kids wearing the same shirt in the Lake Marion dormitories, kids with overbites and cowlicks and shy, squint-eyed ambitions—LMAS! he thought, a kind of heaven. Had he worn the shirt with the custard-thing to his own school, it would have been a request for a punch in the mouth.

But then one day his mom came home from work and said she was being scapegoated by the Paradise Nursing Facility for what management was calling "a distressing oversight." Her superiors recommended that she not return to work. But for almost two weeks Nal's mother would set her alarm for five o'clock, suit up, take the number 14 bus to Paradise. Only after she was officially terminated did she file for unemployment, and so far as Nal could tell this was the last real action she had taken; she'd been on their couch for three months now and counting. Gradually she began to lose her old habits, as if these too were a uniform that she could slip out of: she stopped cooking entirely, slept at odd hours, mummied herself in blankets in front of their TV. What was she waiting for? There was something maddening about her posture—the way she sat there with one ear cocked sideways as if listening for a break in the weather. Nal had been forced to forfeit his deposit at Lake Marion and interview for a job behind the register at Penny's Grocery. He took a pen to the help wanted ads and papered their fridge with them. This was back in April, when he'd still believed his mom might find another job in time to pay the Lake Marion fee.

"Mom, just look at these, OK?" he'd shout above the surf roar of their TV, "I circled the good ones in green," and she'd explain again without looking over that the whole town was against her. Nobody was going to hire Claire Wilson *now*.

All of these changes came about as the result of a single failed mainstay. The windows at Paradise were supposed to be fitted with a stop screw, to prevent what the Paradise manual euphemistically referred to as "elopement." Jailbreak was another word for this, suicide, accidental defenestration—as Nal's mom put it, many of the residents were forty-eight cards to a deck and couldn't be trusted with their own lives. With the stop screws in place, no window opened more than six inches. But as it happened, a stop screw was missing from a sixth-floor window—one of the hundred-plus windows in Paradise—an oversight that was discovered when a ninety-two-year-old resident shoved it open to have a smoke. A visitor found the old woman leaning halfway out the window and drew her back inside the frame. The visitor described the "near fatal incident" to Nal's mother while the "victim" plucked ash from her tongue. According to Nal's mom, the Paradise administrators came to the sudden agreement that it had always been Claire Wilson's responsibility to check the window locks.

She came home that night babbling insincere threats: "They try to pin this on me, boys, you watch, I will quit in a heartbeat." But then the resident's daughter wrote a series of histrionic letters to the newspaper, and the sleepy Athertown news station decided to do an "exposé" of Paradise, modeled on the American networks, complete with a square-jawed black actress to play the role of Nal's mother.

Only Nal had watched the dramatization through to its ending. They'd staged a simulation of a six-story fall using a flour sack dummy, the sack splitting open on the gates and spilling flour everywhere, powdering the inscrutable faces of the stone angels in the garden below. Lawsuits were filed, and, in the ensuing din of threats and accusations, Nal's mother was let go.

Nal had expected his mom to react to this with a froth and vengeance that at least matched his own, perhaps even file a legal action. But she returned home from her final day at work exhausted. Her superiors had bullied her into a defeated sort of gratitude: "They said it was my job, who knows? I'm not perfect. I'm just glad they caught the problem when they did," she kept saying.

"Quit talking like that!" Nal moaned. "It wasn't your fault, Mom. You've been brainwashed by these people. Don't be such a pushover."

"A pushover!" she said. "Who's pushing me over? I know it wasn't my fault, Nal. I can't be grateful that nobody got killed?" She described the "averted tragedy" in the canned language of the Paradise directors: the chance of one of her charges flailing backward out the window and onto the gate's tiny spears. In her dreams the victim wasn't a flour sack dummy but a body with no face, impaled on the spikes.

"That's your body, Ma!" Nal cried. "That's you!" But she didn't see it that way.

"Let's just be thankful nobody was hurt," she mumbled.

Nal didn't want his mom to relinquish her first fury. "How can you say that? They fired you, mom! Now everything's . . . off course."

His mom stroked a blue curl of Nal's hair and gave him a tired smile. "Ooh, we're off course, right. I forgot. And what course was that?"

Nal picked up more shifts at the grocery store. He ran eggs and pork tenderloins down the register, the scanner catching his knuckles in a web of red light. Time felt heavy inside Penny's. Beep! he whimpered along with the machine, swiping a tin of tomatoes. Beep! Sometimes he could still feel the progress of his lost future inside him, the summer at Lake Marion piping like a vacant bubble through his blood.

"Mom, can I still go away to college, though?" he asked her one Sunday, when they were sitting in the aquarium light of the TV. He'd felt the bubble swell to an unbearable pressure in his lungs.

"Sure," she said, not looking over from the TV. Her eyes were like Samson's, bright splashes of blue in an oak-stained face. "You can do whatever you want."

When the bubble in him would burst, Nal would try to start a fight. He shouted that what she called his "choices" about college and LMAS and Penny's Grocery were her consequences, a domino run of misfortune. He told her that he wouldn't be able to go to college if she didn't find another job, that it was lying to pretend like he could.

"I heard you guys going at it," Samson said later in the kitchen, clapping mayonnaise onto two slices of bread. "Give mom a break, kid. I think she's sick."

But Nal didn't think that his mom had contracted any particular illness—he was terrified that she was more generally dying, or disintegrating, letting her white roots grow out and fusing her spine to their couch. She was still sitting in the champagne shadows of the blinds when he got off his shift at six-thirty.

Nal wrote a poem about how his mother had become the sea hum inside the conch shell of their living room. He thought it must be the best poem he'd ever written because he tried to recite it to his bathroom reflection and his throat shut, and his eyes stung so badly he could barely see his own face. She was sitting out there now, watching TV reruns and muttering under her breath. Samson was out drinking that night with Vanessa. Nal gave his mother the poem to read and it was still sitting under a dirty mug, accumulating rings, when he came back to check on her that Friday.

Nal got a second job house-sitting for his high school science teacher, Mr. McGowen, who was going to Lake Marion to teach an advanced chemistry course. Now Nal spent his nights in the shell of Mr. McGowen's house. Each week Mr. McGowen sent him a check for fifty-six dollars, and his mom lived on this income plus the occasional contribution from Samson, wads of cash that Sam had almost certainly borrowed from someone else. "It helps," she said, "it's such a help," and whenever she said this Nal felt his guts twist. Mr. McGowen's two-room rental house was making slow progress down the cliffs; another hurricane would finish it. The move there hadn't mattered in any of the ways that Nal had hoped it would. Samson had buffaloed him into giving him a spare key, and now Nal would wake up to find his brother standing in the umbilical hallway between the two rooms at odd hours:

SUNDAY: "How you living, Nal? Living easy? Easy living? You get paid yet this week? I need you to do me a solid, brotherman . . ." He was already peeling the bills out of Nal's wallet.

MONDAY: "Cable's out. I want to watch the game tonight, so I'll probably just crash here . . ."

TUESDAY: "You're out of toilet paper again. I fucking swear, I'm going to get a rash from coming over here! Some deadly fucking disease . . ."

WEDNESDAY: "Shit, kid, you need to get to the store. Your fridge is just desolate. What have you been eating?"

For three days, Nal hadn't ingested anything besides black coffee and a pint of freezer-burned ice cream. Weight was tumbling from his body. Nal was living on liquid hatred now.

"Hey, Nal," said Samson, barging through the door. "Listen, Vanessa and I were sort of hoping we could spend the night here? She lied and told Mrs. Griga-looney that she's crashing at a friend's spot. Cool? Although you should really pick up before she gets here, this place is gross."

"Cool," Nal said, his blue hair igniting in the flashing light of the TV. "I just did laundry. Fresh sheets for you guys." Nal left Samson to root around the empty fridge and fished clean sheets out of Mr. McGowen's dryer. He made the twin bed with hospital corners, pushed his sneakers and sweaty V-necks under the frame, filled two glasses at the sink faucet and set them on the nightstand. He lit Mr. McGowen's orange emergency candles to provide a romantic accent. Nal knew this was not the most excellent strategy to woo Vanessa—making the bed so that she could sleep with his brother—but he was getting a sick pleasure from this seduction by proxy. The bedroom was freezing, Nal realized, and he reached over to shut the window—then screamed and leapt a full foot back.

A giant seagull was strutting along Nal's sill, a bouquet of eelgrass dangling from its beak. Its crown feathers waggled at Nal like tiny fingers. He felt a drip of fear. "What are you doing here?" He had to flick at the webbing of its slate feet before it moved and he could shut the window. The gull cocked its head and bored into Nal with its bright eyes; it was still looking at him as he backed out of the room.

"Hey," Vanessa greeted him shyly in the kitchen. "So this is McGowen's place." She was wearing thin silver bracelets up her arm and had blown out her hair. She had circled her eyes in lime and magenta powder; to Nal it looked as if she'd allowed a bag of candy to melt on her face. He thought she looked much prettier in school.

"Do you guys want chips or anything?" he asked stupidly, looking from Samson to Vanessa. "Soda? I have chips."

Vanessa kept her eyes on the nubby carpet. "Soda sounds good."

"He's just leaving." Samson said. He squeezed Nal's shoulder as he spun him toward the door. "Thank you," he said, leaning in so close that Nal could smell the spearmint-and-vodka mix on his breath, "Thank you *so much*"—which somehow made everything worse.

❧

"Nal drives the lane! Nal brings the ball up court with seconds to play!" Nal whispered, dribbling his ball well past midnight. He dribbled up and down the main street that led to Strong Beach, and kept spooking himself with his own image in the dark storefront windows. "Nal has the ball . . ." he continued down to the public courts. "Jesus! Not you again!" A giant seagull had perched on the backboard and was staring opaquely forward. "Get out of here!" Nal yelled. He threw the ball until the backboard juddered, threw it again and again, but the bird remained. Maybe it's sick, Nal thought. Maybe it has some kind of neurological damage. He tucked the ball under his arm and walked farther down Strong Beach. The seagull flew over his head and disappeared into a dark thicket of pines, the beginnings of the National Reserve forest that lined Strong Beach. Nal was surprised to find himself jogging after it, following the bird into those shadows.

"Gull?" he called after it, his sneakers sinking into the dark leaves.

He found it settled on a low pine branch. The giant seagull had a sheriff's build—distended barrel chest, spindly legs splayed into star-shaped webbed feet. Nal had a sudden presentiment: "Are you my conscience?" he asked, reaching out to stroke the vane of one feather. The gull blatted at Nal and began digging around the under-side of one wing with its beak like a tiny man sniffing his armpits. OK, not my conscience, then, Nal decided. But maybe some kind of omen? Something was dangling from its lower beak—another cigarette, Nal thought at first, then realized it was a square of glossy paper. As he watched, the gull lifted off the branch and soared directly into one of the trees. In the moonlight, Nal saw a hollow there about the size of his basketball: gulls kept disappearing into this hole. Dozens of them were flying around the moon-bright leaves—they moved with the organized frenzy of bees or bats. How deep was the hollow, Nal wondered? Was this normal nocturnal activity for this kind of gull? The birds flew in absolute silence. Their wingtips sailed as softly as paintbrushes across the night sky; every so often single birds descended from this cloud. Each gull flapped into the hollow and didn't reemerge for whole minutes.

Nal chucked his basketball at the hollow to see if it would disappear like in that terrible TV movie that he secretly loved, *Magellan Maps the Black Hole*, winking into another dimension. The basketball bounced back and caught Nal hard against his jaw. He winced and shot a look up and down Strong Beach to make sure that nobody had seen. The hollow was almost a foot above Nal's head, and when he pushed up to look inside it he saw nothing: just the pulpy reddish guts of the tree. No seagulls, and no passage through that he could divine. There was a nest in the tree hollow, though, a dark wet cup of vegetation. The bottom of the nest was lined with paper scraps—a few were tickets, Nal saw, not stubs or fragments but whole squares, some legible: Mary Gloster's train tickets to Florence, a hologram stamp for a Thai Lotus Blossom day cruise, a roll of carnival-red ADMIT ONEs. Nal rifled through the top layer. Mary Gloster's tickets, he noticed, were dated two years in the future. He saw a square edge with the letters WIL beneath a wreath of blackened moss and tugged at it. My ticket, Nal thought wonderingly. WILSON. How did you get that? It was his pass for the rising sophomore class's summer trip to Whitsunday Island, a glowing ember of volcanic rock that was just visible from the Athertown marina. He was shocked to find it here; his mother hadn't been able to pay the fee back in April, and Nal's name had been removed from the list of participants. The trip was tomorrow.

Nal was at the marina by 8 a.m. He was sitting on a barrel when his teacher arrived, and he watched as she tore open a sealed envelope and distributed the tickets one by one to each of his classmates. He waited until all the other students had disappeared onto the ferry to approach her.

"Nal Wilson? Oh dear. I wasn't aware that you were coming . . ." She gave him a tight smile and shook out the empty manila envelope, as if trying to convince him that his presence here was a slightly embarrassing mistake.

"'S OK, I have my ticket here." Nal waved the orange ticket, which was shot through with tiny perforations from where the gull's beak had stabbed it. He lined up on the waffled copper of the ferry ramp. The boat captain stamped his ticket REDEEMED, and Nal felt that he had won a small but significant battle. On the hydrofoil, Nal sat next to Vanessa. "That's my seat," grumbled a stout Fijian man in a bolo tie behind him, but Nal shrugged and gestured around the hold. "Looks like there are plenty of seats to go around, sir," he said, and was surprised when the big man floated on like some bad weather he'd dispelled with native magic. He could feel Vanessa radiating warmth beside him and was afraid to turn.

"Hey, you," Vanessa said. "Thanks for letting me crash in your bed last night."

"Don't mention it. Always fun to be the maid service for my brother."

Vanessa regarded him quietly for a moment. "I like your hair."

"Oh," Nal said miserably, rolling his eyes upward. "This blue isn't really me—" and then he felt immediately stupid, because just who did he think he was, anyway? Cousin Steve refused to shave it off, saying that to do so would be a "violation of the Hippocratic Oath of Beauty Professionals." "Unfortunately you have an extremely lumpy head," Cousin Steve had informed him, stern as a physician. "You need that blue to hide the contours. It's like you've got golf balls buried up there." But Vanessa, he saw with a rush of gratitude, was nodding at him.

"I know it's not you," she said. "But it's a good disguise."

Nal nodded, wondering what she might be referring to. He was thrilled by the idea that Vanessa saw past this camouflage to something hidden in him, so secret that even he didn't know what she was seeing there.

On the long ride to Whitsunday, they talked about their families. Vanessa was the youngest of five girls, and, from what she was telling Nal, it sounded as if her adolescence had been both accelerated and prolonged. She was still playing with dolls when she watched her eldest sister, Rue Ann, guide her boyfriend to their bedroom. "We have to leave the lights on, or Vanessa will be scared. It's fine, she's still tiny. She doesn't understand." The boyfriend grinning into her playpen, twaddling his fingers. Vanessa watched with eyes round as moon pies as her sister disrobed, draping her black T-shirt over the lampshade to dim it. But she had also been babied by her four sisters, and her questions about their activities got smothered beneath a blanket of care. Her parents began treating her like the baby of the family again once the other girls were gone. Her father was a Qantas mechanic and her mother worked a series of housekeeping jobs even though she didn't strictly need to, greeting Vanessa with a nervous "Hello!" at the end of each day.

"Which is funny, because our own house is always a mess now . . ."

Nal watched the way her mouth twitched; his heart and his stomach were staging some weird circus inside him.

"Yeah, that's pretty funny." Nal frowned. "Except that, I mean, it sounds really awful too . . ."

He tried to get one arm around Vanessa's left shoulder but felt too cowardly to lower it all the way; he stared in horror at where his arm had stopped, about an inch above Vanessa's skin, like a malfunctioning bar in a theme park ride. When he lifted his arm again he noticed a gauzy stripe peeking out of Vanessa's shirt.

"I'm sorry," Nal interrupted, "Vanessa? Uh, your shirt is falling down . . ."

"Yeah," she tugged at it, unconcerned. "This was Brianne's, and she was never what you'd call petite. She's an air hostess now and my dad always jokes that he doesn't know how she maneuvers the aisles." Vanessa hooked a clear nail under her neckline. "My dad can be pretty mean. He's mad at her for leaving."

Nal couldn't take his eyes off the white binding. "Is that . . . is that a bandage?"

"Yes," she said simply. "It's my disguise."

Vanessa said she still held onto some childlike habits because they seemed to calm her parents. "I had to pretend I believed in Santa

Claus until I was twelve," she said. "Did Sam tell you that I was accepted to LMAS, too?"

"Oh, wow. Congratulations. When do you leave?"

"I'm not going. I mentioned that the dorms at Lake Marion were coed and my father didn't speak to me for days." Why her development of breasts should terrify her parents Vanessa didn't understand, but she began wearing bulky, loose shirts and wrapping Ace bandages over her bras all the same. "I got the idea from English class," she said. "Shakespeare's Rosalind." Her voice changed when she talked about this—she let out a hot, embarrassed laugh and then dove into a whisper, as if she'd been trying to make a joke and suddenly switched gears.

"Isn't that a little weird?"

Vanessa shrugged. "Less friction with my parents. The tape doesn't work as good as it did last year but it's sort of become this habit?"

Nal couldn't figure out where he was supposed to look; he was having a hard time staying focused in the midst of all this overt discussion of Vanessa's breasts.

"So you're stuck there now?"

"I don't see how I could leave my folks. I'm their last."

Vanessa wanted out but said she felt as though the exits had vanished with her sisters. They'd each schemed or blundered their way out of Athertown—early pregnancy, nursing school, marriage, the Service Corps. Now Vanessa rumbled around the house like its last working part. Nal got an image of Mr. and Mrs. Grigalunas sitting in their kitchen with their backs to the whirlwind void opened by their daughters' absence: reading the paper; sipping orange juice; collecting these old clothes like the shed skins of their former daughters and dressing Vanessa in them. He thought about her gloopy makeup and the urgency with which she'd kissed his brother, her thin legs knifing over the dune. Maybe she doesn't actually like my brother at all, Nal thought, encouraged by a new theory. Maybe she treats sex like oxidizing air. Aging rapidly wherever she can manage it, like a cut apple left on a counter.

"That's why it's easy to be with your brother," she said. "It's a relief to . . . to get out of there, to be with someone older. But it's not like we're serious, you know?" She brightened as she said this last part, as if it were a wonderful idea that had just occurred to her.

What do I say now? Nal wondered. Should I ask her to explain what she means? Should I tell her Samson doesn't love her, but I do? The homunculus typed up frantic speeches, discarded them, tore at his green sweater in anguish, gnashed the typewriter ribbon between his buckteeth. Nal could hear himself babbling—they talked about the insufferable stupidity of this year's ninth-graders, his harem of geezers at Penny's, Dr. J's jump hook, Cousin Steve's bewildering mullet. More than once, Nal watched her tug her sister's tentlike shirt up. They spent the rest of the afternoon exploring Whitsunday Island together, cracking jokes as they filed past the flowery enclosure full of crocodiles; the dry pool of Komodo dragons with their wispy beards; and finally, just before the park's exit, the koala who looked like a raddled veteran of war, gumming leaves at twilight. They talked about how maybe it wasn't such a terrible thing that they'd both missed out on Lake Marion, and on the way back up the waffled ramp to the hydrofoil Vanessa let her hand slide inside Nal's sweating palm.

That night Nal had a nightmare about the seagulls. Millions of them flew out of a blood red sunset and began to resettle the town, snapping telephone wires and sinking small boats beneath all their weight. Gulls covered the fence posts and rooftops of Athertown, drew a white caul over the marina, muffled every window with the static of their bodies—and each gull had a burgled object twinkling in its split beak. Warping people's futures into some new and terrible shape, just by stealing these smallest linchpins from their presents.

The next day, Nal went to the Athertown library to research omen birds. He was the only patron in the reading room. Beneath the painting of the full orange moon and the plastic bamboo, he read a book called *Avian Auspices* by Dr. Carlos Ramirez. Things looked pretty grim:

CROW: AN OMEN OF DEATH, DISEASE
RAVEN: AN OMEN OF DEATH, DISEASE
ALBATROSS: AN OMEN OF DEATH AT SEA

Screech owls, Old World vultures, even the innocuous sounding cuckoo, all harbingers of doom. Terrific, Nal thought, and if an enormous seagull followed you around and appeared to be making a blithe feast of your life, pecking at squares of paper and erasing whole futures, what did that mean? Coleridge and Audubon were no help here, either. Seagulls were scavengers, kleptoparasites. And, according to the books he found, they didn't portend a thing.

Nal began going to the nest every day. He woke at dawn and walked barefoot on the chilly sand down to the hollow. By the second week he'd collected an impressive array of objects: a tuxedo button, a scrap of paper with a phone number (out of service—Nal tried it), a penny with a mint date one year in the future. On Friday, he found what appeared to be the disgorged, shimmering innards of a hundred cassette tapes, disguised at first against the slick weeds. The seagulls had many victims, then—they weren't just stealing from Nal. He wondered if the gulls had different caches, in caves or distant forests. Whenever he swept his hand over the damp nest he found new stuff:

An eviction notice, neatly halved by the gull's beak.

Half a dozen keys of various sizes—car keys, big skeleton keys and tiny ones for safes and mailboxes, a John Deere tractor key, one jangling janitor's ring.

A cheap fountain pen.

A stamp from a country Nal didn't recognize.

An empty vial of pills, the label soaking and illegible.

Most disturbingly, on the soggy bottom of the nest, beneath a web of green eider, he found the disconnected wires of a child's gleaming retainer.

Nal lined these objects up and pushed them around on the sand. He felt like the paleontologist of some poor sod's stolen fate—somewhere a man or a woman's life continued without these tiny vertebrae, curving like a spine knocked out of alignment. Suddenly the ordinary shine of the plastic and aluminum bits began to really frighten him. He drew the tiny fangs of the tractor key through the sand and tried to imagine the objects' owners: A shy child without his retainer, with a smile that would now go unchaperoned. A redhead with pale eyelashes succumbing to fever. A farmer on his belly in a field of corn, hunting for this key. What new direction would their lives take? In Nal's imagination, dark stalks swayed and knit together, obliterating the stranger from view. Somewhere the huge tractor wheels began to groan and squeal backward, trampling his extant rows of corn. A new crop was pushing into the spaces that the tractor had abandoned—husks hissing out of the earth, bristling and green, like the future sprouting new fur.

We have to alert the authorities, he decided. He zipped the future into his backpack and walked down to the police station.

"What do you want me to do with this sack of crap, son?" Sheila, the Athertown policewoman, wanted to know. "The pawn shop moved; it's down by the esplanade now. Why don't you take this stuff over there, see if Mr. Tarak will give you some quarters for it. Play you some video games."

"But it belongs to somebody." Nal hadn't found the courage to tell her his theory that the new seagulls were cosmic scavengers. He tried to imagine saying this out loud: "The seagulls are stealing scraps of our lives to feather this weird nest I found in a tree hollow on Strong Beach. These birds are messing with our futures." Sheila, who had a red lioness's mane of curls bursting from an alligator clip and bigger triceps than Nal's, did not look as if she suffered fools gladly. She was the kind of woman who would put DDT in the nest and call it a day.

"So leave it here then," she shrugged. "When somebody comes to report the theft of their number two pencil, I'll let you know."

On Saturday he found a wedding invitation for Bruce and Nancy, in an envelope the color of lilac icing. There was no return address. On Tuesday he checked the nest and found the wrinkled passport of one Dodi Watts. Did that mean he was dead, or never was? Nal shuddered. Or just that he'd missed his flight?

His guesswork was beginning to feel stupid. Pens and keys and train tickets, so what? Now what? Sheila was right. How was he supposed to make anything out of this sack of crap?

The giant seagull, who Nal now thought of as his not-conscience, appeared to be the colony's dominant gull. Today it was screaming in wide circles over the sea. Nal sat on a canted rock and watched something tiny fall from its beak into the waves, glinting all the way down. Beneath him the waves had turned a foam-blistered violet, and the sky growled. The whole bowl of the bay seethed around the rocks like a cauldron. Nal shuddered; when he squinted he could see something fine as salt shaking into the sea. Rain, he thought, watching the seagull ride the thermals, maybe it's only raining . . .

Later, when the sky above Strong Beach was riddled with stars, Nal got up on shaky legs and entered the woods. The gulls had vanished, and it was hard for him to find the tree with the hollow. He stumbled around with his flashlight for what felt like hours looking for it, growing increasingly frantic until he felt near-hysterical, his heart drumming. Even after he'd found what he thought was the right tree Nal couldn't be sure, because the nest inside was damp and empty. He sunk his hands into the old leaves and at first felt nothing, but digging down he began to find an older strata of plunder: a leather bookmark, a baby's rusting spoon. The gulls must have stolen this stuff a while ago, Nal thought, from a future that was now peeling away in ribbons, a future that had already been perverted or lost, a past. At the very bottom of the nest he saw a wink of light. Nal pinched at the wink, pulled it out.

"Oh God," he groaned. When he saw what he was holding he almost dropped it. "Is this some kind of joke?"

It was nothing, really. It was just a dull knuckle of metal. A screw. Nal closed his fist around the screw, opened it. Here was something indigestible. It was a stop screw—he knew this from the diagram that had run with the local paper's story "Allegations of Nursing Home Negligence," next to a photograph of the two-inch chasm in the Paradise window made lurid by the journalist's ink. They'd also run a bad photo of his mother. Her face had been washed out by the fluorescent light. She was old, Nal realized. It looked like the "scandal" had aged her. Nal had stared at his mother's gray face and seen a certain future, something you didn't need a bird to auger.

He wouldn't even show her, he decided. What was the point of coming back here? The screw couldn't shut that window now.

Nal was shooting hoops on the public court half a mile from Mr. McGowen's house when Samson found him. A fine dust from the nearby construction site kept blowing over in clouds whenever the wind picked up. Nal had to kick a crust of gravel off the asphalt so that he could dribble the ball.

"Hey, buddy, I've been looking everywhere for you. Mom says you two had a fight?"

Nal shoots, whispered the homunculus. He turned away from Samson and planted his feet on the asphalt. Shooter's roll—the ball teetered on the edge and at the last moment fell into the basket. "It was nothing; it was about college again. What do you need?"

"Just a tiny loan so I can buy Vanessa a ring. Mr. Tarak's going to let me do it in installments."

"Mr. Tarak said that?" Nal had always thought of Mr. Tarak as a CASH ONLY!!! sort of merchant. He had a spleeny hatred of everyone under thirty-five and liked telling Nal his new haircut made him look like the Antichrist.

Samson laughed. "Yeah, well, he knows I'm good for it." He was used to the fact that people went out of their way for him. It made strangers happy to see Samson happy and so they'd give him things, let him run up a tab with them, just to buoy that feeling.

"What kind of ring? A wedding ring?"

"Nah, it's just . . . I dunno. She'll like it. Tiny flowers on the inside part, what do you call that . . ."

"The band." Nal's eyes were on the red square on the backboard; he squatted into his thin calves. "Are you in love?"

Samson snorted. "We're having fun, Nal. We're having a good time." He shrugged. "It's her birthday, help me out."

"Sorry," Nal said, shooting again. "I got nothing."

"You've got nothing, huh?" Samson leaned in and made a playful grab for the ball, and Nal slugged him in the stomach.

"Jesus! What's wrong with you?"

Nal stared at his fist in amazement. He'd had no idea that swing was in the works. Wind pushed the ball downcourt and he flexed his empty hands. When his brother took a step toward him he swung wide and slammed his fist into the left shoulder—pain sprang into his knuckles and Nal had time to cock his fist back again. He thought, *I am going to really mess you up here*, right before Samson shoved him down onto the gravel. He stared down at Nal with an open mouth, his bare chest contracting. No visible signs of injury there, he saw with something close to disappointment. The basket craned above them. Blood and pebbled pits colored Nal's palms and raked up the sides of his legs. He could feel, strangest of all, a grin spreading on his face.

"Did I hurt you?" Nal asked. He was still sitting on the blacktop. He noticed that Samson was wearing his socks.

"What's your problem?" Samson said. He wasn't looking at Nal. One hand shielded his eyes, the sun pleating his forehead, and he looked like a sailor scouting for land beyond the blue gravel. "You don't want to help me out, just say so. Fucking learn to behave like a normal person."

"I can't help you," Nal called after him.

Later that afternoon, when Strong Beach was turning a hundred sorbet colors in the sun, Nal walked down the esplanade to Mr. Tarak's pawnshop. He saw the ring right away—it was in the front display, nested in a cheap navy box between old radios and men's watches, a quarter-full bottle of Chanel.

"Repent," said Mr. Tarak without looking up from his newspaper. "Get a man's haircut."

"I'd like to buy this ring here," Nal tapped on the glass.

"On hold."

"I can make the payment right now, sir. In full."

Mr. Tarak shoved up off his stool and took it out. It didn't look like a wedding band; it was a simple, wrought iron thing with a floral design etched on the inside. Nal found he didn't care about the first woman who had pawned or lost it, or Samson who wanted to buy it. Nal was the owner now. He paid and pocketed the ring.

Before he went to catch the 3:03 bus to Vanessa's house, Nal walked back to the pinewoods. If he was really going through with this, he didn't want to take any chances that these birds would sabotage his plan. He took his basketball and fitted it in the hollow. The gulls were back, circumnavigating the pine at different velocities, screeching irritably. He watched with some satisfaction as one scraped its wing back against the ball. He patted the ring in his pocket. He knew this was just a temporary fix. There was no protecting against the voracity of the gulls. If fate was just a disintegrating blanket—some fraying skein that the gulls were tearing right this second—then Nal didn't see why he couldn't also find a loose thread, and pull.

‧‧‧

Vanessa's house was part of a new community on the outskirts of Athertown. The bus drove past the long neck of a crane rising out of an exposed gravel pit, the slate glistening with recent rain. A summer shower had rolled in from the east and tripped some of the streetlights prematurely. The gulls had not made it this far inland yet; the only birds here were sparrows and a few doll-like cockatoos along the fences.

Vanessa seemed surprised and happy to see him. "Come in," she said, her thin face filling the doorway. She looked scrubbed and plain, not the way she did with Samson. "Nobody's home but me. Is Sam with you?"

"No," said Nal. For years he'd been planning to say to her, "I think we're meant to be," but now that he was here he didn't say anything; his heart was going, and he almost had to stop himself from shoving his way inside.

"I brought you this," he said, pushing the ring at her. "I've been saving up for it."

"Nal!" she said, turning the ring over in her hands. "But this is really beautiful . . ."

It was easy. What had he worried about? He just stepped in and kissed her, touched her neck. Suddenly he was feeling every temperature at once, the coolness of her skin and the wet warmth of her mouth and even the tepid slide of sweat over his knuckles. She kissed him back, and Nal slid his hand beneath the neckline of her blouse and touched the bandage there. The Grigalunases' house was dark and still inside, the walls lined with framed pictures of dark-haired girls who looked like funhouse images of Vanessa, her sisters or her former selves. An orange cat darted under the stairwell.

"Nal? Do you want to sit down?" She addressed this to her own face in the foyer mirror, a glass crescent above the door, and when she turned back to Nal her eyes had brightened, charged with some anticipation that almost didn't seem to include him. Nal kissed her again and started steering her toward the living room. A rope was pulling him forward, a buried cable, and he was only able to relax into it now because he had spent his short lifetime doing up all the knots. Perhaps this is how the future works, Nal thought—nothing fated or inevitable but just these knots like fists that you could tighten or undo.

Nal and Vanessa sat down on the green sofa, a little stiffly. Nal had never so much as grazed a girl's knee but somehow he was kissing her neck, he was sliding a hand up her leg, beneath the elastic band of her underwear . . .

Vanessa struggled to undo Nal's belt and the tab of his jeans and now she looked up at him; his zipper was stuck. He was trapped inside his pants. Thanks to his recent weight loss, he was able to wriggle out of them, tugging furiously at the denim. At last he got them off with a grunt of satisfaction and, breathless and red-faced, flung them to the floor. The zipper liner left a nasty scratch down his skin. Nal began to unroll his socks, hunching over and angling his hipbones. It was strange to see the splay of his dark toes on the Grigalunases' carpet, Vanessa half-naked beyond it.

She could have whinnied with laughter at him; instead, with a kindness that you can't teach people, she had walked over to the windows while Nal hopped and writhed. She had taken off her shirt and unwound the bandage and was shimmying out of her bra. The glass had gone dark with thunderheads. The smell of rain had crept into the house. She drew the curtains and slid out of the rest of her clothes. The living room was a blue cave now—Nal could see the soft curve of the sofa's back in the dark. Was he supposed to turn the light on? Which way was more romantic? "Sorry," he said as they both walked back to the sofa, their eyes flicking all over one another. Vanessa slid a hand over Nal's torso.

"You and Samson have the same boxer shorts," she said.

"Our mother buys them for us."

Maybe this isn't going to happen, Nal thought.

But then he saw a glint of silver and felt recommitted. Vanessa had slipped the pawnshop ring on—it was huge on her. She caught him looking and held her hand up, letting the ring slide over her knuckle, and they both let out jumpy laughs. Nal could feel sweat collecting on the back of his neck. They tried kissing again for awhile. Vanessa's dark hair slid through his hands like palmfuls of oil as he fumbled his way inside her, started to move. He wanted to ask: Is this right? Is this OK? It wasn't at all what he'd imagined. Nal, moving on top of Vanessa, was still Nal, still cloaked with consciousness and inescapably himself. He didn't feel invincible—he felt clumsy, guilty. Vanessa was trying to help him find his rhythm, her hands just above his bony hips.

"Hey," Vanessa said at one point, turning her face to the side. "The cat's watching."

The orange tabby was licking its paws on the first stair, beneath the clock. The cat had somehow gotten hold of the stop screw—it must have fallen out of Nal's pocket—and was batting it around.

The feeling of arrival Nal was after kept receding like a charcoal line on bright water. This was not the time or the place but he kept picturing the gulls, screaming and wheeling in a vortex just beyond him, and he groaned and sped up his motions. "Don't stop," Vanessa said, and there was such a catch to her voice that Nal said, "I won't, I won't," with real seriousness, like a parent reassuring a child. Although very soon, Nal could feel, he would have to.

JULIA SLAVIN

Drive-Through House

A pair of twin boys in a Porsche Boxster drove into the house, skidding to a stop in the middle of living room, where I picked up Pabst cans and McDonald's bags off Mother's hand-knotted rug.

"We heard there might be a viewing . . ." the driving twin said.

"Of the body," the passenger twin completed.

"No viewing." I beat the dust from Mother's sampler pillows, their ethereal particles falling like dandruff on the road.

"Do we still gotta pay?" the driving twin asked.

"It's a donation," I said. "We never ask folks to pay." The boys sped off through the gift shop without leaving a cent. A few minutes later I was surprised to see the Ladies of Tuesday Antique Auto Club rolling through the kitchen. Miss Cutler's '52 DeSoto still smelled like Holsteins on a clover diet at dusk. I walked alongside the car as she inched through the front hall and parlor. She used the old hand crank to roll down the window.

"You were good to come," I said. "And on a Wednesday, no less."

"You won't sell to Walt Sleigh, will you?" Miss Cutler asked.

"I'll go under the steamrollers before that," I said. Miss Jones took my hand as her Hudson Wasp rolled through Mother's bedroom. Pink spread, pink dust ruffle, pink pillows and rug.

"Yogis say pink is the color of compassion," Miss Jones said.

"She was a cranky old bag," Miss Lowry said out the window of her '59 Cadillac, tail fins like two sharks stalking a stingray. "Never satisfied. And did she ever hate this house. Would have signed those papers weren't it to piss off the Sleigh men. But we will miss her."

"You will come back?" I asked Miss Bradley. Her Lincoln Mark II made the kitchen look like a billionaire's showroom. "Even with Mother gone?"

"Unless the Lord stops making Tuesdays." She then pressed a burgundy leather-clad Bible into my hands. "Read this, Shell. It helps." The ladies drove out through the laundry room. I waved good-bye, mourning the passing of each car, until they were swallowed up by the thick, wet heat mirage hanging over the road ahead. Sprigs of crabgrass came through cracks in the back lot, the lines delineating spaces now faded. I looked at the house, which seemed to lean west, wanting no part of the thuggish sun that beat it down day after day. Hoping for relief, I turned to the north, only to face more sand-swept road. But then through a wavy aura I saw the shape of a walking man. At first I thought it must be Sheriff Walt Sleigh, coming with the papers his grandfather had failed to get my grandmother to sign so many decades ago. But Walt would come in the county-issued Nova, never on foot. Soon the heat stopped pulsing and I recognized the gait from more than fifty years before.

As soon as my brother, Sinclair, was old enough to avoid the war, he had pulled himself out of his sickbed and joined the merchant marine. Every few months we got a photo of him in good health, with writing on the back that read, *Here I am by the cargo hold, and look, Ma. No car sickness!* And another, *Here's me and my buddies, port o' call Tokyo, and how 'bout that? A belly full of ship fumes and not one case of the cars!* Mother scoffed at each one, saying Sinclair had become better-than-thou, that travel was supposed to broaden but in his case it seemed to have narrowed. As he stood before me now, I tried to find a point of reference in his face, anything I knew.

"You got old on me, Shell," my brother said.

"How long can you stay?" I asked, wanting him to leave.

"I'd like to see Mother," he said.

"She's at Stokley's getting taped up." I took a broom from the back porch and swept sand. "It wasn't a clean job, I should tell you."

"Never is when you get run down. And in our own home." He looked the house over disapprovingly, taking hold of a post on the porch to help him walk straight. "Smells like fumes. I'm carsick already. Where is everybody?"

"Things have changed since you left, what with the highways. We still get the Ladies Club on Tuesdays. The shit-faced shift starts at eleven. It's picked up a smidge since Mother . . . folks wanting a viewing. As though they deserve it for patronage."

"Maybe they do." He limped down the center of the road, careful not to cross the yellow line, to the parlor, dropping his duffel by the card table.

"I can warm some leek soup," I offered.

"God no," he said. "I'll take a sucker if you got one." He dropped himself in a folding chair, crossing his arms over his middle and hanging his head with a case of the cars.

I walked down the road to the pantry. A lady in a Grand Prix once suggested that Sinclair suck on hard candy when he was sick from fumes. Calcium, magnesium, potassium, a tincture of brewer's yeast, and fresh-grated nutmeg, nothing worked. I searched the larder but the only suckers I could find were horehound in the old tin box we'd been given for Christmas decades before. Sinclair moved the candy around in his mouth, the stick wagging out of his lips like a mouse tail. "Tastes like something I don't want to remember." He coughed, then looked around at the rotting floorboards in the parlor and the smudged paint on the walls.

"We may have seen the best of this house." He'd been home a matter of minutes and already I wanted to break his teeth.

"The past thirty-plus years I've done nothing but walk Mother to the can, collect food stamps—"

"Don't get yourself tied in a clove hitch. I'm going over to Stokley's to see Mother. Come if you like."

"I have seen enough of Mother." I clicked the TV on to the *Triage* channel and lit a pipe of Captain Black. Sinclair was shocked. "Not used to seeing a lady smoke?" I asked.

"Not used to seeing a lady anything." He turned his attention to *Triage*. "He won't live with his organs out like that," Sinclair commented on the latest casualty brought into the green zone.

"You would be surprised at what they can fix," I said. A 1971 Chevelle SS drove through in a blanket of smog so thick that black particles covered the furniture.

"Ever heard of the Clean Air Act, buddy?" Sinclair coughed into a handkerchief. The car screeched through, leaving tracks on the road.

"Don't you talk to my customers that way," I snapped at Sinclair.

"That muscle car gets eight miles to the gallon."

"Not my problem."

"And that's my customer too." He stepped into the road, walking like a cardboard puppet, a full-body jerk with every step.

"Wait and hitch a ride," I said. "The lost come in at noon. This heat will bury you."

"The house will kill me first." He headed north. If we'd had a door I'd have told him not to let it hit him on his way out.

❧

"Rise and shine, Miss Valentine." Miss Chatwin leaned out her window and switched off *Triage*. I could hear the high pitch of her engine running too fast. People always seemed so satisfied to find me asleep in a chair in front of the TV. Embarrassing moments kept the Drive-Through alive, like the time Mother got caught hooking on her minimizer. Business picked up a thousand percent when they saw me kiss Sunny-Side Up McCray's image on *Rock 'n' Roll Hoopla*.

"Now, Shell," Miss Chatwin began. "About the viewing. I've been driving through two times a week since you were crawling. Christmas, Thanksgiving . . ."

"Even for you, Miss Chatwin," I said.

"A lot of folks are sorrowing," she said. "Would help seal 'em up if they could see her."

"I cannot soil Mother's memory by allowing folks to gawk at her crushed bones. You're running hot as well as fast, I should tell you. Would you like a Drive-Through hair coloring? I could cover up those roots in a jiff." She screeched out through the pantry in a blue cloud of exhaust. Jeffrey from the grocer drove into the kitchen right after. I handed him the envelope of food stamps. He passed me the bags out his window. The skin on his hand had become so transparent you could see the blood traveling through his veins, white and red cells stumbling over each other, barely able to make the trip. I gave him the very last of the Drive-Through cookies. "Come for a ride with me, Shell," he said. "It'll do you good to get away for an hour." But I had never left the Drive-Through. I had no need. Nothing existed out there but contestants buzzing in and people eating spiders in order to survive. No thank you.

I waited for Sinclair before eating lunch but he had still not returned at two. I gave his tuna fish sandwich to a lady driving through to her grandson's graduation in Keensville who was too afraid to go on the north-south highways. We ate our sandwiches and drank iced tea as she idled in the parlor, talking about the best routes when I-98 was jammed. We watched *Triage* and wept together when they brought in a boy who fought so hard and then didn't make it. I gave her a mini-manicure and she drove on, her puff of exhaust leaving me with a melancholy so black I put on my eye mask and went to bed, waking each time a car came through, the passengers so pleased at catching me lazy. At five, Sinclair had still not returned. Maybe he'd hitched a ride back to the merchant marine. But then at seven, Mr. Michael from the hardware store stopped his GMC half ton in the parlor and set about unloading supplies.

"I didn't order any of that," I said.

"Sinclair was in." He made two even stacks of long boxes. "Says he's doing some fix-ups. Happy to have your brother back?"

"So happy." I picked a poppy seed out of my front teeth.

I woke after midnight, leaning out of bed to look up the road. Sinclair and Mr. Lennox from Stokley's were talking beside a gray Tundra parked in the mudroom. I tried to go back to sleep but all night Sinclair and Mr. Lennox hammered away outside the parlor. When the banging stopped, I drifted off only to have it start right up again. I woke at five to wonderful silence and though it was still dark, I got up to enjoy the peace. But I was not alone. I looked up the road and saw cars backed up to Darnesville, another line coming from the north. No one noticed me as I stepped out into the road in my nightgown, skittering down the curb like a terrier.

"Now you just hold on to your seat, Mr. Camry," I shouted at the car that slammed on its brakes to avoid me. I could see that all the fuss was over a large glowing box outside the kitchen that Sinclair and Mr. Lennox had spent the night building. I smacked the rear of a Volkswagen Bug that ran right over my foot, and then hopped to the Plexiglas box. "Mother!" I cried. And that was all I could say, because no words could adequately express my horror and delight besides a scream like a badger pulled from its set. "Mother." She lay half-curled to one side on a large quilted cushion, her reading glasses in her hand, *Gulliver's Travels* nearby. Sinclair had prepared her as she had been years before I came along, when she was already old with stiff joints, and near blind. Her hair was copper again, not the white I had known, blown back in loose curls, and her peach-colored face was once again smooth. She wore a tweed pencil skirt and green sweater, no shoes. *Maybe this is what my father saw*, I thought, *the day he drove through and gave her a ride, back door to front, honking the horn as he left.* Sinclair stepped up beside me.

"I got a plastic surgeon down from Greensville. Stokley did her nails." He then became shy. "I did her hair. I was okay at haircuts in the merchant marine."

"Okay?" I said. "Virtuoso."

"You never knew her like that, Shell, but that's who she was, what *my* father saw when *he* drove through the house." I could easily have put my knuckles in his eye for a footnote like that but now I put my hands against the Plexiglas and again, from the deepest space inside me, whispered, "Mother." But soon the cars began sounding their horns.

∽❧∽

While Sinclair worked at restoring the drive-in theater, I dug in at the ovens, trying to re-create Mother's Drive-Through-House cookie.

"We are making mon-ey!" Sinclair slammed an overflowing crate on the kitchen table, fives, tens, and twenties spilling onto the floor. I put a cookie in his mouth.

"A little pulpy," he said. I began again, this time with less candied fruit and a higher concentration of sugars.

"Chalky," Sinclair said. Less sugar and a higher concentration of fats.

"Stringy." Sinclair spit into the trash.

"Damn it to all hell and under." I smashed the tray into the sink. Then we looked into the road where two men stood, blocking traffic. Nobody dared blow a horn at Sheriff Walt Sleigh and his cube-shaped deputy, Alan. They looked over Mother in the case. Then Walt had the cube-shaped deputy produce a document.

"We're not selling to you, Walt," Sinclair said. "Build your freeway elsewhere." People in cars cowered, looking for ways to back up out of the house. Walt Sleigh was known to lock folks up for busted taillights. He spit the shell of a sunflower seed onto the pavement.

"I'd like to see your license and permit," Walt said.

"We don't charge people," Sinclair said. "We ask for donations. For the upkeep of this historical dwelling."

"The Glover Historical Society does not have the Drive-Through House of Horrors in its register, my carsick friend," Walt said. "The only place you're likely to find the Drive-Through House listed is in the textbook of the sick and weird." The cube-shaped deputy bent back from the ribs and let out a horselaugh. Walt took out his pad and wrote two citations: "Code violations." One for "maintaining a non-living human in a residentially zoned neighborhood" and another for "displaying a non-living human female without appropriate license."

"A charm, your little theme park here." Walt handed over the tickets to Sinclair.

"Theme, *attraction*," Sinclair corrected.

"My *home*," I stepped in. Sinclair glared at the two of them, hocking carsick bile onto the road.

"That corpse will begin to rot," Walt said. "You bury it. We got laws against stench too. But I been letting that slide for years." Walt and the cube-shaped deputy headed through the house to the town-issued Nova parked in the lot. As they drove off we saw yellow paint on the tires from where they'd driven over Sinclair's newly drawn lines for the drive-in theater.

A bad day. Got caught dressing in the lights of a Mercedes and then a Land Rover broke down in the kitchen. I sensed it was the serpentine belt but Mother had been the mechanic in the family and I had mechanical shortcomings. "Fixing a ship is not like fixing a car!" Damn, Sinclair was defensive when I asked him for anything traditionally male. We had to get a tow to back up through the house, which filled with fumes so thick I had to put Sinclair in a cold bath. I noticed Mother's hair was coming in white and her manicure was growing out. Sand kept piling up on the road and all night the shit-faced shift cars kept getting stuck. Mr. Lennox and I had to push them out since Sinclair was sick and no use to anybody. The cookie recipe wasn't coming along either. "Sandy," Sinclair said. "Dusty," Sinclair said. "Tastes like the inside of a bass fiddle." I prayed that the pencil I threw would gore him in the neck but he was already down the street to finish work on the theater.

"Any good?" I asked Mr. Lennox, who sat on the front stoop with the flask of whiskey that hadn't left his side in a lifetime.

"Killed Mother Theresa," he said. I took a hard swig, then looked up at the sky to see a pelican that had made the catastrophic mistake of flying overhead.

"Oh my," I said. "Such a wrong, wrong turn." The bird would never live in this heat.

"Best not to look." Mr. Lennox stared at his work boots. "Stew these meats too long, you get a pot full of crust." I lit a pipe, offering a puff to Mr. Lennox. A woman drove up in a Civic and handed me a recipe for Drive-Through cookies she swore Mother had given her. I said thank you, I'd been looking all over, knowing full well the recipe had never been written down or spoken.

"People want something bad enough, they'll find a way to believe it," I said. Mr. Lennox toyed with a loose tooth in the front of his mouth and inhaled some pipe smoke.

"Some boxes come in for the gift shop." He took a few gulps of whiskey. "Globes, but mostly playing cards."

"Mother's face is starting to fall," I said.

"Got some new shelving. Stainless, but Sinclair wants wood."

"Only so far formaldehyde will take you," I said. "When God calls it's an order, not an invitation."

"I got no feeling in my feet," Mr. Lennox said. He stood to go back to work. I could hear every bone in his body snap back into place. He headed down the road. Empires have risen and fallen, stars have been born and turned to supernovas, in the time it took him to walk to the gift shop.

❧

That Tuesday we buried Mother. We had no choice. Walt Sleigh was right. Even the living rotted in the heat. A dozen or so cars shined their headlights on our ceremony. Mr. Michael from the hardware store gave the eulogy.

"She . . . ordered a lot of lumber. I'll sure miss her." Then the men from Stokley's lowered her into the sand. The ladies of the Tuesday Club waved handkerchiefs out their windows and beat on their horns in celebration of, I don't know, a life, I suppose.

❧

"Got something you might want to try." I slammed a plate of cookies down on the card table in the parlor, where Mr. Lennox and Sinclair sat playing canasta after the funeral. Sinclair was untrusting, but took a bite anyway.

"Not a cookie man," Mr. Lennox said, turning down my offer. We sat and watched Sinclair chew with his front teeth. After a pause a smile stretched across his pale face.

"I do believe you have done it, Shell. Tastes just like half a century ago."

"Ex-actly," I snarled. "Mother *did* give out the recipe. There was no secret."

"You live in a drive-through house," Sinclair said. "You don't know about secrets."

"I got secrets."

"Mother wrote to me in the merchant marine."

"She didn't read minds."

"Apparently yours was spread wide open." He attempted a private laugh with Mr. Lennox.

"Let's put the cookies in the grave, Shell," Mr. Lennox said. "Your momma is crossed the bar, dead and gone, lost her teeth, metaphorically speaking."

"Old Sunny-Side Up McCray." Sinclair wouldn't drop the issue.

A yellow Skylark with volunteer-fireman plates jerked to a stop beside us. "You think you pick from a higher tree?" the man in the Skylark yelled at Sinclair. "I know what goes on in the merchant marine."

"Move on, pyro." Sinclair swung his arm in the direction of out.

"Draft dodger!"

"You call getting torpedoed nine times draft dodging? Who brought you ammo and food? How'd you get the boots on your feet?" The Skylark man spit on Sinclair's shoes. Sinclair kicked his hubcap.

"Take this, Shell." The fireman tossed me a white Bible. "When you live in a drive-through, the vermin get in." He sped off. Behind the Skylark the Ladies of Tuesday came through. Miss Cutler offered her hand, white as bleached cow bones.

"The most exciting news, Shell," Miss Cutler said. "They opened the new north-south freeway. Hapsburg to Coolfont in six minutes!"

"Twenty for us, but who's counting?" Mrs. Lowry laughed. I moved car to car, grasping each lady's hand.

"You're not built for the freeways. None of you."

"Oh, Shell, you worry yourself blind."

"The statistics," I begged. Then, seeing there was no dissuading them, I let go of Miss Cutler's hand, sitting back on my bed and weeping.

"There now, Shell," Miss Cutler said. "We'll always have Tuesdays."

"Since the day you were born," Miss Jones said. "In an invasion of headlights. Our grillwork smiling down on your birth."

"You're our girl," Miss Lowry said. I walked the ladies down to the gift shop, giving them each a key chain and a few decks of cards. But then I became aware that Miss Jones's Hudson was idling rough. I could hear air sounds from the Lincoln. The DeSoto was running too fast.

"Miss Jones, you need to clean your throttle bore. Miss Bradley, please." I chased them as they zoomed out of the gift shop, across the theater lot. "Your spark plug wires!" I cried. But they disappeared deep into the heat.

❦

While Sinclair was busy with the theater I took the precious time to sit in Mother's rocker, read, and smoke a pipe of Captain Black. Toyota, Toyota, Toyota, Honda. Where had the Americans gone?

"Whatcha reading?" A man stopped his Lexus in the parlor.

"It's a book about a man with an endless memory," I answered.

He looked away, thoughtful.

"I don't remember a thing," he said. "Not one little thing. Whatcha reading?"

"It's a . . ."

"I'm giving you the left-handed yank. Come to the show with me."

"No."

"Why not?"

"I don't."

He drove over to the theater. Cars drifted by, revving their engines in flirtation, and then speeding up toward the theater. All night long I heard men's voices, pistons slamming in their cylinders, glass breaking. Around two, I tiptoed out on the back porch, leaning around a post. From here I was able to view the screen from a twenty-degree angle. What I saw made no sense. Pinkness, moving like an impeller with arms and legs attached. After a pause the scene clarified into the shape of a man, pushing, like he wanted to break down a door, into a woman on her knees. The woman squeezed a mattress, her knuckles turning white, to keep steady for the man's insistence. I backed up and hurried down the road.

"Oh, unfurl yourself," Sinclair said, though I had not said a word when he came back into the house at three. He shopped in the fridge for something to eat, approving of nothing. "You were living on week-old bread when I came back. Some thanks."

"I guess that's what goes on in the merchant marine?" I asked. "Besides moving crates?" He slammed the refrigerator door. "I spent six days in a life raft—"

"I don't want to hear about that life raft anymore."

"People are tired of watching *Triage*, Shell. Folks are sick of head injuries and doctors saying, 'He fought hard.' We are supplying a service, unloading a ship full of goods." Sinclair fell back into a chair, taking short breaths to keep from upchucking.

"I can make you some eggs."

"I'm going to bed. Go clean the back lot."

"It's the middle of the night," I said.

"And we never close," Sinclair said.

Every night from my hiding place on the back porch I watched more of the movie. The scenes always involved forcing and hanging on for dear life. Sinclair and I went about our days without a word sometimes. He worked the gift shop, I manned the ovens, leaning out the kitchen window, passing out bags of Drive-Through-House cookies like I was offering kisses to sailors. But throughout the day I became impatient, checking the height of the sun, breathless at dinnertime. By dark my heart was pounding. After a certain number of scenes, I was able to piece together a plot. Women from the tenth planet had come to Earth to have sex with humans and take home their offspring. It worked out for everybody. The men got sex, the women got the kids. And every night Sinclair came in sicker and more irritable than before, accusing good people of stealing globes from the gift shop, calling Mr. Lennox "slow as stalagmites in a drought." I was ready to bust my seams, the way he left a spoon on top of the peanut butter, cleared his throat all the time, and said, "Whoop-whoop-de-do," when he read the society page in the *Gazette*.

"Quit singing 'Heave Ho, My Lads,'" I hissed as we dumped Hefty bags into a Dumpster.

"You got no sense of country, Shell."

"I live in a drive-through house, Sinclair. I got a pretty good sense of country." I pushed down the bags in the Dumpster to make room for more. "Only thing we do right is air-conditioning."

"Your problem is, you've never been to sea, never unloaded in wartime, never spent six days in a—"

"AHHHHHHHHHHHHHHHHH . . ."

"You can hear me."

"AHHHHHH, no I can't. AHHHHHHHHHH . . ." When I took my fingers out of my ears and opened my eyes, there was a sackful of garbage that Sinclair had picked up and dropped in front of me to dispose of.

It was a white, sunless afternoon, too hot for the kitchen. Sinclair had gone to Glover with Mr. Lennox for supplies and the Drive-Through was gloriously empty. Through the wet-road mirage coming from Darnsville, I saw the black Lexus, license plates blue as a deep crater lake.

"How's that book you were reading?" the man asked.

"What book?" I asked.

"The book about the man with the endless . . . aw, now you're giving *me* the left-handed yank."

I stepped down from the porch. The man moved the front seat back far enough for me to get on his lap, facing the windshield, leaning my head back. But then he pushed me forward, my chest against the steering wheel. "This is the only road I know that goes through a house," the man said. I grasped the wheel to keep from sounding the horn. When we got to the gift shop, I untangled myself and eased out of the car. I gave him a snow globe and two packs of cards. He asked for some cookies. As I walked down the road to the kitchen, I noticed my gait was off, as though my right foot carried a ten-pound weight, and my eyes had trouble focusing. And then a gigantic thump of nausea that came with only one diagnosis: car sickness.

I tried a horehound sucker but it gave me bad memories. A puff of Captain Black made me so dizzy I had to lie on the floor.

"Try this." A woman in an Odyssey gave me a roll of antacid tablets. It worked for a second but then I was retching into the kitchen sink.

"Call the doctor," I told Sinclair as he knocked sand out of his boots on the porch.

"The only cure for motion sickness is to stop moving," he said. "And we ain't."

∼◉∼

In the morning, as I scraped up condoms and Pabst cans from the theater lot, sucking on a grape Jolly Rancher to ease my case of the cars, Sinclair shuffled out the back. I could tell something bad was up.

"Mr. Lennox crossed the bar," he said. Cars sped by us, not even slowing down to examine the house.

"Well," I said, dragging the Hefty toward the Dumpsters, my sandals making sucking sounds on the black tar. "Folks will be wanting a viewing, I suppose."

"That's all you got to say?" Sinclair asked. "Our old friend?"

I dropped the trash bag. "I shoveled six feet of sand out of the gift shop this morning. I got a case of the cars so bad I can't swallow. Mr. Lennox got out of the heat, went inside for a cool drink."

"I'm going to Stokley's." Sinclair headed up the road.

"Hitch a damn ride, Sinclair. You'll fry in the sun." He didn't get far, because Walt and his cube-shaped deputy drove up, circling around us twice. Walt got out of the car and stood facing the movie screen, twisting his back side to side, like an athlete before a triath-lon. His cube-shaped deputy then produced a copy of an ordinance.

"Section 10b-5," Walt said, "which prohibits the public display of pornographic images without redeeming social value. Wouldn't that be a barn burner of a headline in the *Glover Gazette*."

"Come on, Walt," Sinclair said. "It's just folks doing what folks do."

"With the curtains wide open," Walt said. "Consider your blinds pulled." Sinclair lifted his hands in objection, but then let them fall gracefully to defeat. "How 'bout it, Sinclair?" Walt said. "Let's close the house down. Do it for your sister if not for your ramshackle self. They turned the old glove factory into three-bedroom assisted-living units. You could afford ten of those. The streets are full of boutiques. Shell could update her style."

"We're not selling to you, Walt," Sinclair said.

"*Suture* yourself," Walt said. "But pull the plug on the theater, Canker Sore, and board up the gift shop. Unlawful sale of memo-rabilia carries a thousand-dollar fine. Now, I would just love a bag of those Drive-Through-House cookies that made Shell so famous."

I headed down the road to the kitchen. Sinclair limped up behind me.

"Give him the pulpy ones," he whispered. "Let him pull the strings out of his razor teeth."

But I picked out ten fresh cookies, the ones with the hand-squeezed cane juice and not one thread of bagasse.

"What did I miss?" Sinclair came in the living room as I watched a rebroadcast of *Triage*.

"Six wars, a hundred thousand casualties," I said.

"Some of us work during the day and don't get to watch first run," Sinclair said. "I wanted to see that dead kid come back to life and I'd have seen the first run if I hadn't been busy unloading in the damned merchant marine." He put his head in his hands.

"Are you crying, Sinclair?" I asked. "Sinclair?"

"I should never have taken that deferment." He rocked himself on the wicker footstool. "Whether that war was right or wrong. If boys my age were going, I should have gone."

"We're old now," I said. "War's up to the young." He staggered through the room.

"I need to leave this house." He stepped into the road and began heading north.

"You're in your pajamas," I called after him, chasing him up the street. "It's two o'clock in the damn morning, Sinclair." I sped across the back lot in pursuit, begging him to wait. He walked out into the desert. I stood at the edge, calling to him, and just before he walked into the black I summoned the courage. My feet sank to my ankles in the cold sand as I trudged through the darkness. This land used to be a shady street, vital with front porches and kids racing door-to-door for buttered bread before the road cut us in half.

"Sinclair." I found him in the sand on his back, spread like a starfish.

"Put me in the ground in this spot, Shell. No closer to the house. No farther away. Lean down sometimes. Tell me secrets."

"Nobody ever died of car sickness, Sinclair. Put your tongue on the roof of your mouth, halfway back." He stared up at the stars. "Sinclair?" I leaned over him. He wasn't moving. "Are you dead?"

"Maybe a little," he said.

"Damn it to hell," I said. "Now I got to get up again." I helped him to his feet. We headed back to the house. On our bad knees and backs, nothing was simple.

"There are folks," he said, "who feel a need to spread untrue stories about the merchant marine."

"Is that right?" I noticed cars were backed up at the kitchen, wanting their cookies. They'd have to settle for bags from the deep freeze.

"I can tell you there is not one case on record that we refused to unload. No matter what the danger, we'd unload."

"I thought Mr. Lennox would go on forever," I said.

"Me too," Sinclair said. Finally we got to the porch, out of breath and overheated. "After you," Sinclair said.

"You go first," I said back. Even indoors, the road is a lonely place.

⁂

Walt handed a check to Sinclair, who looked at it like it was an artifact from an archaeological dig that he couldn't identify.

"My road will be so wide in parts you can't see from one curb across to the next," Walt said. "Think of the Nile and the life it gave to the Egyptians." The last car to drive through was a white Infiniti.

"The Nile was filled with snakes," I said.

"Snakes that slid up next to the body for warmth at night in the frozen desert." Walt took my hand. I remembered Sunny-Side Up McCray, on *The Mitch Barker Show*, saying that you could tell that a boy liked you if his hand got damp when he held yours. Walt's were dry as cornmeal in the sand.

"You'd have to be mighty careful getting up in the morning," Sinclair said, "without waking those snakes." Down our road I saw the fleet of steamrollers come out of a migraine of heat, the leadman waving his arm like a rodeo cowboy.

"Mother," I said.

"You can't climb down in the grave with her," Walt said.

Sinclair and I got in the back of Walt's Nova. "Take a last look at the miserable remains of your house," Walt said. "Synchronize your watches and over the hills we go." The cube-shaped deputy began to drive.

"Assisted living," Sinclair said.

"I could use some myself," Walt said, "what with my degenerative-disc disease."

"I supposed we could knock down a few walls in the units?" Sinclair asked.

"Your place," Walt said. "Do what you want."

"And we'd have plenty of assistance, wouldn't we." Sinclair made rude gestures behind Walt's back. I turned so I was facing away from Sinclair, out toward the desert. On the horizon I saw a city. As we got farther from the house my car sickness seemed to subside and Sinclair too had more color in his face. After a while, Sinclair began to kick the back of Walt's seat. Just lightly, not enough for Walt to ask him to stop but enough to make you crazy and never know why. Farther along, Sinclair put pieces of torn tickets on Walt's head—again, not enough to notice, just enough to make him uneasy. Walt whipped around to find out what was funny. And still, the scraps of paper clung to his last three strands of hair.

GINA ZUCKER

Big People

One afternoon, a small man came to my apartment. He looked in some ways like a dwarf and in other ways like a midget, though he claimed to be neither. When I opened the door to his knock, I looked straight over his head at first, not seeing him. I noticed him finally when he fluttered his hands in front of his face. He was short all over, except for an outsized head shaped like an egg. He appeared to be wearing a jester's suit underneath his regular clothes, the one-piece kind with a harlequin pattern.

Also he had an issue with his left foot. To say he had a "clubfoot" does not accurately describe the state of it, although that's how he referred to the problem. For all anyone knew the foot itself could have been okay, if it wasn't stuck inside a metal bucket of cement that had apparently hardened around his ankle. I didn't question him about the bucket other than to ask, as I let him into the apartment, if he needed help getting it off. I suggested calling the fire department, but he said, "It's my clubfoot, there's nothing anyone can do." It seemed to me this man had enough on his plate, what with the jester suit and his large head and his small body; from that moment on I decided to ignore the foot problem.

We sat down at my kitchen table and I offered him a cup of coffee—I'd just brewed a fresh pot. He accepted, thanking me. I could see at once that he suffered from depression. He kept his head down when he drank his coffee and kicked his free foot rigidly under his chair. The other foot hung low, pulled by the weight of cement. I asked him some questions about his present circumstances; he answered in vague, meandering sentences from which I gathered he was unemployed, living in a flophouse, and without family. He said he'd quit the circus about six months ago to try theater, and when that didn't work out, television, but wherever he went he was typecast.

"They didn't want *me*," he said, raising his eyes to mine. "They just wanted a dwarf, which I'm not. You know: *Look, a dwarf, everything's all* peculiar *now*." To emphasize his point, he swiveled his eyeballs around and wiggled his fingers, like on an imaginary keyboard. "It is a lazy way for artists to make a statement," he said. When he spoke, his voice seemed to pitch from octave to octave, one word high and squeaky, the next guttural, as if he were going through puberty. He was not; he told me his age: twenty-five, the same as my own. "I had to get away," he said. "I wanted to be . . . I wanted . . ." He trailed off, sighing, and looked down.

I patted one of his hands. Moon slivers of dirt lined the inside of his fingernails.

"It's not what I imagined for myself," he said.

"It sounds like you did what you had to do." I spoke gently.

"I suppose," said the small man. He squeaked a little and swiped at his nose with a fist. "I'm hungry."

I gave him a yogurt; he ate neatly and without hesitation, yet also with an air of shame about him. When he'd finished the container of yogurt I put some cheese and crackers on a plate and set it between us. I picked at a cracker, wanting him to feel we were sharing the food, though in fact he ate everything.

We kept talking, and as we warmed to each other I found the small man a thoughtful, if somewhat slow, conversationalist. He had a sweetness about him that made me feel protective.

I left him briefly to check on the baby. Caroline was still napping vigorously, her pink fists resting on either side of her head. Her chin made an adorable crease that I had to restrain myself from tickling. She wore a one-piece suit, pink. It's true, what they say about having children: you love them so much it can take your breath away.

When I returned to the kitchen my guest was sitting just as I'd left him. We drank another cup of coffee, and he asked about me.

"What you see is what you get," I said.

"I like that," said the small man. "You seem to be a very nice, nonjudgmental person, the kind of girl I would have liked to marry."

Blushing at this bald compliment, I asked quickly, "Have you ever been in love?"

"Oh." The small man took a deep, shuddering breath. "Tara. She had little black pigtails. I liked to watch her do aerial somersaults, she'd flip around so fast she looked like a spinning yo-yo, with braids. We did everything together, we sang, we napped, we ate our sandwiches on the grass. One day, out of nowhere, she said she wouldn't see me anymore. I said, 'Why?' She just cried, and said she couldn't explain. I called her a pantywaisted coward. She went to work for the Flying Trotsky Sisters. I saw her perform for the last time when our troupes crossed paths at the Champlain Valley Carnival. At the end of her routine she took a great leap and floated through the air, high above the straw, and when she landed on the shoulders of Ivanovya Trotsky she flung out her arms as if to invite the love of the whole world. And from the sound of the people screaming and clapping, it seemed the whole world did love her. That's how I remember Tara."

"It's sad," I said. "That you couldn't be together." I didn't want to state the obvious.

The small man grimaced; his teeth, large, square, and white, startled me. "I will love again." He squeaked on the word "love."

"Yes, you will," I said. I looked around. Everything in the kitchen was in order: the spice jars on the spice rack, arranged by use, with those I used most frequently on the right and those I used the least on the left. My new set of copper pots hung from the ceiling. The stove top gleamed from the bleach solution I'd scrubbed into it earlier in the day. My maturation as a homemaker was progressing in fits and starts: sometimes I did the errands and cleaning and cooking and had Caroline to bed by seven, and if Gordon was home early, he'd look with sly pleasure at the laid table and the open bottle of wine. But more often than not I didn't manage to get it all done, especially the cooking—though it didn't matter so much since Gordon rarely made it home in time for dinner anyway. On bad days I didn't even leave the apartment, let alone shop for groceries.

The small man's story had put me in a melancholy mood. When I heard my mother's key in the lock I was surprised at how much time had passed. She always came promptly at four thirty—at least two hours had gone by since the small man had arrived. "She comes every day to see the baby," I explained, over the sound of my mother rattling hangers in the foyer. This was true, though my mother didn't limit herself to grandmotherly duties—sometime between the death of my father and the birth of Caroline she had decided that I needed daily reminders on how to conduct myself and run a household. Ordinarily I didn't mind giving her something to do. Now I could hear her in the dining alcove, rummaging through the mail on the sideboard; then she moved on to the living room, calling out in her ringing voice if I had done the things on my to-do list. Had I picked up my prescription at the drugstore? I had, not that it was her business. Had I called Dr. Iger to reschedule the appointment for the baby? I had. Had anyone remembered to retrieve the clean clothes from Moon Laundry? I decided not to answer that, as the dirty clothes had not as yet been dropped off. As usual, she didn't bother coming to find me, preferring to yell through the walls to be heard.

The baby woke up and began to cry; immediately I heard my mother scurry down the hall to the nursery. Although every particle of my being wanted to go to the nursery myself, I decided it was better to let Mother be distracted. I pressed my teeth into my bottom lip, hard. My guest had gone still. Before I could apologize for the intrusion and all the racket, a strange thing happened. I heard another key in the lock: Gordon, my husband. I knew it was him not only because he was the only other person with a key to our apartment, but from the absolute stealth with which he moved, the quiet click of the door closing, the whispery step of his smooth leather soles on the foyer rug. My husband might have been a dancer or a spy, he moved with such grace. In fact he practiced corporate law at a firm where recently he'd become one of their youngest partners. Gordon never came home this early—something had to be wrong. I excused myself to the small man, who was now blinking rapidly. He had long eyelashes, I noticed. Clearly, he sensed my anxiety, and I could tell this had counteracted the therapeutic effect of our conversation.

"I'll be just a moment," I assured him.

My guest made a fluttery-sweeping gesture at the door, urging me along.

I stepped into the foyer. "Gordon!" I said. "What a surprise!"

My husband smiled at me, then walked straight by, flinging his coat at the carved-mahogany secretary we kept next to the closet (the coat slumped to the floor—an uncharacteristically careless move for Gordon). He strode through the dining alcove into the living room, sat down in one of the matching armchairs, and began to read a magazine.

I followed him partway into that room; we had decorated it after our wedding two years ago with a combination of aesthetics, mine and his, that worked well together, we thought. I was responsible for the handwoven rugs from Morocco and Egypt (from my travels with my parents), the exotic plants and small objets d'art placed on side tables; he'd hung on the walls a series of framed satirical cartoons from eighteenth-century newspapers, featuring bulbous-nosed men with wigs, and donkeys, pigs, and elephants with sacks of coins, that he'd bought at auctions. He had also designed the floor-to-ceiling bookcases flanking the fireplace. The shelves were lined with hardcovers sorted by genre and, within genre, alphabetically by author. He had arranged the spices on the spice rack as well. My husband's knack for putting things in order inspired many people to say he had a good head on his shoulders.

"Gordon?" I hovered next to a bookcase.

He looked up from his magazine and sighed. His face, though a little gray from winter, struck me now, as it did each time I saw it, as more handsome than I remembered: his features, like his thoughts, lined up in perfect relation to each other, as right as a professional portrait artist could have designed, with its wide forehead, straight eyebrows, upturned nose, and square chin. His only flaw was that his eyes became slightly bloodshot at times, particularly when he was tired, but even that looked good on him.

"Your mother called me at work this morning," said Gordon. "She said you've been having—" here he paused, and rubbed his eyes. "She said you've been having visitors."

"Did she?" I said.

In the pause following my question we could hear the infant babbling from the nursery down the hall, and the lower, more nasal babbling of my mother in turn.

Gordon sighed again, making a frond on the miniature palm behind his chair bounce a little. Sighing did not become him. It did something prissy to his demeanor.

"She said you've been taking in people off the street. She says she's walked in on you talking to them in the kitchen a few times, and that you act like it's normal and say they're friends of yours, but she thinks you've never seen them before in your life. She's concerned."

At this moment I felt another deep pull to the nursery, but instead I pressed my top teeth into my bottom lip and squeezed my thumbs equally hard with my fingers.

"You're irritated," Gordon said.

"She's overreacting," I said. I tasted some blood from my lip. Still, I maintained the gentle, controlled tone I had used earlier with my guest, about whom I was beginning to worry, imagining him alone in the kitchen. "I hope you'll agree with me that it's not a crime to have guests from the other side of the tracks, as it were."

Now Gordon's pink-tinged eyes had locked onto me with an intensity that made me falter.

"Well, it's nothing to *worry* about," I said. "They're harmless. They never leave the kitchen. I give them a cup of coffee, we talk for a while, they leave. That's all."

"That's all?" Gordon closed his magazine. He put it on the side table by his chair, covering a small brass paperweight of a reclining nude. "Where do you find them, your visitors?"

"I despise that tone," I said. "I hope you don't use it with your clients."

"Don't change the subject, Bettine," said Gordon.

"What does it matter where they find me? Maybe I'm found."

"How do they get our address?" Gordon had softened the interrogative edge to his voice; nonetheless I could see he wasn't about to stop questioning me.

"How does anyone know anyone's address?" I laughed. "If someone has a positive experience, they pass on the information. Isn't that how it works?" I took a step closer to my husband's chair.

"We have so much," I continued. "They have nothing. Why not give something?"

Gordon didn't answer. He rubbed his eyes for a long time, making a revolting sticky noise. Then he began to speak, slowly. "Help me out with this, Bettine. I'm having trouble getting my mind around this."

"Around what?"

"This idea that you are inviting total and complete strangers into the privacy of our home. Could you explain it to me one more time?"

"Fuck yourself, Gordon." This was not what I'd meant to say. This was not who I was. I felt tears hot in my eyes.

For a moment Gordon seemed about to stand and reach for me, but a noise made us both turn. My forgotten guest was dragging his pail across the Moroccan rug, making his halting way toward us.

Feeling the blood rush to my head, I stepped quickly out of Gordon's reach and spoke to my friend. "Please, come in. I'm so sorry for my rudeness." I placed my hand on his shoulder, bending my knees slightly. "This is Gordon, my husband." I tilted my head at Gordon, who was standing now, his arms folded.

I realized then that I didn't have the small man's name. "And this," I said, avoiding Gordon's eyes, "is our guest."

Gordon said nothing. I raised my eyes just enough to see that he was scrutinizing the small man coldly. His nostrils were flared. The small man had fixed his own gaze on a spot under the side table; when I touched his shoulder again, I saw, on the tip of one of his eyelashes, a tear. It beaded and dropped, slowly.

It would be a lie to say that I gave what I did next a lot of thought. Like swearing at my husband, I did it on impulse. I'd not brought any of my previous guests into any room other than the kitchen. Of these handful of sad, often smelly men and women, none of them had asked to see more of the place, and only two had needed to use the bathroom.

"Please come with me," I said. I turned my back on Gordon and led my charge down the hall, ignoring the sound of his bucket scuffing the parquet floors. I showed him the den, with its two computers and the thirty-six-inch flat-screen television Gordon had bought *la famille* for Christmas. We looked in on the spare room, the bathrooms, the master bedroom; I opened closets, revealing my pairs of shoes in their labeled boxes, and Gordon's racks of suits and stacks of shirts; I even invited my new friend to try out the King (our name for the bed) but realized too late it would be impossible for him to leverage himself onto the mattress. I told him where things were, towels and lightbulbs and rubbing alcohol. Through all of this, my guest offered appreciation, bobbing his egglike head, smiling widely. Caught up in his enthusiasm, I pulled out my underwear drawer. Although my guest continued to nod and smile, I realized what I'd done and, feeling my cheeks prickle, I explained that I needed to do laundry and wanted to see how many clean pairs I had left. "Let's go to the nursery," I said.

We crossed the hall.

"Thank you for showing me your lovely home. But I'm afraid I'm messing up your floors." He pointed at a whitish scrape where he'd pulled his bucket along.

"What? No." I waved this away. "A little oil soap and it's gone." By this time I'd expected my mother or Gordon to appear, but they hadn't.

I had only one clear thought as I stood outside the closed nursery door that separated me and the small man from Caroline and my mother: This was not how I wanted my child to be raised. I threw open the door and pulled my guest in beside me. Near the window that looked out on a pretty little garden on the roof of a shorter neighboring building, my mother was feeding the baby in the rocking chair. In contrast to the downy orb of my daughter's head, my mother seemed made of angles. Her cheekbones jutted out beneath her eyes, her thin neck supported a small pointy head, emphasized by the ponytail into which she pulled her hair. We had the same stark coloring, me and my mother, and similar body types. People said we were the spitting image, but my mother liked to point out that she was French, whereas I was half American. "It is why she is so much bigger," she would sometimes remark, as if this were charming.

"Hi, Mom."

Without missing a beat in her rocking, she shot me a vicious glare. Her eyes narrowed, as mine do when I'm angry. Then she returned her gaze to the baby. Caroline waved her little paws and looked back at her grandmother as she suckled the bottle rhythmically.

"She's beautiful," whispered the small man.

"Thank you," I said. "I think so, too."

"*Mon dieu*," my mother said. "What on earth is wrong with you?"

The small man looked alarmed. "Madam, I—"

"I meant no offense to you, Monsieur; I was speaking to my . . . daughter." She managed to make the word "daughter" sound as though it were being ground into dust under her heel. Still, she spoke softly so as not to disturb Caroline. "Forgive me, Monsieur, but I must speak to her." Her eyes went back to the baby. "I don't think it's a good idea to allow unknown persons into your home. Not when you have a child, not when you're alone, not ever. It's time to use common sense." She shifted her gaze away from Caroline, to the small man. "I'm sure you're a very fine person, Monsieur . . ."

"Carlos, I just go by Carlos." He spoke his name clearly. I looked at him. He smiled at me, and winked.

"*Monsieur* Carlos. But I'm going to have to ask you, in lieu of my daughter's sense, to leave right away. It's simply not a good time."

I felt the urge to lie down on the floor. I said, "This is my home. You don't have the right to order my guests around. You don't have the right—"

"It's okay," said Carlos. "She's right. You've been very hospitable. More so than anyone I've ever met."

"Thank you," I said. "But I am the decision maker in this household, not her, and I have not asked you to leave." Pointedly, I looked at him, acting as though my mother were now invisible. "I like your company. In fact, I'd like you to stay for supper."

"Bettine," my mother said. "Stop being irrational."

"Please," said Carlos huskily. "That's too kind."

"Not at all," I said. "Do you like chicken?" I put my hand on the doorknob. It was a good thing my mother was stuck in the rocking chair; otherwise, from the look on her face she might have tried something physical.

"Bettine!" my mother called after us.

Briskly, I walked back down the hall with Carlos chinking behind me. We moved through the living room without pause; from the corner of my eye I glimpsed Gordon in his chair—he appeared to be reading his magazine again.

"Listen, Carlos," I said, once we were in the kitchen. "I need to do some grocery shopping." I felt a little out of breath. I thought of lying on the couch in the living room, with my own magazine and a glass of wine. I thought of Caroline.

"We have to go out, you know, to get the food."

Carlos nodded.

But when we entered the foyer he dropped to his knees. And then he crawled underneath the mahogany secretary, pulling my husband's coat up over him. I was amazed by how quickly he'd moved. I stood there for a minute, unsure of what to do.

"Carlos?" I knelt down and tried to see under the desk. My father, who didn't live to meet Caroline, had brought it from Africa when I was a child. It had a masklike face carved into the center of the fold-up lid, a visage with downward-pointing eyebrows and a beak nose; flowers, birds, and vines were carved across the drawers and the legs, which rested on claw feet. Carlos seemed to have curled up tightly under Gordon's coat, though his bucket foot was sticking out. I had the feeling he just wanted to sleep. I understood. But I couldn't leave him there. I couldn't let him stay.

There was no response, and I peered further under the desk. He had the coat pulled up to his chin like a blanket. "Carlos, I'm sorry. You really need to come out now."

Carlos sniffed and closed his eyes. He had jammed himself well in. "I know," he said. "I know."

"Please," I said. "You can come back anytime. Tomorrow, if you like. I'll make more coffee." I knew then that this wouldn't happen. "This is really not a good time for this," I said. I was panting.

Carlos lay silent. We both stayed where we were, breathing, for several moments.

Sometimes, when I think back on that day, I see Carlos's foot sticking out from under my father's desk and I can't breathe and I feel I have to lie down. Given another chance, I might have chosen differently. I might have, I might have.

"Gordon!" I called. Now it was my voice that sounded shrill and uneven. "I'm sorry. I need your help here."

Within moments my husband stood at the entrance to the foyer. He took in the scene: me, crouched on the floor, Carlos wedged under the secretary with the coat. I got to my feet and walked over to Gordon. We were nearly the same height.

I thought he would be angry with me, but instead he looked into my eyes with his whole face, in that way he had when I first knew he loved me. He'd asked me to go swimming in the ocean. I wore a two-piece bathing suit and splashed him with my feet although I'd known him for only a short time. When I stopped splashing I saw he was looking at me not just with his eyes but with all his features open and shimmering in a kind of abandon, hiding nothing, seeing everything, inviting me to float across that plane of water, high above the fathoms, and glide into his life.

In our foyer, I gazed back at my husband. His blue eyes veined with pink seemed the most familiar colors on earth. We didn't have to say anything. Together, Gordon and I lifted the antique secretary off Carlos. Together, we carried him, his form motionless, stunted, heavy, through the door and onto the elevator. He didn't struggle, nor did he help us. He said nothing; he barely breathed. We rode down from our floor, silently, our burden between us, and bore him across the flagstone lobby. We delivered the small man outside, onto the street.

About the Authors

AIMEE BENDER is the author of four books; the most recent, *The Particular Sadness of Lemon Cake*, was the recipient of the SCIBA award and an Alex Award. Her short fiction has been published in *Granta*, *GQ*, *Harper's*, *Tin House*, the *Paris Review*, and other publications, as well as heard on PRI's *This American Life* and *Selected Shorts*. She lives in Los Angeles, where she teaches creative writing at USC.

KATE BERNHEIMER is the author of three novels, including *The Complete Tales of Lucy Gold*, and the story collection *Horse, Flower, Bird*, which is illustrated by Rikki Ducornet. She also edits fairy-tale anthologies, including *My Mother She Killed Me, My Father He Ate: Forty New Fairy Tales*.

JUDY BUDNITZ is the author of two story collections, *Flying Leap* and *Nice Big American Baby*, and a novel, *If I Told You Once*.

SARAH SHUN-LIEN BYNUM is the author of two novels: *Ms. Hempel Chronicles*, a finalist for the 2009 PEN/Faulkner Award, and *Madeleine Is Sleeping*, a finalist for the 2004 National Book Award and winner of the Janet Heidinger Kafka Prize. Her fiction has appeared in several magazines and anthologies, including the *New Yorker*, *Tin House*, the *Georgia Review*, and *The Best American Short Stories* 2004 and 2009. The recipient of a Whiting Writers' Award and an NEA Fellowship, she directs the MFA program in writing at the University of California, San Diego. She lives in Los Angeles and was recently included on the *New Yorker*'s 20 Under 40 list.

LUCY CORIN is the author of the short story collection *The Entire Predicament* (Tin House Books) and the novel *Everyday Psychokillers: A History for Girls* (FC2). Her stories have appeared in *American Short Fiction, Conjunctions, Ploughshares, Tin House, New Stories from the South: The Year's Best*, and a lot of other places. She's been a fellow at Breadloaf and Sewanee, and a resident at Yaddo and the Radar Lab.

LYDIA DAVIS is the author of *Varieties of Disturbance*, which was a National Book Award finalist; *Samuel Johnson Is Indignant; Almost No Memory; The End of the Story*; and *Break It Down*. Her latest book is *Collected Stories*. Her work has appeared in *Conjunctions, Harper's*, the *New Yorker, Bomb*, the *Paris Review, Tin House, McSweeney's*, and many other magazines and literary journals. Davis has translated works by the French writers Maurice Blanchot and Michel Leiris; she has also completed a highly acclaimed new translation of Marcel Proust's *Swann's Way* for Penguin Classics and a new translation of Gustave Flaubert's *Madame Bovary*. Among other honors, she has been awarded a MacArthur Fellowship, a Guggenheim Fellowship, and a Lannan Literary Prize and has been named Chevalier of the Order of Arts and Letters by the French Government. In 2003, she won the French-American Translation Prize, and in 2005 she was inducted into the Academy of Arts & Sciences. She lives in upstate New York with her family.

The author of eight novels, three collections of short fiction, a book of essays, and five books of poetry, RIKKI DUCORNET has twice been honored by the Lannan Foundation. She has received the Bard College Arts and Letters Award and, in 2008, an Academy Award in Literature. Her work is widely published abroad. Recent exhibitions of her paintings include the 2007 solo show Desirous at the Pierre Menard Gallery in Cambridge, Massachusetts, and the group shows O Reverso Do Olhar in Coimbra, Portugal, in 2008, and El Umbral Secreto at the Museo de la Solidaridad Salvador Allende in Santiago,

Chile, in 2009. She has illustrated books by Jorge Luis Borges, Robert Coover, Forrest Gander, Kate Bernheimer, Joanna Howard, and Anne Waldman, among others.

JULIA ELLIOTT teaches English and Women's and Gender Studies at the University of South Carolina. She sings and plays keyboards for the band Grey Egg. Her fiction has appeared in *Tin House*, the *Georgia Review, Conjunctions, Puerto Del Sol*, the *Mississippi Review, Fence*, the anthology *Best American Fantasy 2007*, and other publications.

SAMANTHA HUNT's second novel, *The Invention of Everything Else*, was a finalist for the Orange Prize and winner of the Bard Fiction Prize. Her first novel, *The Seas*, won a National Book Foundation award for writers under thirty-five. She lives in Tivoli, New York, and teaches at the Pratt Institute in Brooklyn.

MIRANDA JULY is a writer, performer, and moviemaker living in Los Angeles.

KELLY LINK is the author of three collections: *Pretty Monsters, Magic for Beginners*, and *Stranger Things Happen*. Her short stories have won three Nebula awards, a Hugo, a Locus, and a World Fantasy Award. She was born in Miami, Florida, and once won a free trip around the world by answering the question "Why do you want to go around the world?" ("Because you can't go through it.") Link lives in Northampton, Massachusetts, where she and her husband, Gavin J. Grant, run Small Beer Press and play ping-pong. In 1996 they started the occasional zine *Lady Churchill's Rosebud Wristlet*.

LYDIA MILLET is the author of eight books, including a story collection called *Love in Infant Monkeys* (2009), which was a finalist for the Pulitzer Prize, and a novel, *How the Dead Dream*, the first in a series whose second and third installments, *Ghost Lights* and *Magnificence*, will come out from W.W. Norton in fall 2011 and fall 2012. Her first novel for young readers, called *The Fires Beneath the Sea*, was published by Small Beer Press in May 2011.

ALISSA NUTTING is author of the short story collection *Unclean Jobs for Women and Girls*, selected by Ben Marcus for the Starcherone Prize for Innovative Fiction. A Cobain Fellow in fiction at the University of Nevada, Las Vegas, she is fiction editor of the literary magazine *Witness* and managing editor of *Fairy Tale Review*. Her work has been published in literary journals such as *BOMB, Fence, Mid-American Review*, and others, as well as in multiple magazines relating to history, art, and culture. Say hello at http://alissanutting.com.

GINA OCHSNER is the author of two collections of short stories, *People I Wanted to Be* and *The Necessary Grace to Fall*, both of which won the Oregon Book Award, and a novel, *The Russian Dreambook of Color and Flight*, which was longlisted for the Orange Prize. Her work has appeared in the *New Yorker, The Best American Nonrequired Reading, Glimmer Train, Tin House*, and numerous other publications. She is a recipient of the Flannery O'Connor Award, the Ruth Hindman Foundation Prize, Guggenheim and NEA grants, and the Raymond Carver Prize. She lives in Keizer, Oregon.

STACEY RICHTER is the author of two short story collections: *My Date with Satan* and *Twin Study*.

KAREN RUSSELL, a native of Miami, has been featured in the *New Yorker*'s debut fiction issue and on the *New Yorker*'s 20 Under 40 list and was chosen as one of *Granta*'s Best Young American Novelists. In 2009, she received the 5 Under 35 award from the National Book Foundation. A former fellow at the New York Public

Library Cullman Center for Scholars and Writers, she has taught creative writing at Columbia University and Williams College and is currently writer-in-residence at Bard College. She is the author of the collection *St. Lucy's Home for Girls Raised by Wolves* and the novel *Swamplandia!*, both published by Knopf.

JULIA SLAVIN is the author of *The Woman Who Cut Off Her Leg at the Maidstone Club and Other Stories* and the novel *Carnivore Diet*.

JOY WILLIAMS is the author of four novels—the most recent, *The Quick and the Dead*, was a finalist for the Pulitzer Prize—and two collections of stories, as well as a book of essays, *Ill Nature*, a finalist for the National Book Critics Circle Award.

GINA ZUCKER has published short stories, essays, and articles in a variety of magazines, journals, and anthologies, including *Elle*, *GQ*, *Cosmopolitan*, *Rolling Stone*, *Salt Hill*, *Opium*, and *Tin House*. She teaches creative writing at Pratt Institute and lives in Brooklyn with her family.

About the Editor

ROB SPILLMAN is the editor of *Tin House* magazine. He has written for publications such as *Salon*, *Bookforum*, the *Baltimore Sun*, *British GQ*, *Details*, *Nerve*, the *New York Times Book Review*, *Premiere*, *Rolling Stone*, *Spin*, *Sports Illustrated*, *SPY*, *Vanity Fair*, *Vogue*, and *Worth*, among others.

Copyright Notes